Smokin' Hot

More Erotic Romances by Lynn LaFleur

Nightshift

(with Kate Douglas and Crystal Jordan)

Hot Shots

(with Anne Marsh and Stacey Kennedy)

Flaming Hot

(coming soon!)

Smokin' Hot

LYNN LaFLEUR

APHRODISIA

KENSINGTON PUBLISHING CORP.
www.kensingtonbooks.com

APHRODISIA BOOKS are published by

Kensington Publishing Corp.
119 West 40th Street
New York, NY 10018

All Kensington titles, imprints, and distributed lines are available at special quantity discounts for bulk purchases for sales promotion, premiums, fund-raising, educational, or institutional use.

Special book excerpts or customized printings can also be created to fit specific needs. For details, write or phone the office of the Kensington Special Sales Manager: Kensington Publishing Corp., 119 West 40th Street, New York, NY 10018. Attn. Special Sales Department. Phone: 1-800-221-2647.

Aphrodisia and the A logo Reg. U.S. Pat. & TM Off.

ISBN-13: 978-1-61773-088-7
ISBN-10: 1-61773-088-2
First Kensington Trade Paperback Printing: April 2014

eISBN-13: 978-1-61773-089-4
eISBN-10: 1-61773-089-0
First Kensington Electronic Edition: April 2014

10 9 8 7 6 5 4 3 2 1

Printed in the United States of America

CONTENTS

Singe

1

Lanville, Texas, was a blip on the highway southwest of the Dallas–Fort Worth Metroplex. Small, picturesque, slow-paced. That's why Julia Woods decided it would be the perfect place to settle.

It hadn't been easy for her to decide to leave the home she'd always known in Northern California. She'd lived her entire life among the Sierra Nevada mountains. But the last incident left her no choice. The pain had been too severe to ever experience again. She needed a fresh start someplace far away from horrible memories.

Now, she sat in a booth at Burger King in Lanville, ready to begin the next chapter of her life.

Munching on a French fry, Julia studied the directions Dolly Mabery had e-mailed on how to get to her place. Dolly and Julia's mother, Cathy, had gone to college together and remained friends for the past thirty-plus years. Dolly had offered Julia a job at her bar to help her until she decided exactly what she wanted to do with the rest of her life.

While thankful to Dolly for her generous offer, Julia had

waitressed in her early college days at a diner that hadn't exactly been at the top of the food critics' must-go-to list, and hadn't liked it. The tips could be very generous, yet Julia had quickly grown tired of men's groping hands and sexist remarks about her big breasts. She'd heard them called every slang term ever created to describe that part of the female anatomy, from balloons to cantaloupes to tatas.

Some men could be such jerks.

Besides, she didn't think she could stand on her feet for long periods of time now, not with her bum knee, so she had turned down Dolly's offer.

Masculine laughter at the main doors had Julia raising her head to see who entered the fast-food place. Four men sauntered in, all of them wearing jeans and dark blue T-shirts with a gold-and-red logo over their left pectorals. Two had dark hair, two blond, and all four possessed amazing good looks. The blonds had to be brothers, possibly twins since they favored so much, and appeared to be in their mid-twenties. Cute, but nothing to make her heart beat faster. One of the brunettes looked to be in his early forties. Very good looking, but again he did nothing for her.

The other brunette . . .

She guessed him to be twenty-six or twenty-seven. He stood at least six feet tall with wide shoulders and a muscled body. Olive skin gave him the appearance of a year-round tan. A couple of days' worth of stubble covered his lower face. His thick mane of dark brown hair fell over his forehead, ears, and nape in waves that would wrap around a woman's fingers. Julia could easily imagine her fingers in his hair while his full, shapely lips moved over hers in a ravenous kiss.

Mmm, nice thought.

But one she knew wouldn't come true. She had no intention of dating for a long, long time, much less getting involved with anyone.

That didn't mean she couldn't enjoy the scenery.

The man she had momentarily drooled over let the other three step up to the counter before him. He turned his back to her as he studied the menu, giving her an excellent view of the way his jeans molded to his ass. Such a nice ass, with just the right amount of fullness so a woman could grip it while he slid his cock into her pussy.

The bite of French fry stuck in her throat. Julia picked up her cup of iced tea to wash it down, but she'd already drunk all of it. She could get a refill, except the beverage dispensers sat right by the counter where the four men stood. She'd be within a few feet of them if she refilled her cup.

So? You're a big girl. You can ignore them.

The decision made, Julia rose from the booth and headed for the dispensers. She refilled her cup with tea, chose another lemon slice, and dropped it into her beverage. Taking a sip, she turned to go back to her booth.

And looked directly into a pair of eyes the color of aged cognac.

She froze in place. Her throat closed, which kept her from choking on her tea. She watched the hunky brunette's gaze dip down her body to her hips before making the return journey to her face. A slow smile lifted the corners of his mouth.

"Stephen, you're up," the older man said.

" 'K." He winked at her, then stepped to the counter.

The temperature in the room shot up at least twenty degrees. Julia stopped herself before she fanned her face. She had no idea how a simple wink could drive up her blood pressure.

She turned and made her way back to her booth. It didn't surprise her to feel that pull, that awareness, toward the handsome man. She'd left Cole's bed a month before she made the decision to leave California. After a very healthy sex life, weeks of abstinence had her thinking of cool sheets and hot skin.

Shaking off the thought of sex—or lack of sex—Julia concentrated on what she needed to do. A job came before anything else. Dolly had warned her that finding a job in Lanville wouldn't be easy. The small-town businesses tended to keep their employees for years instead of having a quick turnover. At least Julia didn't have to search for a place to live right away, since Dolly had offered her guest room for as long as Julia needed it.

An online search had garnered some ideas of places to apply for work. The Inn on Crystal Creek occupied the spot at the top of her list. Although she hadn't found an ad listing open positions, Julia hoped there would be something available in housekeeping. It would be physical work with a lot of standing, yet she enjoyed cleaning and might be able to take more rest breaks than if she waitressed.

Gathering her personal items and the tray with her lunch trash, Julia rose and headed for the exit. She had to pass the table where the four men sat. They all gave her a quick glance and she returned their attention with a small smile. She emptied her tray in the trash and turned toward the door. Before she pushed it open, she glanced over her shoulder at the table of men. The sexy brunette stared at her with interest in his eyes.

Julia held his gaze a few seconds longer before she managed to look away from him and leave.

"Damn," Kory said, "did you see the centerfold tits on that blonde?"

Stephen McGettis most certainly had. He'd noticed everything about the beautiful woman—the short, blond hair that curled over her head, her heart-shaped face, her huge blue eyes. Her full breasts, rounded hips, and perfect ass almost cried out for a man's hands to caress and fondle.

He looked across the table at the Wilcox twins. Kory always said exactly what popped into his head, which sometimes got him in a lot of trouble. Kirk had more control, more finesse. He wouldn't describe the beautiful breasts on a woman as tits. Neither would Stephen. He believed a woman's body should be worshipped, treasured.

He wouldn't mind spending about three days worshipping that woman's body.

"You should watch your mouth," Luis Galendez said, pointing a finger at the younger man.

"What did I do?" Kory asked, confusion obvious in his voice.

"You need to be more respectful of women."

Kory spread his arms wide. "Hey, I *love* women."

"They don't love you back, bro," Kirk said. "Maybe they would if you grew up."

"What is this, pick on Kory day?" he asked with a frown. "And you're the same age I am."

"I'm just sayin' there's a reason why the women around here turn you down when you ask them out."

Kory's lips thinned and a red flush colored his face as he glared at his brother. "You aren't exactly burning up the sheets, *bro*."

"I burn 'em more often than *you* do."

Stephen bit back a grin. He looked at Luis seated to his right. The older man's eyes gleamed with laughter. The twins could be very entertaining. "Okay, I think we can all safely say none of us have been successful in the sex department lately."

"Speak for yourself," Luis said with a grin.

Stephen chuckled. "Okay, I'll rephrase my statement. None of us *single guys* have been successful in the sex department lately."

"Not without lack of trying," Kory mumbled.

"Yeah," Kirk added. "Celibacy sucks."

The call of his order number kept Stephen from responding, although he agreed with the Wilcoxes. It had been at least two months since he'd experienced the feel of a woman's soft body next to his, the slide of his hard dick into her wet pussy. Yeah, almost two months to the day since he'd fucked one of the gals in his skydiving class. The sensation of flying through the air had only been eclipsed by the incredible sex after the jump. Sex after an adrenaline rush always seemed hotter, more intense.

He wondered if the blonde who had recently left had ever parachuted from a plane.

Picking up the tray holding his Whopper and fries, Stephen made his way back to the table. He had to forget all about the beautiful woman who had stolen his breath when he looked into her blue eyes. More than likely, she'd stopped long enough to eat on her way through Lanville and had already left the city limits. He'd never see her again.

Julia looked around the welcoming sitting area at The Inn on Crystal Creek. Cushy chairs arranged by the rock fireplace made the room appear cozy and homey. The room's furnishings combined a touch of yesterday with a bit of the present. If the rest of the bed-and-breakfast gave her the same comfortable feeling, it would be a pleasure to work here.

If she got the job.

She stood as a lovely, slim woman approached. "Julia?"

"Yes."

The woman smiled and offered her hand to shake. "Hi, I'm Kelcey Ewing, the manager. Thanks for waiting. Let's go to my office where we'll have some privacy."

Julia followed Kelcey past the check-in counter and down a short hallway. She inhaled deeply of the scent of chocolate and vanilla wafting from the kitchen.

"Our chef is baking cookies," Kelcey said. "I made her promise she'd bring some to us as soon as they come out of the oven." She motioned to a chair at the side of her desk. "Please sit down."

Julia did as suggested and set her large purse on the floor between the chair and desk. She saw her résumé and application lying on Kelcey's desk, so she knew the manager had already read them.

"Would you like something to drink, Julia?" Kelcey asked.

"No, thanks. I'm fine."

Picking up the paperwork from her desk, Kelcey swiveled her chair to face Julia. "You worked for the U.S. Forest Service in California?"

"Yes. I worked part-time while going to college, then went to full-time five years ago when I graduated."

"So you lived in Northern California all your life?"

"Yes, in the Sierra Nevada foothills, east of Sacramento."

Kelcey glanced at the résumé again before returning her gaze to Julia. "That's the only job you've ever had?"

"The only major job. I waitressed for a while in college, but that didn't last long." Julia stopped herself before she bit her bottom lip. She'd been worried her lack of experience would be a hindrance in finding a new position.

"Why did you leave?"

Thinking about leaving the job she'd loved so much made her stomach churn, but she had to be honest with a potential employer. She decided it would be easier to give a simple explanation that another woman could understand. "Man trouble."

"That explains a lot. I doubt if there's a woman anywhere in the world who hasn't had man trouble." Kelcey tilted her head. "It must have been really bad for you to move halfway across the country."

Without warning, a huge lump formed in Julia's throat . . . the first sign that tears would fall soon. She blinked quickly to hold them back. She couldn't break down in front of the manager. Kelcey would show her to the door with a polite don't-call-us-we'll-call-you and a pat on the shoulder. "Things got . . . intense between us," she managed to get out past the lump.

Julia thought she saw sympathy flash through Kelcey's eyes. She didn't want pity, she wanted a job.

"It takes a lot of courage to move away from home, and even more courage to move to a completely different state." Kelcey laid the paperwork on her desk. "A housekeeping position doesn't pay much. There are benefits, such as all the cookies you can eat, but not a huge salary. Surely you could find a position similar to what you did in California. Isn't the U.S. Forest Service nationwide?"

"It is, but I . . ." Julia stopped. She didn't know how much to tell Kelcey, or how much she *wanted* to tell Kelcey. The wound still festered deep inside. She couldn't handle ripping it open again. "I need something different. I thought a new job should go along with my new place to live."

"Do you already have a place to live in Lanville?"

Julia pointed to the personal references line on her résumé. "Dolly Mabery offered me her guest room until I can find a permanent place."

"Is Dolly a friend?"

"Of my mother's. They went to college together. I've never met her in person, but I've spoken on the phone with her dozens of times."

A sinking feeling formed in the pit of Julia's stomach at the realization that Kelcey probably wouldn't hire her. Desperation gave Julia the strength to plead her case. "You can check with my former boss. She'll tell you I'm dependable and honest and a hard worker. I'm a little anal about order and like to clean. I'll take day shifts, night shifts, weekends . . . wherever you need me. I promise I'll do a good job for you."

Great. Why don't I get on my knees, as long as I'm begging? Kelcey probably thinks I'm a whiny weakling.

Kelcey studied Julia's face for several seconds. "Yes, I think you will."

Julia blinked, not sure if she'd been given the job or not. "Does that mean I'm hired?"

"It means you're hired." Kelcey smiled. "How soon can you start?"

Eager to make a good impression, Julia said, "Today. Right now."

Kelcey laughed. "I like an employee willing to work. How about if you start Monday? That'll give you the weekend to get settled at Dolly's and learn a little about the town."

"Monday works for me."

"Be here by eight. You can fill out the necessary forms before I show you around The Inn."

"I'll be here." She stood as Kelcey did and offered her hand. "Thank you so much."

"You're welcome." Smiling again, Kelcey shook Julia's hand. "See you Monday at eight."

2

Voices outside her window slowly dragged Julia from dreams to reality. Through one eye, she peered toward the sliver of light shining through the curtains. It hit the hardwood floor, highlighting dust motes dancing in the air.

She couldn't believe any dust motes existed in Dolly's house, not the way it sparkled. Julia had always considered herself to be neat and organized. The house she'd rented in California resembled a sty compared to Dolly's immaculate home.

The voices drew closer to her window. She couldn't quite make out the words, but she recognized Dolly's tone. A masculine voice blended with Dolly's . . . a nice, deep, sexy-as-sin masculine voice. For some crazy reason, an image of the guy from Burger King yesterday popped into her head. The guy with Dolly had the same type of voice she imagined her hunky brunette would also possess.

Julia rolled to her side and looked at the digital clock on the nightstand. 9:07. She blinked and looked again. She hadn't slept this late in . . . she didn't think she'd *ever* slept this late. But she hadn't fallen asleep until almost three o'clock. Since Dolly's bar, Boot Scootin', wasn't open on Wednesdays, Julia and Dolly had talked until well after midnight. After that, Julia's mind had been too full for her to fall asleep. She worried about starting over in a new state. She worried about finding a place to live in a small town where rentals were scarce.

She ached to feel Cole's arms around her, hungered for the taste of his kiss.

Leaving him had been the hardest thing for her to do. But she'd had no choice. After what he'd done . . .

Julia threw off the covers and sat on the edge of the bed. Her stomach rumbled. Not surprising, since she hadn't eaten anything since a snack at nine last night. Dolly had told her to make herself at home, that she could cook whatever she wanted, do her laundry, hibernate in the guest room when she desired privacy. Dolly wanted Julia to think of this as her home for as long as she stayed.

She understood why her mother loved Dolly so much. The woman had a caring heart as big as the state where she lived.

Discarding the large T-shirt and panties she'd slept in, Julia donned underwear, jeans, and a loose, short-sleeved blouse. After a quick trip to the bathroom to brush her teeth and hair, she followed the scent of coffee to the kitchen. No more than two steps into the room, she stopped in her tracks. The hunky brunette from Burger King sat at the round wooden table.

He looked her way. Surprise flitted across his face before he smiled and stood. "Hello."

Dolly straightened from peering into the refrigerator. "Oh, good, you're awake. How did you sleep?"

"Great," she answered her hostess while still looking at the man she never expected to see in Dolly's kitchen.

"Are you hungry? I promised Stephen an apple crêpe to go with his coffee."

Julia's stomach gurgled loudly. Warmth crept into her face and she covered her tummy with her hands. Dolly laughed.

"I'll take that as a yes. Why don't you get your coffee and sit down?" She motioned to the hunk. "This is Stephen McGettis. He and his cousin are going to repair my roof. I had quite a bit of hail damage last week when a bad thunderstorm blew through Lanville. Stephen, this is Julia Woods. She just moved here from California."

"It's nice to meet you, Julia."

"Nice to meet you, Stephen."

He remained standing while she got her coffee, not sitting again until she sat in the chair across from him. His politeness impressed her. After working mainly with men who treated her like a kid sister, she enjoyed the bit of chivalry.

Julia watched Dolly place the crêpe ingredients on the counter. "Can I help?" she asked.

"No, I'm fine. I already have the apple mixture and it won't take me a couple of minutes to whip up the batter. I've made these so many times, I can almost do them with my eyes closed." She glanced at Stephen over her shoulder. "Stephen, you and Julia have something in common."

He turned those amazing cognac-colored eyes on Julia. "Oh?"

Her breath hitched and she had to tighten her grip on the coffee mug before her lax fingers dropped it. The sun shone through the window and touched his long, dark hair, giving it reddish highlights. She doubted if this man spent very many Saturday nights alone. Or any other night of the week.

"She was a firefighter in California for the U.S. Forest Service."

A crooked smile turned up one corner of his lips. "No shit?" His smile quickly disappeared. "Uh, I mean, really?"

Julia hid a smile behind her mug as she sipped her coffee. She thought it cute that he didn't want to curse in front of her and Dolly. "My main job was in research, but I fought fires when the call went out for extra help."

"Stephen is a firefighter on our volunteer fire department."

Another point for Stephen. Julia had always admired the

men and women who worked on volunteer fire departments. They put their lives on the line without any pay or compensation other than the desire to help others. "How many volunteers on your fire department?"

"Twenty-four men and three women. Are you interested in joining? We can always use another pair of hands."

Part of her wanted to say yes, that she would love to help. Another part of her didn't think her knee could handle fighting fires yet. "I'll think about it."

The skin at the outer corners of his eyes tightened a bit, as if he could read her thoughts and knew she had personal reasons for not jumping in to immediately volunteer. "If you change your mind, Dolly knows how to get in touch with me."

Dolly set a small plate holding a large crêpe in front of each of them. The scent of apples and cinnamon drifted from the pastry, making Julia's stomach gurgle again.

"There are two more crêpes on the stove," Dolly said. "I have a couple of things to do, then I have to head to the bar in time for my delivery." She touched Julia's shoulder. "Come by later. I'll fix you one of my famous cheeseburgers."

"Apple crêpes now and cheeseburgers later? I don't need to gain any weight, Dolly."

"*Pffft*. You're perfect. A man doesn't want to hold a pile of bones. Isn't that right, Stephen?"

A look of apprehension flashed through his eyes. He obviously didn't want to comment on what Dolly said. "I, uh, think I'll refill my mug. You want more coffee, Julia?"

She struggled not to laugh at how quickly he changed the subject. "Please."

Julia and Dolly exchanged grins while Stephen carried the two mugs to the coffeemaker. Then Dolly pushed Julia's hair behind her ear, the way Julia's mother did so often. "I meant what I said. This is your home for as long as you need to stay here."

Hugs last night and touches this morning meant Dolly had

to be a physical person. Julia didn't mind that at all. The affection made her miss her mother a bit less. Smiling, she squeezed Dolly's hand. "Thank you."

Dolly left the room as Stephen returned with the full coffee mugs. Not sure what to say to him since she'd only met him twenty minutes ago, she dug into her crêpe instead. One bite and she couldn't stop the moan deep in her throat. Realizing it seemed similar to a sound made while making love, she lifted her gaze to Stephen. She caught him staring at her, his eyes narrowed, his nostrils flared. He quickly looked down at his plate, cut into his crêpe.

She took advantage of his lowered head to study him. He had gorgeous hair. She'd dated guys with short hair, long hair, and various lengths in-between. It had never mattered to her as long as the guy kept it clean and neat. Stephen's hair fell to his shoulders in gentle waves. She remembered noticing it when she first saw him in Burger King yesterday and thinking how the waves would wrap around a woman's fingers.

Her gaze continued over his face. Oval in shape. A straight nose. Mouth a little wide, with full, well-shaped lips that made her think of kissing for hours.

She could see his mouth better if not for the stubble. He obviously hadn't shaved in at least three days, perhaps longer. Julia had never been a fan of stubble, but she had to admit it gave him a dangerous, bad-boy appearance.

Cole had been a bad boy. Julia never wanted to get involved with one of them again.

Stephen scooped up the last bite of his crêpe. "I'm ready for seconds. How about you?"

Julia looked down at the remaining piece on her plate. "I don't think I can eat a whole one."

Rising from his chair, Stephen walked over to the stove and returned with the plate holding two crêpes. He set it on the table between them. "Take what you want and I'll eat the rest."

She divided a crêpe into halves and placed one on her plate. Stephen pulled the plate in front of him. She watched his hand as he cut into the half she'd left. Long, thick fingers, bare of any hair. Short, clean fingernails surrounded by cuticles a little ragged . . . probably from the physical work he did as a roofer. She couldn't see his palm, but she wouldn't be surprised if callouses existed there.

She wondered how those callouses would feel scraping over her nipples.

Warmth swept through her body at the forbidden thought. Just because Stephen looked hot didn't mean she would get involved with him. Her messed-up life had to be straightened out before she could have any kind of physical relationship with a man again. Besides, just because she found Stephen attractive didn't mean he felt the same way about her.

"Why Lanville?" he asked.

The image of Stephen's calloused fingers touching her vanished at his question. "What?"

"Why did you move to Lanville? Do you have relatives here?"

"No, I only know Dolly. Well, actually, I didn't know Dolly until I met her yesterday, but I've talked to her many times on the phone. She and my mom went to college together and have been friends for years."

"Dolly's the best. There isn't a woman more caring in this whole town." He laid his fork on his empty plate. "Where did you live in California?"

"East of Sacramento, in the Sierra Nevadas."

"No mountains around here, just hills. Lanville is probably a lot different than what you're used to."

Julia shrugged one shoulder. "I needed a change. Dolly offered me a place to stay and a job."

"You'll be working at Boot Scootin'?"

"No, I turned down her job offer. I'm starting work as a housekeeper at The Inn on Crystal Creek Monday."

His eyebrows shot up, as if what she said surprised him. "You'd rather clean rooms than make great tips?"

"I like to clean."

Pushing his plate aside, he leaned forward and rested his folded arms on the table. "Are you looking for outside work? I lost my cleaning lady a month ago when she cut back her hours. I'd rather eat raw frog's liver than clean a bathtub or oven."

Julia wrinkled her nose at the mental picture his statement created. "Eww."

"Exactly."

She laughed when he grinned. The charm oozed off this man. "I don't know what my hours will be yet. I wouldn't feel right taking other jobs if they'll interfere with my main job."

"Well, if you decide you want to pick up some extra money . . ." He reached into the breast pocket of his T-shirt and withdrew a white card. After flipping it over, he took the pen from on top of his clipboard that lay on the table and wrote something on the back. "Here's my cell number. That's the best way to reach me."

He held out the business card to her. Their fingers brushed when she took it, sending a pleasant tingle up her arm and straight to her nipples. They tightened inside her bra.

Ignoring her body's response, she looked at the front of the card. A cute cartoon man hammering a shingle onto a roof drew her attention before she read *McGettis Roofing, Dusty and Stephen McGettis, Owners.*

"Is Dusty your brother?"

"My cousin, but we're as close as brothers. He's three years older and we grew up together."

"Do you have any brothers or sisters?"

"Two brothers, both older. One is a lawyer, one is a college professor." He shrugged and flashed her a grin. "They got the brains, I got the brawn."

A single glance at Stephen's broad shoulders, muscular arms, and wide chest proved he definitely got the brawn. However, she had no doubt he had as much intelligence as his brothers. She could tell that from the way he spoke and carried himself.

"How about you?" Stephen asked.

Julia shook her head. "Only child. That was cool while I was growing up since I had all my mom's attention. Now, I wish I had a brother or sister. That's a bond that can never be broken."

"No father?"

She'd known Stephen for less than an hour. Personal stuff shouldn't even enter into their conversation, yet for a reason she didn't understand, she wanted to be honest with him. "I'm the result of my mother's one-night stand with—according to her—the most handsome man she'd ever seen. He didn't bother to give her anything but his first name. He snuck out of her apartment before she woke up the next morning."

A little uncomfortable at what she'd revealed to Stephen, she decided to change the subject the way he had earlier. "Would you like more coffee?"

"No, thanks. I need to go. I have another appointment in . . ." He checked the thick watch on his wrist. "Fifteen minutes."

Julia rose as he did. He headed toward the back door, so she assumed that's the way he had come into the house. She followed him, holding the door open after he crossed the threshold. Two steps onto the porch, he stopped and faced her.

"Dolly is right."

Confused, she tilted her head and asked, "About what?"

"Your body is perfect."

His gaze dipped to her breasts for a second before he turned and walked down the porch steps, leaving her a little breathless and a lot scared of such a strong reaction to Stephen McGettis.

3

Julia Woods stayed on Stephen's mind all day. Due to the hail damage a week ago, he and his cousin had been busy giving estimates on roof repairs. Stephen focused on work while with a potential customer, but Julia popped back into his mind as soon as he finished.

She fascinated him . . . and he didn't know why.

Sure, she had a gorgeous body with full breasts, wide hips, and a well-shaped ass. He'd always preferred long hair on women, but her short, blond curls looked perfect on her. She had huge blue eyes the color of cornflowers. He could make that comparison only because his mother had planted all kinds of flowers and shrubs around his parents' home and made sure her sons knew the name of every one. Not sure how that would help him in his life, he and his brothers still obeyed her and learned the species, colors, when each one bloomed, how long it bloomed, and if it was an annual or perennial. He'd be set if he ever decided to go into the florist or nursery business.

His current business kept him plenty busy. In fact, he should've left to meet Dusty at Boot Scootin' fifteen minutes ago.

A quick text to let his cousin know he'd be late and Stephen took off. His heart beat a little faster the closer he got to the country bar. If Julia had decided to accept Dolly's offer for a cheeseburger, he'd get to see her again. He'd kicked himself more than once ever since he left Dolly's house for not asking Julia out when he had the chance.

Stephen pulled into the parking lot of the bar. Few vehicles filled the spaces at five-thirty on a Thursday evening. He knew that would change, as soon as more people got off work and hit the bar for a cold beer and some of Dolly's amazing cooking. She featured chicken enchiladas on Thursday nights. Stephen's mouth watered just thinking about them.

Pulling open the heavy wooden door, he stepped into a large room filled with tables, chairs, and booths. The Texas Rangers played on the big-screen TVs, the clack of pool balls sounded from the back room. Dolly stood behind the bar, along with her weeknight bartender, Mel. Keely wove her way through the tables, her round tray loaded with bottles of Bud and Coors. He nodded to the people he knew, which included almost everyone. Living in a small town and being on the volunteer fire department meant he knew most of the residents.

A quick glance around the main room produced no Dusty, so Stephen headed for the pool room. He heard his cousin's laugh as he stepped through the archway. Dusty stood next to one of the pool tables, holding a cue stick with its butt resting on the floor, talking to Julia.

The sight of her had his balls tightening with lust.

As if she sensed his presence, she turned her head and looked at him over her shoulder. Stephen definitely felt something pass between them. Impossible to ignore that "something's" lure, he walked toward Julia and his cousin. She stared into his eyes as he approached her, keeping that tether between them.

He wondered if his fingers would get singed when he touched her.

"Hi," he said once he stood before her.

"Hi," she said with a hint of a smile.

"Hey, y'all already know each other?" Dusty asked.

"I met Julia when I did Dolly's estimate this morning."

"How'd that go?"

"Dolly gave us the thumbs-up for the job."

Dusty smiled. "Great." His smile quickly faded as he met Julia's gaze. "Uh, not great that she had hail damage, but great that she gave us the job to fix her roof."

Julia smiled. "I knew what you meant."

Stephen let his gaze wander over Julia while she had her attention focused on Dusty. She wore a blouse the color of ripe raspberries, faded jeans, and running shoes so white, it had to be the first time she'd worn them. Silver studs adorned her earlobes. A single strand of silver hung down the front of her blouse to below her breasts. She wore little makeup, but whatever she used on her eyes made them look huge.

My God, you're stunning.

Two sizzling plates of chicken enchiladas passed by Stephen on the waitress's tray. The enticing aroma made his stomach growl. "Man, those smell good. Have y'all eaten yet?"

"I was waiting for you," Dusty said.

Stephen looked directly at Julia. "How do you feel about chicken enchiladas?"

"Love them."

The waitress, Monica, stopped by them and smiled at him. "Hey, Stephen, ready for a beer?"

"Yeah. And how about three plates of those enchiladas?"

"One, two, or three per plate?"

"How many can you eat, Julia?" Stephen asked.

"I'm really hungry. Probably two."

"Two for the lady, three for Dusty and me," Stephen told Monica.

The waitress smiled. "You got it." She looked at Julia. "Ready for another glass of wine?"

"Please."

Once the waitress left them, Stephen motioned toward a table for four in the corner that he knew had to be Dusty's from all the paperwork spread over it. "How about if we sit down?"

"Hey, Dusty," Quade Easton called out from one of the pool tables, "you're up."

"Y'all go ahead," Dusty said. "It's my turn to beat Quade."

Stephen snorted with laughter. "In your dreams."

Dusty frowned. "It could happen."

"Maybe when the sun rises in the north."

"I won't tell you what you can do with that comment with a lady present."

Stephen motioned for Julia to precede him to the table. The mess his cousin always left made Stephen glad that Dusty's wife, Hannah, took care of the office and billing. As organized as Dusty was messy, she kept their business running smoothly.

Julia slipped into the chair next to the wall and he took the one opposite her, facing the room. They'd barely taken their seats when Monica arrived with their drinks, along with a basket of tortilla chips and three small bowls of salsa. "Food up in five."

"Thanks, Monica," Stephen said.

Picking up all the paperwork on the table, he stacked it into a pile for Dusty to figure out later. He waited for Julia to take a sip of her blush wine before he drank from his beer bottle. Although he couldn't call this an official date, he planned to take the opportunity to get to know Julia better. "Are you getting settled in at Dolly's?"

She nodded. "Dolly's been great. I understand why my mom loves her so much."

"Did you try the cheeseburger for lunch?"

"No, I didn't get here until about ten minutes before you did." She pushed a blond curl behind her ear. It immediately popped forward to touch her temple. *Lucky curl,* Stephen thought. "Dolly yelled out my name to everyone and they all said hi. I followed the sound of the pool balls back here. Dusty was the first to approach and welcome me to Lanville, so I stood and talked with him until you arrived."

"Did you do any exploring today?"

"I did." She cradled the stem of her wineglass in both hands. "Dolly gave me a map and I drove around, checking out the town. I love the courthouse square. I didn't do any shopping, but plan to in the next couple of days, especially in the bookstore."

Something they had in common. Stephen loved to read. "I thought a modern California gal like you would have one of those electronic readers."

"I do, but I love print books, too. There's something so satisfying about holding a book in my hands and breathing in the scent of the paper." She wrinkled her nose. "You probably think that's silly, don't you?"

No, it gave him a hint to the sensual woman he expected her to be. "Not at all. I'm a reader, too, so I understand what you're saying."

He must have said the right thing, for she smiled and took a chip from the basket. "What do you like to read?"

"Mysteries, mostly. I like psychological thrillers, a little bit of sci-fi." Beer bottle in hand, he leaned back in his chair. "I'll bet you like romances."

"Guilty." She broke her chip and ate half of it. "But I also like mysteries, too. I want a satisfying ending, no matter what I read."

He could add "romantic" to the list of words he'd use to describe Julia. He already had "beautiful" and "charming" and "sexy" on that list.

Stephen saw Dolly walking toward them, carrying a large tray. "Hey, boss lady, you playing waitress?"

"Only for y'all." She set three platters of food on the table, then rested the tray on her hip. "I had to be sure you're taking care of Julia."

"I'm being a perfect gentleman."

She switched her gaze to Julia. "Is he?"

"He is," Julia said with a smile.

"Good." She pointed one finger at Stephen. "Be sure it stays that way."

He gave her a sharp salute. "Yes, ma'am."

Once Dolly left, Stephen picked up one of the bowls of salsa and poured it over his Spanish rice. He forked up a big bite, along with the refried beans. The mixture of heat and spices slid over his tongue and he almost moaned in pleasure.

He ate in silence with Julia for a few moments before speaking again. "So what're your plans for tomorrow?"

Before she said anything, he heard *beep-beep* from the pager on his belt. A grass fire. Part of him cringed at the possible loss while part of him savored the quick adrenaline rush at the thought of being in the middle of the action and danger.

He gobbled the last two bites of his supper. "I gotta go."

"Go? What—"

"There's a grass fire somewhere." He glanced at Dusty's untouched plate. He hated that his cousin didn't get to eat, but knew Hannah would take care of him. He also hated leaving Julia when they'd been getting along so well.

Knowing the fire wouldn't wait, he pushed back his chair and stood. He dug two tens and a five from the front pocket of his jeans and tossed them on the table next to his platter. "Catch you later." He rushed toward the exit, along with the four other guys who also belonged to the fire department.

* * *

Julia turned in her chair and watched the men leave Boot Scootin'. Apparently most of the ones here tonight belonged to the volunteer fire department. She remembered many times when she'd dropped everything in a second and hurried out to fight a forest fire. Even worse, hurrying out to fight a house fire and hopefully save some of the family's mementoes that could never be replaced.

Worry formed a knot in her stomach. Stephen said it was a grass fire, but those could get out of control so quickly.

"Gets quiet when the guys leave," Dolly said as she touched Julia's shoulder.

"Stephen said it's a grass fire."

"Doesn't surprise me. We're in a bad drought and the smallest spark can set off a blaze. Course, you already know that."

"Yeah." She pushed her half-full plate to the side, next to Dusty's pile of paperwork. "Dusty left all his stuff."

"I'll call his wife and let her know. She'll come by and get it." Dolly picked up the untouched platter. "I'll fix this to go, plus a plate for her. She runs the office for Dusty's and Stephen's company, but also works part-time at the hospital. She gets off at seven on Thursdays." She touched the side of Julia's plate. "Want that to go? It makes a great midnight snack."

"I'll come with you and take care of it."

Julia followed Dolly to the kitchen. She nodded to Dolly's helper, Rosa, who she'd met when she first arrived at Boot Scootin'. To Julia, Rosa looked like a Mexican version of Alice from the old sitcom, *The Brady Bunch*.

Dolly handed Julia a Styrofoam container for her food, then gave Dusty's platter to Rosa. "Make this to go and fix another container the same way. Hannah McGettis will pick them up on her way home from work."

"Chips and salsa, too?" Rosa asked in her lovely accent.

"Yes. Double on the salsa. Hannah really likes it." Dolly

turned to Julia. "She's expecting her and Dusty's first child in two months. Once her morning sickness phase ended, she started craving hot and spicy."

"I crave hot and spicy, too, but I can't blame that on pregnancy."

Dolly laughed out loud. "Well, then, you'll be happy to know there are chips in my pantry and salsa in the fridge."

"Great." She closed the lid to her container. "Thank you for the delicious meal."

"You heading out?"

Julia nodded. "I'm a little tired. I think I'm still recuperating from the long drive."

"I'm sure you are." Dolly gave her a quick hug. "Go home and relax. I'll see you in the morning."

Two couples entered as she left the bar. The dark-haired men looked so much alike, they had to be brothers. One dipped his head in greeting while he held the door open for her. The other man and the two women smiled at her.

One thing Julia could say about the people in Lanville—everyone had been incredibly friendly to her.

Once inside her car, she draped her arms over the steering wheel while trying to decide what to do with the rest of her evening. She hadn't lied to Dolly about being tired, but it wasn't the kind of tired where she'd fall asleep if she went to bed early. She felt . . . restless, edgy, as if she needed to do something but had no idea what.

Julia started her car, backed out of her parking space. More vehicles entered the lot while she made her way to the exit. It appeared what had started out as a slow night at Boot Scootin' would soon turn livelier.

Meeting a lot of people might jerk her out of her restlessness, but Julia didn't have the energy to smile and make small talk tonight. She simply wanted to be alone.

She entered Dolly's house through the back door into the

kitchen. After putting her container of food in the refrigerator, she wandered into the living room. The sun would set soon, so she turned on a couple of lamps to fight off dusk's gloom.

In no mood to watch television, she went to her bedroom to retrieve the book she'd started reading last night. After helping herself to a glass of white wine from the kitchen, she returned to the living room and curled up in a corner of the couch.

No more than ten minutes passed when she saw the flash of headlights through one of the windows. How odd. Dolly told her the bar closed at two a.m., so she usually didn't get home until almost three-thirty. She shouldn't be home for hours yet.

Deciding Dolly must have forgotten something and came home to get it, Julia turned her attention back to her book. A moment later, footsteps crossed the wooden porch, then the doorbell rang.

A shiver of fear galloped up and down her spine. Dolly lived in the country on land surrounded by trees. Julia had no idea how close a neighbor lived, or how quickly she could get help if she needed it.

Laying her book on the end table, Julia rose and walked to the front door. No peep hole. Dolly might trust everyone in Lanville, but Julia didn't know the people here well enough to do that. She leaned close to where the door met the frame. "Who is it?"

"Hey, Julia, it's Stephen."

As quickly as the fear formed, it disappeared. She flipped the deadbolt and opened the door. "Hi."

"Hi," he said with a smile. "Am I disturbing you?"

"No, I was just reading. Is the fire out already?"

Stephen nodded. "It wasn't very big. Someone was burning brush on his property and it got out of hand, but we caught it before it spread too much."

She opened the door wider. "Come in."

"I can't. I smell like smoke."

His comment came right before a breeze brought the scent of smoke to her from his clothing. The smell threw her back to her job in California and the many fires she'd helped fight. "I don't mind."

He glanced past her in the direction of the end table. "Tell you what. How about you bring your wineglass and one for me out here on the porch? Then I won't stink up Dolly's house."

She liked that idea a lot. "Sure. I'll be right out."

Julia hurried into the kitchen, poured a second glass of Riesling, and returned to the living room. She paused before stepping over the threshold onto the porch and took a moment to admire Stephen from the back. He stood with his legs braced apart, looking out into the night. She couldn't see his hands, so she decided he must have them in the front pockets of his jeans. Or perhaps with his thumbs hooked over the pockets. Whatever he did made the worn denim tighten over his ass.

The man had a first-class booty.

Giving her head a shake to chase away the sexy thought, she stepped behind him. "Here's your wine."

He faced her, accepted the glass she held out to him. "Thanks."

Once she had a free hand, she closed the front door. It threw them into darkness, except for the bit of light shining through the windows. Julia led the way to the two chairs and small table at the edge of the porch. Unsure what to say since she didn't know why he'd come to see her, she chose a neutral subject. "Dolly packaged Dusty's dinner and called his wife to pick it up."

"Good. I hated the thought of him missing out on Dolly's enchiladas. He loves them."

"I saw a Mexican restaurant on the main road through town when I went exploring today, but didn't see any cars. Is it closed?"

"Only on Thursdays. Several of the restaurant owners got

together and decided on their operating hours so they wouldn't all be closed on the same days. It's not good for tourist business if someone can't find anything to eat. Course the fast-food places are open seven days a week, but sometimes people want something other than fast food."

"True." Julia sipped her wine. "Is the Mexican restaurant good?"

"Very. I haven't eaten anywhere in town where the food isn't good. O'Sullivan's looks like an English pub and serves great fish and chips. It's a block off the square. Mona's Place is a family-style restaurant with a different plate-lunch special every day. The Purple Onion serves incredible hamburgers. It's right off the square, too. And you haven't lived until you've eaten barbecued brisket from Bunkhouse."

It all sounded wonderful, even though she'd eaten a short while ago. "You're making me hungry."

"Sorry." He swirled the wine in his glass before taking a drink. "Speaking of eating, that's the reason I'm here. Will you have dinner with me tomorrow?"

Julia didn't speak right away since she didn't know how to answer his question. She liked Stephen, yet had no desire to get involved with anyone.

One date didn't mean involvement. Stephen would be a lot of fun on a date. She had no doubt about that. "I'd like that," she said softly.

Her eyes had adjusted to the dimness so she could see him smile. "Great. Café Crystal is the nicest place in town. I'd like to take you there."

"I don't need the nicest place in town, Stephen. I don't have expensive tastes. One of those other restaurants you mentioned would be fine."

"Hey, let a guy impress you on the first date, okay?"

She thought it sweet that he wanted to impress her. "Okay."

"I'll make reservations for . . . six? Six-thirty?"

"Six-thirty is good."

A cool breeze whipped over them. Now that the sun had set, the temperature began to steadily drop. Julia was about to excuse herself to go and get her sweater when Stephen spoke again.

"My shower is calling me to get rid of this smoky smell." He drained his glass and set it on the table between them. "I'll pick you up a little after six."

"Okay."

She started to rise when he did, but remained in her chair when he motioned for her to do so. "Enjoy your wine. I'll see you tomorrow."

She watched him walk across the porch and down the first two steps. He stopped on the third one, turned, and came back to her. Placing his hands on the arms of her chair, he leaned over and pressed his lips to hers.

His soft, warm lips moved slowly over hers, tempting, enticing. Her heart sped up, her breath hitched. She caught the scent of smoke on his skin, mixed with his masculine aroma. The flavor of the wine he'd drunk lingered on his mouth.

Julia gripped her wineglass to keep from reaching for him. He didn't deepen the kiss, but he didn't have to. The gentle kiss sent pleasure zipping up and down her spine.

Stephen lifted his head so their lips no longer touched, but still close enough for her to stare into his eyes. She couldn't clearly see the emotion in them due to the dim light, but the sound of his increased breathing proved he had enjoyed their kiss as much as she.

"Oh, yeah," he said, his voice husky. "Definitely singed." He ran his thumb across her chin. "See you tomorrow."

Singed? She didn't understand what he meant by that. Turning in her chair, she watched him walk to his pickup and drive away. She lightly touched her lips with her fingertips. She didn't think a simple kiss had ever affected her so strongly. If they ever made love, she would probably self-combust.

Her heart may not be ready for a relationship, but apparently her hormones had other ideas.

4

Stephen checked once more to be sure his shirt was tucked into his pants before he pressed the doorbell. He fought the urge to run his hands through his hair. He didn't want to muss it since he'd taken a lot longer with it tonight than he usually did. Normal for him meant washing it and letting it dry however it wanted to. Tonight he'd used a hair dryer and brush to tame the natural waves.

Normal also meant not bothering to shave but once or twice a week. He'd made sure to shave tonight, wanting his face to be smooth for Julia. If he kissed her after dinner—which he hoped to do, more than once—he didn't want to leave whisker burns on her skin.

Two seconds before he rang the doorbell again, the front door opened. Stephen caught himself before his mouth dropped open. A vision from a dream stood before him. Julia wore a sleeveless white dress with splashes of purple, blue, and green in it. The V-neck gave him a hint of cleavage. The skirt hit right below her knees, letting him admire her tanned and shapely calves. Her white shoes consisted of little more than a strap across the top of her foot and around her ankle.

"Wow," he breathed.

Delight filled her eyes, a tinge of pink colored her cheeks. "Thank you. I could say the same thing about you."

He dipped his head to acknowledge her compliment. "Think we'll be the best looking couple at Café Crystal tonight?" he gently teased.

She smiled, which made her look even lovelier. "I'd be willing to bet I'll have the most handsome escort."

"You'd better stop with the compliments or my head won't fit through the doorway."

Her musical laugh made him grin. "Okay, no more compliments." She moved away from the door, returning a moment later with a small white purse hung over her shoulder and a silky-looking white wrap draped over her forearm. "I'm ready."

Stephen waited while she closed and locked the door, then placed his hand on the small of her back to lead her toward his car. They'd taken no more than a few steps when she suddenly stopped.

"What's wrong?" he asked.

"You have a Mustang Fastback?" she asked with awe in her voice.

It pleased him that she recognized the model. "I do."

She hurried over to the hood of the car. "V8 289?"

"V8 302."

"What year?"

"Sixty-five."

She slowly ran her hand over the smooth, black surface, similar to the way a woman would touch her lover's skin. Stephen swallowed at the mental image of her stroking him instead of the car. "How do you know the model?"

"My best friend's brother had one, only it was a 289 engine. It sat in the garage more than he drove it. There was always something wrong with it. I think he tinkered more than repaired." Still touching the car, she looked at him. "All original?"

"Most of it. It took Dusty and me months to get the necessary parts because I wanted as much of it original as possible. The carpet isn't original, but it still has the AM radio. And it works." He walked over to her, leaned against the side of the Mustang. "Then he bought a fifty-seven T-Bird in February for us to repair. Our roofing business keeps us busy, but we hope to have the car finished by the end of summer."

"Will it be black, too?"

"Nope. Candy-apple red. Dusty has a thing for red cars." He leaned closer to her and lowered his voice. "Want to drive it?"

She bit her bottom lip, but he could still see her grin as she nodded.

"Can you drive a stick shift?"

"Yes."

He dug the keys out of his pocket, dangled them in front of her. "Then let's go."

With a squeal of delight, she grabbed the keys and hurried to the driver's side door. Chuckling, Stephen rounded the car to the passenger side and settled into the seat. He'd suspected his date with Julia would be fun, but he had the feeling it would far surpass his expectations.

The inside of Stephen's car smelled like leather mixed with the clean scent of the woodsy soap he must use. She hadn't noticed the scent on the way to the restaurant because she'd been so excited to drive the classic muscle car. Now, in the dark and quiet, the combination of masculine smells made desire curl in her stomach.

Julia didn't think more than five minutes passed the entire evening without her smiling. She couldn't remember ever enjoying a date more. There hadn't been any of those dreaded dead moments of a first date when she had no idea what to say.

Conversation had flowed easily and steadily between them, almost as if they'd known each other for years instead of only a couple of days.

She looked down at the Styrofoam container sitting on her lap. She'd had to try the bread pudding drizzled with caramel sauce, but hadn't been able to eat more than a bite after the amazing dinner of honey citrus pork chops. Stephen had polished off all of his turtle cheesecake despite the huge slice of prime rib he'd eaten and teased her about stealing her bread pudding. She'd teased right back that he wasn't getting one bite of her dessert.

She wondered if she should invite him in for coffee and to share the rest of her dessert. If she did that, they could easily end up in her bed. After the kiss he'd given her last night, she had no doubt he wanted her. Plus, she saw awareness in his eyes every time he looked at her.

She'd never slept with a man after one date . . . not only because of morals, but because it usually took her a few dates to get to know a guy before she wanted that special closeness with him. With Stephen, she'd felt that closeness almost from the moment she'd seen him at Burger King two days ago.

"Did you enjoy your meal?" he asked.

"Very much. The food was amazing."

He glanced at the container on her lap. "Still hoarding your bread pudding, I see."

The dim light from the dash let her see his lips quirk. His teasing helped her make the decision about whether or not to continue their date inside Dolly's house. "Actually, I was thinking of sharing it with you. Are you interested?"

"With or without coffee?"

"With, of course."

"Deal."

He pulled into the driveway and parked to the side of the garage. By the time Julia gathered her purse from the floorboard, he'd opened her door and held out his hand to help her from the car.

Everything about Stephen screamed gentleman. She couldn't help wondering why he wasn't married or involved with anyone. The ladies of Lanville had to be nuts not to go after this guy. Either that, or he had something wrong with him that she hadn't discovered yet.

He walked by her side to the porch. She'd left one lamp burning in the living room, so the muted light greeted them when she unlocked the door. "Sit down and I'll start the coffee."

"I'll help you."

Since they'd been so easy with each other all evening, Julia decided to continue to tease him as she led the way to the kitchen. "You're following me because you're afraid I'll eat the pudding before you get any."

"You got it."

"I can't believe you don't trust me."

"Not when it comes to sharing your dessert. You could change your mind while making the coffee."

"I could." She motioned toward the round table. "Go ahead and sit down. I promise I won't change my mind about sharing."

Julia started the coffee brewing, then transferred the pudding to a small plate for warming in the microwave. By the time she set the plate on the table, along with two forks and napkins, the scent of fresh coffee filled the air.

"Black, right?" she asked as she poured the hot brew into two mugs.

"Right."

She carried the mugs to the table and took the chair opposite Stephen. She noticed he hadn't picked up his fork yet. He could've snitched a bite of bread pudding while she poured the coffee, but didn't.

Her admiration for him rose another notch.

She tore off a small bite with her fork, which must have

given him permission to do the same. Picking up his fork, he cut into the fluffy treat. "Wow, that's good," he said after chewing the bite.

"Better than the turtle cheesecake?"

"Different than the turtle cheesecake." He took another bite, licked the caramel sauce from the fork. Seeing his tongue swirl over the tines sent a jolt directly to her clit. She imagined his tongue licking her feminine folds instead of the fork. . . .

Giving herself a mental shake, Julia sipped her coffee. She hadn't loved Cole, but she'd cared deeply for him and still missed him. He'd been an incredible lover and she missed sex a lot. Despite what her body craved, she couldn't see herself becoming involved with another man so quickly.

A night in bed didn't mean a relationship.

But it did. Sex had always meant caring about the man she chose to share her bed, not simply a way to satisfy her body's temporary needs.

"You okay?" Stephen asked after eating the last crumb of bread pudding. "You're quiet."

She gazed into his eyes. Her heart flipped over in her chest. Looking at Stephen gave her a great deal of pleasure because of his handsome face and hunky body, yet the attraction she felt also had a lot to do with Stephen, the man—the charming, courteous, quick-witted man.

His beard stubble and long mane of hair had given her the impression of him as a bad boy when she first saw him. She wouldn't call him that now. He held a steady job, worked on the volunteer fire department. Everyone she'd met so far who knew Stephen had nothing but good things to say about him.

He'd shaved the stubble, letting her see the small cleft in the center of his chin. She couldn't help but be attracted to him, yet didn't know whether or not to act on that attraction.

She smiled to reassure him. "Sorry. I let my mind wander."

"Someplace good, I hope."

She thought again of his tongue between her thighs. "Yes, someplace very good."

His eyes narrowed a bit, making her wonder if he guessed her naughty thoughts. "Tell me about it. I like good places, too."

"Would you like more coffee?" she asked, hoping to divert him to another subject.

His eyes narrowed even more. "Why do I get the feeling you don't want to tell me what you were thinking?"

"You're way too suspicious, do you know that?"

"Not suspicious, just curious." He propped his folded arms on the table and leaned forward. "So share with me. Especially if it was something dirty."

He bobbed his eyebrows, which made Julia laugh. She had the feeling that's exactly what he wanted her to do. "Sorry, no dirty thoughts."

"Damn. You just burst my bubble."

"I'm pretty sure you'll survive."

He gave her a devilish grin before leaning back in his chair. His relaxed position made his shoulders look even broader. "You kept steering the conversation back to me over dinner. It's your turn to tell me all about you."

"I thought guys like to talk about themselves."

"I get tired of talking about myself. I want to know more about you."

Julia glanced at his empty coffee mug. "If I'm going to bore you with my life story, you'll need something stronger than coffee."

"I won't be bored, and I'll drink whatever you're having."

Deciding Merlot would be appropriate for soul-baring, Julia carried their dishes to the sink and removed two wineglasses from the cabinet. Stephen appeared beside her as she removed the corkscrew from one of the drawers.

"I'll open it for you."

Accepting his offer, she handed the corkscrew to him before

choosing a bottle from the wine rack at the corner of the counter. He looked at the label first, then proceeded to remove the cork from the bottle. She watched his hands as he did so, noting his sure, efficient movement.

He'd be an incredible lover.

Julia held the glasses while Stephen filled them half full. After she handed one glass to him, he took her hand. "I vote for getting comfortable."

He led her from the kitchen to the living room. Julia curled up in a corner of the couch. Stephen sat and turned toward her, one leg resting on the couch. The lamp behind her cast a golden light across his face. The inside of a person mattered more than the outside, but Julia had to admit she liked Stephen's outside very much.

"Why the Forest Service?" he asked after taking a sip of wine.

"I love the outdoors. I'd rather be outside than inside. Working for the Forest Service gave me that opportunity." She tilted her head. "Why a roofing company?"

"Nuh-uh," he said, waving one forefinger back and forth. "We're talking about you now. Tell me about where you worked."

"I worked out of the Eldorado office in Placerville. That's about fifty miles east of Sacramento on Highway 50. It was a gorgeous area to work with lots of pine trees and rolling hills. I loved it."

"What did you do?"

"I worked in the fire and fuels program. I studied how fire behavior affects fuel types and conditions." She shrugged one shoulder. "Probably sounds boring."

"Not at all. I want to know more."

Julia doubted if he wanted a blow-by-blow account of what she'd done daily, so veered off in another direction. "My boss was a woman, but I worked with mostly men. They were a great bunch of guys."

"If you liked your job and your coworkers, why did you leave?"

Telling him about Cole and the accident would put a huge damper on an evening she'd enjoyed very much. She didn't want anything to destroy her and Stephen's date. "Several reasons that added up to needing a change."

An emotion flashed through his eyes, but it disappeared so quickly she couldn't put a name to it. "No problem. I understand." He swirled the wine in his glass, took a healthy sip. "So tell me something crazy you've done."

Laughter bubbled past her lips before she could stop it. She appreciated the change of subject, but hadn't expected him to say anything like that. "What?"

"Everyone has done something crazy, something they wish they hadn't done. I know you have, too." He stretched his arm along the back of the couch, his fingers barely an inch from her shoulder. "Tell me about it."

Julia sipped her wine while she thought back over some of the things she'd done that she probably shouldn't have. Several things popped into her mind, but one stood out among all the others.

"Okay, I'll tell you, but remember it was for a good cause, so you can't laugh."

"I won't crack a smile," he said, his tone serious, but his eyes twinkling with humor.

A little unsure whether she should tell Stephen something so personal or not, she took another sip of wine for courage. "I . . . posed for a calendar."

Stephen blinked. "Excuse me?"

"It was a fund-raiser for a wing of one of the local hospitals. A bunch of the gals in the Forest Service posed for a calendar three years ago."

"How did you pose?"

"In a pair of really short denim cutoffs and a pink tank top." She stopped and cleared her throat. "A *wet* pink tank top."

She saw his throat work as he swallowed. "Bra or no bra?"

"No undies at all."

He released a low whistle. His gaze briefly dipped to her breasts. "Do you still have any of those calendars?"

"I kept three or four, but they're in storage at my mom's."

"Damn," he muttered.

He sounded so disappointed, she couldn't help but laugh. "Sorry. I guess I shouldn't have told you without being able to show you."

"You can model your outfit for me any time."

He sounded like a little boy asking for a puppy for Christmas. Julia struggled not to laugh again. "You're much too eager."

"Well, you can't blame a guy for trying." He took another sip of his wine. "I guess since you told me a secret, I should tell you one, too."

"I love secrets."

"Do you have a computer?"

His question threw her for a moment. She didn't understand what a computer had to do with telling her a secret. "I have a laptop in my room."

"Great." He set his wineglass on the coffee table, took her hand, and tugged her up from the couch. "I want to show you something online."

Julia set down her glass, then led the way to her bedroom. She stopped by the small desk beneath the window, turned on the lamp, and gestured to her laptop. "Go for it."

"Are you connected to the Internet?"

"Yes, Dolly has wireless."

She stood behind his left shoulder and watched as Stephen opened the computer, started the browser, and keyed in an address. A Web site for something called *Hot Shots* popped up.

"What is *Hot Shots*?"

"It's a magazine published by Maysen Halliday. She's the girlfriend of our fire chief, Clay Spencer. Maysen came here last month to do an article about the fire department. She fell in love with our town, and with Clay." He looked at her over his shoulder and grinned wickedly. "We were voted the sexiest firefighters in Texas by the magazine's readers."

She'd met few of the firefighters so far, but the ones she'd seen in Boot Scootin' last night would definitely qualify for the sexiest something.

Stephen added more letters to the URL address. "She came up with the idea of putting together a calendar as a fund-raiser to help us buy our new tanker truck. It's supposed to come out in September."

A page full of thumbnails appeared when Stephen pressed the return key. "She put all the pictures on a hidden page on her Web site so we can see them." He scrolled down the page, by-passing several photos of hunky men . . . some in full firefighter gear, some in only pants, some alone, some in groups. She got a glimpse of a few pictures of females before he stopped scrolling. "Here it is."

He double clicked on the picture. Stephen's face filled the screen. Julia caught herself before she moaned at how sexy he looked. Several days of stubble covered his lower face; his mussed hair looked as if he'd run his hands through it several times before someone snapped the picture. He gazed directly into the camera lens with an I'm-ready-to-ignite-your-hormones expression.

Very appropriate for a firefighter.

Stephen pressed the tab key. In the next photo, he stood with three other men next to a fire truck. They wore pants, but no shirts. Stephen casually held an ax on one shoulder, which made his biceps bulge. He had tribal-band tattoos on both biceps. His pants rode low on his hips, letting her see he had no hair on his chest, but did have an impressive set of abs and an enticing happy trail of dark hair that ran down from his navel.

The next picture showed Stephen in the foreground with other firefighters in the background while they battled a brush fire. He tabbed through several more pictures, until he reached one of another man.

"That's it for me. I'll leave this page open if you want to look at some of the other pictures later."

She would definitely look at the pictures of Stephen again . . . over and over and over.

He turned in the chair, braced his arm along the back. "So we have something in common. We've both posed for calendars." His gaze once again briefly passed over her breasts. "Although I'm sure your picture is much sexier."

"I don't know. The picture of you shirtless with that ax on your shoulder is pretty sexy."

A slow grin turned up his lips. "Yeah?"

Julia nodded. "Definitely."

His grin slowly faded, as did the playfulness in his eyes. "I'm glad you think so," he said softly.

He continued to stare into her eyes, making her tummy flutter. When several seconds of silence passed, Julia broke it with a simple question. "Is something wrong?"

Stephen shook his head. "I'm thinking about how much I want to kiss you."

He hooked one forefinger beneath her chin and gently urged her to bend closer. She did, until her lips brushed his.

5

Her lips tasted of Merlot, with a hint of caramel mixed with the unique flavor of Julia. Stephen didn't deepen the kiss or use his tongue. He kissed her softly, gently, touching her with only his lips and fingertip.

Since discovering how nice sex could be shortly after he turned sixteen, he'd indulged whenever possible and probably fucked more than his share of women in the last eleven years.

He'd never wanted any of them with the fierceness that he wanted Julia.

With his lips still pressed to hers, Stephen slowly stood. Julia gripped his shoulders, tilted her head to the side. He took that as a silent request for him to deepen their connection. He slipped his arms around her waist, splayed his hands over her back. The tip of his tongue slid over the seam of her lips. They parted, blessing him with an intimate taste of her.

The tiny taste made him crave more.

He dropped kisses on her cheek, her jaw, beneath her ear. "I want you, Julia."

Instead of responding with words, she kissed him. Her lips

were so soft, so satiny, so warm. Desire galloped through his veins. All the blood in his body headed to his dick, filling it in only moments.

Stephen wanted her naked and beneath him as soon as possible, but his first time making love with Julia should be special. Taking her hand, he led her the few steps to the bed. Pushing gently on her shoulders, he silently asked her to sit on the edge of the bed. He dropped to one knee before her and slipped off her high-heeled sandals.

Before he could rise again, she leaned over and kissed him.

A groan formed in his throat. She ran her hands into his hair, held his head while she took control of their kiss. Her tongue swiped across his lips before darting into his mouth. Their tongues met, danced together, before she withdrew. Tilting her head the other direction, she gave him another kiss that caused him to stop thinking and simply absorb all the sensations of their mouths touching.

Stephen laid his hands on her thighs on top of her dress. He longed to feel the bare skin of her legs, yet knew if he touched them he wouldn't stop until he stripped her naked.

"Make love to me, Stephen," she whispered against his lips.

Her husky plea traveled straight to his cock, making it surge in his briefs. How easy it would be to unfasten her dress so he could get to her flesh with his hands and mouth. If he did that, going slow would be impossible. Pleasing Julia meant everything to him. He wanted her to be so sated, she wouldn't be able to move even a finger for the rest of the night.

He clasped her wrists, tugged her hands out of his hair. "Do you have any idea how much I want to be inside you?"

Her eyes burned with desire. "I want that, too."

He kissed each of her palms. "Let me give you pleasure first."

A soft whimper flowed past her lips. "Only if I can do the same for you."

Stephen thought of her hands coasting over his body, followed by her lips. Pushing the erotic images from his brain, he released her hands and stood. "Lie down."

Once she did as he said, Stephen toed off his shoes and reclined beside her. Julia wrapped her arms around his neck and pulled him back to her for another kiss. Stephen slid one leg between both of hers. His action caused her dress to slide upward, giving him a clear path to glide his hand up her smooth leg to mid-thigh. He wanted to keep going, to touch the warm, silky place between her thighs, but ignored his desire to concentrate on hers.

Although from the way she tugged at the back of his shirt, he could change his mind in a hurry.

"Off, please." She nipped the side of his neck. "I want to touch you."

Stephen had to taste her mouth once more before he moved away from her. Rising to his knees, he began unbuttoning his shirt. Julia propped up on one elbow. As he loosened each button, her hand followed his path. When he released the last button, she spread the lapels wide and watched her hand as it traveled over his chest. He hissed when her fingertips skated over his nipple.

"Do you like that?" she asked, caressing his nipple again.

"Yeah." His voice came out sounding rough, guttural. He swallowed.

Her fingers drifted to his stomach, circled his navel twice before venturing along his fly. Stephen spread his knees farther apart so she could touch him however she wanted to. Her fingertips outlined his cock, grazed his tight balls. When she made the journey a second time, he grabbed her wrist to stop her.

"Time for you to take off something."

She gave his balls one more gentle squeeze before she rose to her knees in front of him. Looking him in the eyes, she unfastened the button at her waist. The left side of her dress fell away from her body. Stephen clenched his fists at his sides to keep from helping her. She released a second button on the other side of her waist, letting the right side part to expose the center of her body. Instead of letting the dress slide away, she pushed off his shirt. It fell to the bed behind him.

"You didn't specify what I should remove."

"No, I didn't." Stephen pushed back the sides of her dress so he could see more of her. A lacy bra a shade lighter than her skin barely held her lush breasts. Panties in the same shade rode high on her hips and skimmed her stomach beneath her navel. He laid his hands on her waist, ran them up and down her sides. "Take off your dress."

She held his gaze as she followed his order. She now wore nothing but the sexy bits of lingerie. Although beautiful, it had to go, too. He motioned toward her breasts. "Bra off, too."

She obeyed him without hesitation. Her bra joined her dress on the bed.

"Damn," he breathed.

Large, round, with big pink nipples made for him to suck. Stephen's mouth watered with the need to do exactly that. Unable to resist the lure of her succulent flesh, he cradled both breasts in his palms. Julia inhaled sharply. Her eyes slid closed, her head fell back.

"Do you like this?" he asked as he kneaded her breasts.

"Yesssss."

Stephen lifted both her breasts, leaned over, and pulled one nipple between his lips. Julia arched her back and moaned softly. That sound of pleasure urged him to suckle harder. He moved from one tip to the other, treating each to his tongue, his teeth, his lips.

Julia buried her hands in his hair again. "That feels so good, Stephen. More."

Only too happy to do as she requested, Stephen alternated between sucking on her nipples and licking around the pebbled areolae. The sucking and slurping sounds he made, along with his and Julia's heavy breathing, filled the room. She gripped his hair in both fists, apparently unwilling to let him stop his worship of her breasts.

He had no intention of stopping something he enjoyed so much.

Julia's breathing became more erratic, choppy. Her hold on his hair became almost painful, but Stephen accepted the discomfort and suckled harder. Suddenly she gasped. Her body trembled before she sagged against him. He had the feeling she would've melted to the bed if he hadn't slipped an arm around her waist to hold her upright. Surely she hadn't . . .

"Did you come?" he asked.

"Mmm, yes." She lifted her head from his shoulder, gave him a sleepy-eyed smile. "My breasts are very sensitive."

His cock jerked at her declaration. He loved a woman's breasts. Knowing Julia could come from his sucking made him even more eager to spend a lot of time paying attention to them. He squeezed the firm globes while rasping his thumbs over the tips. "So what other ways can you come?"

Her smile turned mischievous. "Maybe you'll have to experiment and find out. But first . . ." She unfastened his belt. "I need to do some exploring."

He didn't stop her before she unbuttoned his pants, but did catch her hands before she lowered the zipper. Her bottom lip stuck out in a pout. "Why did you stop me?"

"Because if you touch my cock, it'll go off in your hand."

Her smile returned, even more mischievous and wicked. "Maybe I'd like that."

"I'm not nearly done playing with you yet." He reluctantly released her breasts. "Lie down again."

"Only if you take off your clothes. *All* of them."

If his lady wanted him naked, he'd get that way in a hurry. Climbing off the bed, he finished unfastening his pants and let them fall to his feet. Julia lay back as he tugged them over his feet, along with his socks. Clad in only his briefs, he dug the two condoms from his pants pocket that he'd brought in hopes he'd need them. After placing them on the nightstand, he removed the last item covering his body.

Julia's soft moan proved she liked what she saw.

Stephen wrapped his hand around his dick and gave it a couple of slow pumps. Julia's lips parted as her gaze snapped to his hand. She shifted her hips on the bed, as if her pussy felt empty and desperately needed something to fill it.

He had the perfect "something" in his hand.

"Take off your panties."

Julia lifted her ass, slid the panties past her hips, her thighs, and down her legs. She tossed them to the floor. Stephen's gaze wandered to the blond tuft of hair covering her mound. She didn't shave or wax her pussy. He liked that. He enjoyed running his fingers through the soft hair on a woman's cunt.

He enjoyed running his tongue along her slit even more.

Stephen climbed on the bed and crawled to Julia on his hands and knees. He straddled her body, stared down at the perfection beneath him. He couldn't clearly see her eyes in the dim light from the desk's lamp, but he could hear her heavier breathing, feel the touch of her hands on his arms, smell the flowery cologne she wore. "You're beautiful, Julia," he said, looking into her eyes.

He lowered his head so he could kiss her. The bite of her fingernails into his shoulders caused his cock to surge and his balls to draw up closer to his groin. Every hormone in his body screamed at him to take her.

Ignoring his own body's needs, Stephen concentrated on Julia's pleasure. He kissed her again, then began the leisurely journey down her body. He nibbled the pounding pulse in her neck, stroked his tongue across her collarbone. He dropped kisses down the center of her chest until he came to her breasts. Each nipple received a swipe with his tongue, a long suckle with his lips.

Julia arched her back, gripped his shoulders tighter. Those two actions, plus the way she writhed on the bed, gave him the encouragement to continue. More kisses fell on her soft skin as he moved farther down her body. He circled her navel with the tip of his tongue, gave her one long lick from the small indentation to the top of her pubic hair.

"Stephen," she rasped in a husky tone.

He lifted his eyes so he could see her face, but didn't stop licking or kissing her. This close to her pussy, he could smell the musky scent of her desire. He nipped the top of each thigh. "What?"

"I need you inside me."

His dick liked that idea, but he knew he'd come way too quickly if he entered her now. "In a little bit."

"No, *now*."

Ah, a tigress lurked inside his lady. He liked that, too. Gently, he pushed on the inside of her thighs until she spread her legs wider apart. "I think you need to come again first."

Although Julia left the natural bush on her mound, Stephen discovered smooth, hairless skin below her clit. He caressed the swollen labia and wet folds with his thumb, causing Julia to moan loudly.

Needing to be closer to that pretty pussy, Stephen stretched out on his stomach and placed her legs on his shoulders. They fell farther apart, giving him a better whiff of the delicious aroma of her cunt.

He had to taste her.

Spreading her labia with his thumbs, Stephen licked the entire length of her slit from anus to clit. Julia's body jerked and she moaned again. "Mmm, yes."

Her obvious pleasure along with his desire to taste her again spurred him to repeat his action. He gave her a few more long, slow swipes with his tongue before he settled in to feast.

Stephen decided he could easily become addicted to her sweet, salty taste. And her scent. And the sexy little sounds coming from her throat that she probably didn't realize she made.

Stephen concentrated on her clit while he pushed a finger into her channel. Her internal walls surrounded the digit in hot silk. He pressed up in search of her G-spot. Her sharp gasp signaled when he found it. Adding a second finger, he palpated the sensitive area while his tongue flashed over her clit again and again.

"God, Stephen, I'm going to come."

Oh, yeah, that's what he wanted. He wanted the walls of her pussy to clamp around his fingers as the pleasure flowed through her body. Mere seconds passed before she started to tremble. Stephen pushed his fingers as far into her as he could, and smiled to himself when he felt the pulsing deep inside.

Stephen gave her clit one more gentle lick before he rose to his knees. He kept his fingers in her pussy, wanting the intimate connection between them. Julia's chest heaved from her heavy breathing. Perspiration dotted her skin. He laid his other hand over her heart and felt it pounding. "You okay?" he asked.

"No." She opened her eyes barely a slit. "You killed me."

Her words stroked his ego. He loved that he'd made her come so strongly. "Does that mean you're through for the night?"

She lifted her head from the pillow, pointedly looked at his hard cock jutting out from his groin. "*You* obviously aren't done."

"No, but if you're too tired, I can just . . . you know."

Heat filled her eyes when her gaze met his again. "I think I'd like watching you . . . you know."

"Would you?" he asked, his voice low and gravelly. The thought of her watching him get himself off sent a fresh wave of desire through his veins.

"Yes." Rising to one elbow, she held out her hand to him. "But not now. Now, I want you inside me."

6

She tasted herself on his lips when she kissed him. Julia tugged on his hand until he reclined on the bed beside her. With a gentle push to his chest, he rolled to his back and she loomed over him. His body lay before her and she very much wanted to devour it.

The need to have his cock pounding into her pussy overwhelmed her. In two seconds, she could straddle his hips and take him inside her body where he should be. But Stephen had taken his time driving up her desire, so she wanted to do the same for him.

She kissed his mouth again as she slowly ran her hand over the smooth skin and firm muscles of his chest and stomach. She dipped down to caress his cock and balls, but then moved her hand back up his body. His hands also remained busy, one traveling up and down her back and ass, one cradling her breast and thumbing her nipple. Despite two shattering orgasms, each pass over the hard tip sent a zing to her clit.

Remembering how he'd reacted the first time she'd touched his nipple, Julia slid down until her mouth hovered over the small brown peak. Her movement caused him to release her breast and cradle her nape instead. He didn't guide her head, but held her neck while he caressed the sensitive spot behind her ear with his thumb.

Julia touched his nipple with the tip of her tongue. She heard his sharp intake of breath, felt him slowly exhale. She circled the peak several times, laved it with the flat of her tongue. "You're sensitive here, too."

"Yeah."

His voice came out as a choked whisper. Julia switched to his other nipple, giving it the same loving attention as the first. His hand tightened on her nape while he lifted his hips. He didn't say the words, but his actions told her he wanted her mouth on another part of his anatomy.

Stephen sucked in a quick breath when she wrapped her fingers around his cock, pulled it straight up, and squeezed. "You're big," she whispered. Her hand milked him once, twice. "And so hard." She inched farther down his body, blew on the weeping slit in the center of his crown before gathering the liquid with her tongue. Needing more of his essence, she squeezed his shaft again and lapped up the salty pre-cum that formed on the tip. "And you taste so good."

His hand tightened on her head. "*God,* Julia, you're killing me." He slipped his hands beneath her chin and gently pulled her mouth away from him. "I've got to get inside you."

"Not yet. I'm not through."

He barked out a laugh. "*I'll* be through if you keep doing what you're doing."

She licked all the way around the crown. "Are you telling me you're only good for once a night?"

His eyebrows lowered, his eyes narrowed in a scowl. "Hardly."

Julia pressed her lips together to keep from grinning. She'd hit him right in the ego. "Then let me play."

Frustration and lust crossed his face. Julia had a feeling the lust would win out. She made sure by licking around the crown again, then opening her mouth over it and sucking.

"Jesus!"

Stephen's hips jerked. His action pushed half of his shaft into her mouth. Relaxing her throat, Julia took as much of him as she could before moving her lips back to the head. She thoroughly laved the tip, the sensitive area beneath it, and ran her tongue down the heavy veins. By the time she'd licked over every part of his balls, Stephen's breathing sounded as if he'd just completed a marathon.

He touched the top of her head. "Let me inside you. Please."

Julia slithered back up his body, making sure to rub her breasts across his chest while she kissed him. Stephen gripped her butt, ground his cock against her mound.

"Now," he growled. "Ride me now."

Julia reached over to the nightstand, grabbed one of the condom packets. She sat on his thighs while she opened it and slid the latex down his hard length. Holding the base, she raised her hips, then slowly impaled herself.

She didn't know who moaned louder—her or Stephen. Julia closed her eyes and leaned her head back to better savor the sensation of fullness. She dug her fingers into his abs, clenched her internal muscles to grip his cock. Stephen arched his hips, driving his shaft even farther inside her.

"Mmmm." Opening her eyes, she looked into his heat-filled ones. "Feels good."

"Yeah."

She loved the guttural sound of his voice, a sure sign that he felt desire as strongly as she. Bracing her hands on his firm chest, she lifted her hips until his cock almost slipped out of her, then lowered them again.

"That's the way, darlin'," he murmured. "Ride me."

The sweet endearment pleased her, even though she had no

idea if Stephen knew he'd used it. With his help in guiding her, Julia soon established a rhythm with him. She moved slowly at first, but picked up speed as her lust grew stronger. Stephen clasped her hips firmer, pumped into her faster. The aroma of sex strengthened with every thrust.

Stephen released one of her hips, slid his thumb between her legs to caress her clit. "Come for me again."

The extra stimulation to her clit along with his sexy command sent her over the edge. Julia grabbed her breasts as every nerve in her body caught fire. She bucked on Stephen's cock, milked it with the walls of her pussy as he kept fucking her.

"You are so hot," he said in the tone that turned more raspy with each word. "Yeah. *Yeah!*"

He looked gorgeous with his head thrown back and his muscles taut as pleasure swept through his body. Julia tried to remain upright, to keep watching him, but the third orgasm drained her. She wilted on top of him.

Their combined breathing sounded loud in the quiet room. Julia snuggled her head beneath his chin, wanting to be as close to him as possible. His softening shaft remained in her pussy.

Time passed while she tried to recuperate. Stephen caressed her hip, the only movement he made. She began to wonder if he would fall asleep when he kissed the top of her head.

"That was amazing," he whispered.

She smiled. "Yes, it was."

"I . . ."

He stopped. Julia lifted her head and looked into his eyes. "You what?"

"I don't know. My brain is scrambled." He pushed her hair back from her face. "How many times did you come?"

"Three."

A cocky grin turned up his lips. "Yeah?"

She playfully punched him in the side, causing him to release an *oomph*, "Don't be conceited."

"Yes, ma'am." He lifted her fist, kissed the back of her fingers. "Seriously, I want you to be satisfied."

She could tell he meant that by the sincere tone in his voice. It warmed her heart to know her pleasure mattered to him. "I was. I am. I promise."

"Does that mean you aren't interested in seconds?"

Seconds sounded really good. Or maybe she should think of it as fourths since she'd already had three orgasms. "I . . . might be persuaded."

"I'm a pretty damn good persuader."

"You are, huh?"

"Yeah. But before I start any persuading, I think we need a snack."

She couldn't believe he could possibly be hungry. "How can you want something to eat after that huge meal?"

"Hey, I just burned off a lot of calories. I need to replenish my strength."

This time, she couldn't stop her grin. "I'm sure we can find something in Dolly's kitchen for a snack."

She gave him a quick, smacking kiss before moving away from him. Stephen rose from the bed, holding the base of the condom. "I need to make a fast stop in the bathroom."

"First door on the left."

She reached for her robe that lay draped over the footboard. Stephen spoke to her before she touched it. "What are you doing?"

"Putting on my robe."

"Uh-uh." Taking her hand, he tugged her toward the door. "No robe."

"Stephen, I can't walk around Dolly's house naked!"

"Why not? You and I are the only ones here." He touched the tip of her nose. "Be just a minute. Stay here."

Crossing her arms over her stomach, Julia leaned against the wall and glared at the closed bathroom door. She didn't think it wrong for a person to be nude in his or her home, but this wasn't her home. Dolly wouldn't be back for hours, yet Julia couldn't help feeling guilty to be traipsing through the rooms not wearing one stitch of clothing.

Then she laughed. *Why not do something out of character? It'll be fun.*

The bathroom door opened. She watched Stephen's gaze sweep her body. A slow grin played over his lips. He stepped closer, placed his hands on either side of her head. "I like you naked."

"I like you naked, too."

His kiss began the fire building inside her again. Before it could turn into a raging inferno, he pulled away from her.

"Snack first, then sex."

"You have your priorities completely backward."

He leaned over and spoke directly into her ear. "You don't know what I might do with my snack."

Goose bumps erupted across her skin, in contrast with the heat inside her. She would've taken his hand and dragged him back to her bed if he hadn't slipped his arm around her waist and guided her toward the kitchen.

"Any chance there's some of Dolly's salsa in here?" he asked, opening the refrigerator.

"Second shelf, red bowl. I'll get the chips from the pantry. And our wineglasses from the living room."

She returned to the kitchen in time to see Stephen pop a salsa-covered chip into his mouth. He winked at her while he chewed. Shaking her head at his silliness, she walked over to the counter where she'd left the bottle of Merlot and poured more into their glasses. When she turned around again, she caught him looking at her ass.

"Watch it," she playfully scolded.

"I was."

She laughed when he bobbed his eyebrows and grinned. She handed him his wineglass, then reached for a chip.

"No, let me."

Julia waited while he scooped some salsa on a chip. She opened her mouth when he held the chip up to it. Holding his gaze, she chewed and swallowed.

"Good?" he asked.

She nodded.

"Want another?"

"Please."

Stephen slipped his hands beneath her arms, lifted her to sit on the table. The cold surface made her inhale sharply. She soon forgot the cool wood beneath her when he positioned her close to the edge and stepped between her legs. She glanced down at his relaxed cock only inches from her mound.

"Open."

Julia thought he meant for her to spread her legs wider until she looked up again and saw he held a chip. A little disappointed that he preferred food over her, she accepted the chip and slowly chewed. Her chewing abruptly stopped when Stephen dipped his finger into the salsa and spread it over her left nipple.

"What are you doing?" she managed to choke out after she swallowed her half-chewed chip.

"Persuading. I told you I might do something different with my snack." He leaned over, swiped the salsa off her skin with his tongue. "Dolly makes excellent salsa."

Julia sighed when he licked her nipple again, as if making sure he removed every bit of the spicy sauce. He tugged on it with his lips until it became a hard peak. He did the same on her right nipple—adding salsa, licking it off, tugging with his lips. She felt everything he did to her nipples deep in her core.

No longer relaxed, his cock stood up full and hard between them when he straightened. "Lean back on your hands."

Unsure what he planned to do but eager for whatever it might be, she did as he said. Stephen picked up one of their glasses, poured a thin stream of Merlot between her breasts. He lapped it up before it could reach her navel. He repeated his action over each breast. Julia arched her back, silently asking him to keep doing the marvelous thing he did with his tongue.

Stephen set down the wineglass, cradled her breasts in his palms. He lifted, kneaded, pushed them together. With every movement, every caress, his thumbs kept her nipples hard to the point of aching.

"Suck my nipples, Stephen. Please."

She'd barely made the request when he drew one firm tip into his mouth. He encircled her waist with one arm to support her, giving her the freedom to tunnel her hands into his hair. His other hand supported her breast while he licked and suckled the nipple.

The heat built inside her, the prelude to that glorious burst of sensation that would flood her body. She tightened her hold in Stephen's hair, refusing to let him stop the sweet torture. It wouldn't take much more to push her over the edge again.

Seconds away from orgasm, he released her nipple. Julia would have cried out if he hadn't kissed her. His tongue shot into her mouth in a slick penetration, reminding her of the way his cock had penetrated her pussy in her bed.

"Wrap your legs around my waist," he said in a voice thick with passion.

She obeyed him without hesitation. Stephen lifted her against him. His hard cock rode between her thighs as he walked toward her bedroom. Her clit brushed the base, keeping her close to a climax with each step he took.

He deposited her on the bed, reached for the unused condom on the nightstand. Julia sat up and helped him roll it down his length. Their lips met while he urged her to lie back. The kiss continued as he entered her.

Julia met every thrust he made. Stephen slid one hand beneath her ass, hooked her leg over his other arm, and pumped even deeper. The new angle brushed her clit over and over.

"You're so wet, so warm." He nipped her earlobe, blew into her ear. "Come for me again, darlin'. I love to feel you come."

Hearing his husky command along with the direct stimulation to her clit sent her flying to the heavens again. Pleasure shot from her core and traveled to all her limbs. She clutched at Stephen's shoulders and savored every second of ecstasy.

Now that the initial burst of bliss passed, she wanted to concentrate on Stephen's pleasure. She tightened her arms around his neck, nipped his earlobe the way he had hers. "Your turn," she whispered. "Come inside me."

She'd barely said the words when his body jerked and he released a long moan. She could feel his cock pulsing in her channel. Part of her wished the condom didn't separate them for she wanted *all* of him inside her.

He lay on top of her, supporting his weight on his elbows. Julia ran her hands up and down his spine, wiping away the sheen of sweat. His hot breath brushed her neck when he exhaled. She felt warm and content. She'd experienced orgasms with Cole and the few other lovers in her life, but she couldn't say she'd ever been content after lovemaking, as if she belonged in his arms.

Way too soon for her to feel so close to Stephen.

He lifted his head from her shoulder and gave her a sleepy-eyed smile. "Hey."

She returned his smile. "Hey."

"So you don't mind when I play with my food?"

"Not if you keep doing what you did in the kitchen."

"Be happy to." He kissed her forehead, the tip of her nose, her lips. "May I spend the night with you?"

The thought that he might leave after sex had never crossed her mind. "I'd like that."

His smile widened. "Good. I want to spend the night, but would leave if that's what you wanted."

"I'll warn you—I like to cuddle."

"That's perfect, because I'm a cuddler, too."

He slowly rose until his soft cock slipped out of her. "Be right back."

After Stephen left the room, Julia pulled back the covers and slid between the sheets. Fatigue hit her suddenly, the result of all those orgasms. She'd be asleep before he got in bed if he didn't hurry.

She'd almost dozed off when the mattress dipped. Julia managed to open her eyes enough to see Stephen get in bed beside her. He lay on his back, drew her into his arms.

"I cleaned up the kitchen and turned off the lights except for a lamp in the living room."

"Thank you. Dolly doesn't like to walk into a dark house."

She wondered if her words sounded as slurred to him as they did to her. He pulled her a little closer and kissed the top of her head. "Good night," he whispered.

7

Julia looked so beautiful sleeping, Stephen hated to wake her. Yet he didn't feel right leaving without saying good-bye to her.

Sitting on the edge of the bed, he slipped his hand between the sheets and touched her back. Her skin felt warm and smooth beneath his palm. He ran his hand down her spine and over her ass, then repeated the journey to her shoulder blade. Her eyebrows drew together in a frown as she stirred.

"Good morning," he said softly.

She blinked a couple of times before rolling to her back. Her movement caused his hand to shift on her body to her breast. He palmed the firm mound, dragged his thumb over the tip. He smiled when she arched her back as if asking for him to keep touching her.

"Wha' time 'zit?"

"Almost seven. I'm sorry to wake you, but I have to go."

" 'K. I unnerstand." She rubbed her hands over her face before opening her eyes. "Are you working today?"

"No, but I have something planned." He rubbed her nipple

with his thumb again. Damn, he hated to leave her. "I'll call you later, okay?"

"Okay."

Stephen unlocked his cell phone, flipped to his contacts list. "What's your cell number?"

She rattled off the ten digits. He pointed the phone at her, intending to take a picture, but she quickly covered her face.

"Don't you *dare* snap that camera!"

Stephen grinned. He liked teasing her. "How about if I take a picture of you tonight while we're at O'Sullivan's?"

"We're going to O'Sullivan's?"

"Yeah, I'd like to take you there. There's a dart tournament every Saturday night, along with all-you-can-eat fish and chips. I thought you might enjoy it."

Her eyes turned sultry. She laid her hand over the top of his that still caressed her breast. "What I'd enjoy is for you to get naked and come back to bed."

Stephen's cock responded to her sexy invitation. One phone call and he could postpone his plans for the day. However, he'd be messing up the plans of several guys. He didn't want to do that. Plus, his heart drummed heavily in anticipation of what he'd be doing in a short while. He'd looked forward to it all week. "No more condoms, remember?"

She frowned. "Damn it."

He chuckled at her obvious frustration. "Could I have a rain check?"

"Sure."

Her smile reached her eyes, so he knew turning her down didn't make her angry at him. He leaned over and gave her a soft kiss. "I'll call you this afternoon."

He made it halfway to the door before she spoke again. "Better buy a big box of condoms."

Stephen looked at her over his shoulder. She sat up in bed, the covers bunched at her waist to expose her beautiful breasts.

You're an idiot to leave instead of playing with that gorgeous body all day.

"I'll buy the super jumbo size."

She flashed him that sultry look again. "Are you talking about the size of the *box* of condoms, or the condoms?"

"Both," he said with a grin.

She licked the tip of her forefinger, rubbed it over her nipple. "Better make it *two* boxes."

Groaning, Stephen pressed his hand against his burgeoning cock. "You're cruel, do you know that?"

The sultry look disappeared, to be replaced with laughter. "Go. I have things to do today, too."

He winked at her. "See you later."

Stephen hurried out of the house and to his car. He barely had enough time to get home, shower, and grab something to eat before he had to leave to meet the other guys. He tightened his hands on the steering wheel as he peeled out of Dolly's driveway. Racing today and Julia in his arms tonight.

It would be a great day.

Julia nibbled on the sugar cookie that Dolly had removed from the oven barely ten minutes ago. Soft and moist with just the right amount of sugar on top, it almost melted in her mouth. "This is soooo good."

Dolly smiled as she set two glasses of iced tea on the kitchen table. "I'm glad you think so." She sat in the chair opposite Julia and selected a cookie for herself. "Sugar cookies are my favorite to make and to eat."

Julia finished her cookie and took another one from the plate between her and Dolly. "I'm a brownie nut. I could eat them every day. I have to discipline myself not to buy the mixes or I'd always have brownies in the house and then I'd be as big as a barn."

"You're built like your mom, and she's gorgeous."

"I agree she's gorgeous, but we have the body type that could quickly blow up if we aren't careful."

"I told you, men like curves." A mischievous light appeared in Dolly's eyes. "Stephen likes your curves, doesn't he?"

Her supposedly innocent question didn't fool Julia for a moment. "Is that a subtle way of asking me if Stephen and I made love last night?"

"I don't have to ask. I saw his car when I got home. And I found two wineglasses in the sink."

"I probably should've asked you for permission before letting him spend the night."

Dolly waved a hand as if dismissing Julia's apology. "Don't be silly. I told you I want you to consider this your home." She leaned forward, her expression as eager as a woman's in a chocolate store. "So, is he good?"

"A-ma-zing."

Dolly grinned. "I expected he would be. He has that sexy swagger that shouts he'd be great in bed."

"You shouldn't be looking at young men's swaggers," she playfully admonished.

"I'm fifty-six, not dead. I *love* looking at men's asses."

Julia giggled, and Dolly joined her. She couldn't believe how easily she could talk to this woman, almost as easily as talking to her mother. It made her miss her mom a little less.

Julia's cell phone rang. She glanced at it lying on the table. She didn't recognize the phone number, but did recognize the local area code. The burst of excitement that coursed through her body told her it had to be Stephen. She held up the phone so Dolly could see the number. "Is this Stephen?"

"It is."

Another spark shot through her. It ended at her clit, making it throb. She pressed the button to accept the call. "Hello?"

"Hey, sexy lady," he said in his slow Texas drawl. "What are you doin'?"

She looked across the kitchen table at Dolly, who grinned broadly. "Having tea and cookies with Dolly."

"Are we on for O'Sullivan's tonight?"

"We are."

"Great." She could hear the smile in his voice. "I'll pick you up about six. Is that okay?"

"Sure. How should I dress?"

"Naked works for me," he said, his voice low.

Heat crept into her cheeks. She glanced at Dolly, who still grinned. "I think a different outfit would be better for O'Sullivan's."

"You're right. I don't want anyone looking at your beautiful body but me."

His compliment moved the heat from her face all the way down her torso to settle between her thighs.

"Casual is good. It's a fun place, like Boot Scootin'. Ask Dolly. She'll tell you about it."

"I'll do that."

"Then I'll see you in about three hours. Bye."

"Bye."

She disconnected the call and laid her cell on the table. Her heart shouldn't beat so hard, her blood shouldn't run so hot, for a man she met two days ago. It didn't make sense for her to feel such a strong attraction for Stephen.

"Stephen's taking you to O'Sullivan's tonight?" Dolly asked.

Her question snapped Julia from her thoughts. She nodded. "He said it's a fun place."

"It is. There are always several people there on Saturday night for the darts tournament. Whoever wins gets their meal comped and free drinks for the rest of the night." She took a sip of her iced tea. "Sometimes I'll schedule myself off on a Saturday night and play in the tournament." Her grin returned. "I've won twice."

The mental image of the petite Dolly beating all those tall men in darts made Julia laugh. She'd love to see that.

"Stephen will be hard to beat tonight if he won his race today."

Julia paused with her glass raised halfway to her mouth. A sudden chill chased away all the warmth she'd felt after talking with Stephen. "Race?"

"Stephen and four or five other guys race their motorcycles the first Saturday of every month. They each put one hundred dollars into the pot. Stephen usually wins."

Slowly, she lowered her glass back to the table. "Stephen races motorcycles?"

"Oh, yeah. He's good at it, too. Like I said, he usually wins that race every month." She glanced at the clock on the wall. "I'd better clean up in here and shower if I'm going to make it to work by five."

"I'll take care of the kitchen."

Smiling, Dolly reached across the table and squeezed Julia's hand. "Thank you, sweetie."

Julia's mind whirled while she emptied the dishwasher and loaded it with the dirty dishes and utensils from Dolly's baking spree. Stephen raced motorcycles. That didn't mean he was an adrenaline junky like Cole. Dolly said the race occurred once a month. Julia didn't know if someone hooked on adrenaline could wait a whole month for a "fix." Cole certainly hadn't. He'd done something to make his blood thunder through his body every few days.

The more she thought about Stephen's racing, the more she realized she had no right to question anything he chose to do. They barely knew each other. It would be a long time—if ever—that she could call what they had a relationship. They were still in that getting-to-know-each-other stage. Perhaps she'd fallen in bed with him too quickly, yet she'd wanted to make love with him as much as he seemed to want her. As long as they desired each other, she saw no reason for them not to be together sexually.

She added detergent to the dishwasher and started the wash cycle. For now, she planned to enjoy her time with Stephen and not worry about anything but deciding what she would wear on her date tonight.

The way Stephen's eyes lit up when she opened the front door showed her he approved of her choice of white capris, a pale lilac tank top, and a short-sleeved, dark lilac blouse that she left unbuttoned. His gaze swept all the way down to her white sandals and back to her face. "I've changed my mind about going to O'Sullivan's. Let's order a pizza, stay here, and make out."

Julia laughed at the hopeful expression on his face. "No."

"Damn it. I never get nothing."

She reached up and patted his cheek. "You poor baby." Grabbing her keys and purse from the accent table by the door, she pushed him back and stepped over the threshold. "My mouth has been watering all day for fish and chips. You aren't getting out of taking me to O'Sullivan's now."

He slipped his arms around her waist from behind as she locked the door. "I hope you have something in mind for later to make up for my suffering."

She looked at him over her shoulder. "Did you buy the condoms?"

"Two large boxes, just like you told me to." He took her hand, led her toward his Mustang. "Of course, I had to put up with the ribbing from James at Caldwell Apothecary when he said I must have big plans for the weekend."

He opened the passenger side door for her. "You could have told him you were simply restocking," she said after sliding onto the seat.

"A small box is restocking. Two large boxes means plans."

"Is that part of the guy code?"

"I could tell you, but then I'd have to kill you 'cause you aren't a guy." He tapped the end of her nose. "And I'm very glad about that."

Several cars filled spaces in the parking lot of O'Sullivan's. Julia felt as if she'd walked into a family reunion with so many people greeting Stephen when they entered the pub. He kept one hand on the small of her back, waved to the people with the other.

An impression of friendliness and warmth struck her as she glanced around the spacious room. Three dart boards hung on the wall to her left with customers playing a game at all of them. A stone fireplace occupied part of the space by the dart boards, now dark and unlit due to the warm weather. A large, lighted bar with an impressive display of different liquor bottles occupied the place to her right. Tall padded stools surrounded the bar, covered in the same dark leather as the chairs and booths placed throughout the room. The scent of cooking food filled the air, enticing a person to sit down for something to eat and a cold drink to wash it down.

She felt as if she'd stepped into a pub in the United Kingdom.

Stephen led her to a table for four close to the back. A very pregnant woman sat there, drinking a glass of iced tea. Her face lit up with a smile as they approached. "Hey, handsome."

"Hey, gorgeous." He leaned over and kissed her cheek, then playfully rubbed her rounded tummy. "How's my little cousin doing?"

"Kicking up a storm. He's either going to be a punter or a soccer player." She turned her gaze to Julia. "Hi."

"Hannah, this is Julia Woods. She's new to Lanville. Julia, Hannah McGettis, Dusty's wife."

"It's nice to meet you, Hannah."

"Nice to meet you, too. Dusty's told me about you."

The calculating gleam in Hannah's eyes made Julia wonder exactly what Dusty had said.

She sat in the chair Stephen held for her. "I'll go to the bar and get us a drink. What'll you have?"

"White wine."

"Okay." He motioned toward Hannah's half-empty glass. "Want another tea?"

She sighed dramatically. "Yes, since I can't have a Guinness."

Stephen chuckled. "You can make up for the lack of liquor once the baby is born."

Before Stephen could leave the table, Dusty walked up and slapped his cousin on the back. "So? Did you win?"

A wide grin spread across Stephen's lips. "What do you think?"

Dusty grinned, too, then let out an ear-piercing whistle. Once everyone stopped talking and looked his direction, he yelled out, "Stephen won today. Next round's on him."

Applause erupted throughout the pub. Apparently no one had to explain to the crowd exactly what Stephen had won. They already knew.

So did Julia since Dolly had told her about the race, but she wanted to hear the explanation from Stephen. "What did you win?"

"I'll tell you when I get back with the drinks. Guinness, Dusty?"

"I'll go with you."

She watched the two men walk to the bar. They both possessed muscular bodies from the physical labor of their jobs.

Otherwise, the cousins favored little physically—Dusty's light brown hair and blue eyes completely opposite from Stephen's dark brown hair and cognac eyes—but they both had that swagger Dolly mentioned.

She turned her attention back to Hannah. Dusty's wife had fair skin, dark brown hair that curled to her shoulders, and icy blue eyes. Julia could sum up her looks with one word—*stunning*. "When is your baby due?"

"Mid-July. I am so ready to hold him."

"You know it's a boy?"

Hannah nodded. "Dusty and I were going to be surprised, but then we decided we wanted to know for sure. All his little dangly bits showed up clearly on the ultrasound last week."

Julia laughed while Hannah grinned. She liked the open friendliness of the lovely brunette. "Have you picked out a name?"

"Finally. Dusty's real first name is Randall and I wanted to name our son after him. He thinks Randall is a stuck-up name, which is why he goes by Dusty. But he finally agreed on Randall as the first name if our baby's middle name could be Jacob, which is Stephen's middle name. We're going to call him R. J." She swirled her straw through her tea, making the ice cubes tinkle against the glass. "Dusty is an only child and grew up with Stephen and his brothers. He and Stephen have always been tight, even though Dusty is closer in age to Stephen's brother Mark. Dusty and Stephen bonded when they were children and have stayed close ever since."

"Stephen must be honored to have his cousin named after him."

"We haven't told him yet. We're keeping the name secret until after R. J. is born." Hannah's eyes twinkled with mischief. "I can hardly wait to see the look on Stephen's face when we introduce him to little Randall Jacob. He is such a sensitive man with deep feelings. I know he'll cry." Hannah's eyes suddenly filled with tears. She dabbed at them with her napkin. "Just like me. Damn pregnancy hormones."

The men arrived with the drinks at the same time a young waitress stepped up to the table. "Hey, y'all."

"Hey, Nina," Dusty said.

"Does anyone need a menu?"

Stephen looked at Julia as he sat on the chair to her right. "Fish and chips still okay with you? They come with coleslaw and baked beans, too."

"Sounds great."

Stephen turned back to the waitress. "Fish and chips all around, Nina."

"Got it." She made a note on her order pad before she grinned at him. "I've started the tab of drinks for you."

"Gee, thanks."

With a sparkling laugh, she moved on to the next table. Julia decided the mention of Stephen's tab would be the perfect opening to ask him about the race. "What did you win and why are you buying drinks?"

Stephen took a long pull from his mug of Guinness before he spoke. "I'm in a motorcycle race the first Saturday of every month with five other guys. We all chip in one hundred dollars. Whoever wins the race wins the money."

"So you won five hundred dollars today?"

"Yeah."

"What he isn't telling you," Dusty said, "is that he usually wins."

Stephen shrugged. "I've been lucky."

"You're skilled, man, not lucky."

"Hey, McGettis," a man called from the area of the dart boards, "you wanna lose some of that money you won today?"

"Who's supposed to beat me, Greene?"

"Come over here and find out."

"The tournament doesn't start until eight."

"Afraid you'll lose now?"

"Yeah, right." He lowered his voice before he spoke to Julia again. "That's Jaxon Greene. The guy next to him is Bain Duncan. They work at the newspaper."

Julia touched the back of his hand. "If you want to play a game with them, don't feel like you have to entertain me. I was enjoying talking to Hannah."

"Yeah," Hannah said. "Why don't you guys go play until the food comes?"

"I think they're trying to get rid of us," Stephen said.

"They probably want to talk about girl stuff." Dusty gave his wife a quick kiss. "Back in a bit."

Once the men left, Julia leaned forward in her chair. "Tell me more about Stephen."

8

"You're quiet," Stephen said halfway to Dolly's house. "Is something wrong?"

Yes, something was wrong, but she didn't know how to bring it up with him, or whether she should say anything at all. "No, of course not. I'm just full from all the fish I ate."

He reached for her hand, lifted it to his mouth, and kissed her palm. "Good, huh?"

"The best I've ever eaten."

He smiled, kissed her hand again. "I'm glad you liked it."

"I enjoyed everything about tonight, even if you didn't win the dart tournament."

"That damn Jax beats me almost every time."

She could see the smile still tugging at his lips, so she knew losing didn't truly upset him. She studied his profile in the dim light from the dash. Her conversation with Hannah while Stephen and Dusty played darts with Jax and Bain had been very enlightening. Not only did Stephen race motorcycles, he also went white-water rafting and participated in several other activities that could easily put his life in danger.

A true adrenaline junky, just like Cole.

She didn't have the nerve to travel that road again. She should end their relationship now, before her feelings for Stephen deepened.

Stephen pulled over to the side of the road. Leaving the motor running, he turned in the seat to face her. "The road to my house is coming up soon. We can keep going to Dolly's, or you can come home with me. Your choice."

It would be awkward to ask him to take her back to Dolly's house once she told him good-bye. *If* she told him good-bye. "Dolly's."

He touched her cheek with the back of his knuckle. "You got it."

Stephen had sensed Julia's discomfort all evening. She'd laughed and talked and been friendly with everyone he introduced her to, yet he knew something bothered her.

He wanted her fiercely, but perhaps he should tell her good night at the front door and leave.

Deciding he'd take his cue from her, Stephen parked in Dolly's driveway behind Julia's car. He met her at the hood of his car, took her hand, and led her to the porch. Once they reached the door, he released her hand and took a step back, giving her the chance to invite him inside or say good-bye.

Julia unlocked the door, stepped over the threshold. She stood still, her back to him, for several seconds before her shoulders rose and fell with a deep breath. Turning to face him, she held out her hand to him.

Relief surged through him, along with the desire to hold her. He stepped inside, closed the door, and drew her into his arms. He held her close for long moments before he covered her lips with his.

Her soft lips moved, parted, beneath his. She pressed her body close so he could feel her firm breasts against his chest.

He wanted them in his hands, her hard nipples in his mouth. He longed to touch every inch of her skin.

It almost frightened him how much he craved her.

She took his hand and led him to her bedroom. The lamps on either side of the bed came on when she flipped the wall switch. She stopped beside the bed, looked at him with lust burning in her eyes. Taking her quickly would be easy. He had no doubt her pussy already creamed from desire. Fast and furious didn't work for him. He wanted to take his time and savor her.

He kissed the spot beneath her ear that he'd already learned made her breath hitch. "I'm going to undress you."

"Okay," she said, her voice barely above a whisper.

Blood surged in his cock when he heard her breathy surrender. Stephen moved up her neck, dropping gentle, nipping kisses until he reached her mouth. Once again, it softened beneath his. He laid one hand over her heart. It pounded beneath his palm. Moving his hand lower, he cradled her breast and gently squeezed it. Her moan urged him to continue, to give her even more.

He would gladly give her whatever she needed.

He slipped the blouse from her shoulders, let it fall to the floor behind her. The tank top followed. Before he could unhook her bra, she tugged his T-shirt out of his jeans and slid her hands beneath the fabric. Now Stephen moaned when she scratched his nipples.

"You don't like scratching?" she asked.

"*Love* scratching." He proved his words by digging his fingernails into her ass. "And biting." He scraped his teeth across her neck. "And sucking." Placing his mouth over the throbbing pulse in her neck, he sucked hard.

"Are you giving me a *hickey?*"

He'd love to mark her neck so everyone would know she belonged with him, but wouldn't do that when she started a brand-new job in two days. However, he could suck on other parts of her body that no one else would see. And he would love doing that.

Still holding tightly to her ass, Stephen brushed his dick back and forth on her mound. Julia whimpered. She rubbed both thumbs over his nipples, urging them to hardness. Stephen loved her touch, but wanted to give her pleasure before he thought about himself. Grabbing the hem of his T-shirt, he jerked it over his head and dropped it on top of her blouse and tank. Her bra soon followed. He tugged her closer, until her breasts once again flattened against his chest.

She drew back so they no longer touched. "I want to look at you."

Stephen stood still while her gaze moved over him. She glided her hands over his shoulders, across his chest, and down his flat stomach to the waistband of his jeans. She loosened the buckle on his belt before looking back into his eyes.

"Don't stop now," he said, his voice raspy.

Her gaze still locked with his, she unsnapped his jeans and slowly lowered the zipper. Stephen kissed her neck again as she pulled his briefs away from his body. He waited, breath held, for her hand on his hard flesh.

He blew out his breath with a groan when she slid her hand inside to wrap around him. He arched his hips forward, searching for more of her soft hand. "Yeah. Touch me."

She gripped his cock, ran her thumb over the velvety head. He could feel her thumb sliding through the moisture oozing from the slit. Cradling her face, he drove his tongue deep into her mouth as she spread the pre-cum over the tip.

The sensation became too much when she started moving her hand up and down his shaft. He had to stop her before he wouldn't be able to.

"How about if we get rid of the rest of our clothes?" Stephen asked as he pulled her hand out of his briefs. He gently pushed on her shoulders until she sat on the side of the bed. Dropping to his knees, he slipped off her sandals. He massaged one foot, then the other, until her eyes turned slumberous.

She leaned over and kissed him. Her position let her breasts sway away from her body. He couldn't resist cradling them while her lips and tongue played over his mouth.

Her breathing sounded heavy and harsh when she ended the kiss. "I want to watch you take off your clothes."

Happy to do what she requested, Stephen stood. He toed off his shoes, then removed his socks. He liked that Julia's breathing became heavier when he hooked his thumbs in the sides of his jeans. They and his briefs fell to the floor at the same time. He kicked them aside. His cock stood up, thick and long and straight, with moisture still leaking from the slit.

Julia grasped the base of his cock, leaned forward, and licked off the pre-cum.

He couldn't resist indulging in the pleasure of her mouth on him for a few moments. He tunneled his hands into her hair to hold her head in place. "That feels really good."

She circled the rim with her tongue, licked down the entire length to his tight balls. After her third trip, Stephen tightened his hold on her head and gently pulled away from her.

"That's enough. It's your turn to be naked."

Stephen pushed on her shoulders again, this time to get her to lie back on the bed. Julia lifted her hips when he unfastened her capris. He quickly added them to the pile on the floor. She now lay before him in nothing but a pair of tiny white panties.

Looking into her eyes, he gripped the waistband of her panties with his teeth and tugged. Julia helped him by pushing them past her hips. Still holding the elastic with his teeth, he pulled them down her legs.

After dropping them on the floor, he leaned over her, his hands on either side of her waist. His gaze swept the entire length of her body, admiring her ivory skin and generous curves. "Much better."

She wrapped her hand around his cock again and spread her legs, releasing the scent of her arousal. "I want you inside me."

Nothing would please him more than to slide his dick into her wet channel, but not yet. He shook his head. "If I enter you now, we'll fuck."

A confused expression crossed her face. "And that would be a problem . . . why?"

"I don't want to fuck you, Julia. I want to make love to you."

Her eyes softened with so much emotion, his throat tightened. He lowered his head and kissed her gently, slowly, telling her with his lips how much he wanted her. She slid her hands up his arms, over his shoulders, into his hair. She clutched handfuls of it as he coaxed her lips to part for the sweep of his tongue.

Stephen could kiss her all night, but he needed more and knew Julia did, too. Cradling her breast in his palm, he licked and sucked her nipple as his other hand traveled down her stomach to between her thighs. He delved through the creamy folds.

"Mmm, you're nice and wet."

Julia lifted her hips and spread her legs wider. Her action meant she obviously enjoyed his touch, but he longed to do more. "I think you need something other than my fingers."

She grabbed his wrist to keep him from moving his hand. "Your fingers are doing fine."

Her frantic tone made him chuckle. "No, you definitely need more." He dropped to his knees at the side of the bed. Slipping his arms beneath her knees, he dragged her hips right to the edge. "Don't you?"

He spread her labia with his thumbs and licked her . . . a long, slow stroke the length of her folds. She twisted her hands into the bedspread when he stroked her again. He circled her clit, darted his tongue inside her channel. Julia hooked her hands behind her knees and spread her legs even wider. Stephen ran his tongue down to her anus and back to her clit.

He'd never get enough of her scent, her taste.

"Stephen."

Obeying the silent command in that one word, he stood and leaned over her again. She reached between their bodies and grabbed his cock. "Condom. Now."

He pulled back so she could no longer touch his shaft. "Not yet."

Julia released a sound of frustration. "Why not?"

"I want you to come first."

"Trust me, coming won't be a problem."

"Good. That's what I want."

He kissed her mouth and each nipple before dropping to his knees again. This time he feasted, using his tongue and teeth to stimulate every sensitive spot between her thighs. Julia arched her hips again, pushed her mound closer to his mouth. Stephen took her silent request to mean she needed more. He happily gave it, pushing two fingers inside her and pressing upward into her G-spot as he suckled her clit.

Julia gave a long, keening moan. She grabbed his head as her hips bucked and her body trembled. He continued to gently lick all over her pussy until she stilled.

No woman he'd ever been with looked as beautiful in the throes of climax as Julia.

Grabbing his jeans, he located one of the three condoms he'd stuck in his pocket. He stood and watched her while he sheathed his cock. She lay with her eyes closed, her lips parted. Her breasts rose and fell with her rapid breathing. He kissed each thigh, her mound, the center of her stomach. "Move to the middle of the bed."

She slowly opened her eyes, blinking several times as if to bring him into focus. "*Move?* You aren't serious."

He chuckled. "You have a very horny man here who has all kinds of ideas of what to do to you."

"Oh. Well, in that case . . ."

She shifted until she lay lengthwise on the bed, tucked a pillow beneath her head. Stephen followed. With one thrust, he entered her.

Stephen kissed her as he began to move. He heard the catch in Julia's throat, that sexy sound of pleasure. She dug her fingernails into his shoulders, wrapped her legs around his waist. Needing to move faster, thrust deeper, he slipped his hands beneath her ass and lifted it. She made that sound, the one he knew meant she would soon come again.

He straightened his arms and lifted his torso away from her. "I love being inside you." He gazed at her breasts, moved down to where their bodies joined. He watched his wet cock sliding in and out of her slick pussy. "Look at that."

Julia lifted her head and watched him pumping into her. Stephen hooked one of her legs over his arm to raise her hips higher so she could see better.

"It looks good, doesn't it?"

"Yes." Her eyes drifted closed, her head tilted back. "Feels so good."

"What do you need me to do?"

"That. Just . . . that. Keep moving . . . *Ohhhhhhh!*"

Her back bowed, her nipples beaded, a sheen of sweat covered her skin. Stephen pushed his cock all the way inside her. The walls of her pussy milked it, signaling her climax.

She opened her eyes and smiled at him. Stephen kissed her forehead, the tip of her nose, her lips. "You're so beautiful when you come."

She tunneled her fingers into his hair. "You didn't come."

"Not yet. I'm not through with you."

Her sudden burst of laughter made him smile. "Stephen, I'm wiped. That's it. No more."

"Never say never. I might have some tricks you haven't seen."

"I have no strength for tricks."

"Then I'll do all the work."

Holding tightly to her body, Stephen rose to his knees. He arranged her over his lap, his cock still buried deeply in her pussy. Gripping her ass, he started pumping again.

The new position caressed Julia's clit with each movement. It shocked her to feel desire already building again. The shock soon turned into so much pleasure, it brought tears to her eyes. She wrapped her arms around his neck, pressed her breasts to his chest, and let him guide her however he wanted to.

He thrust harder, deeper. The pleasure grew, sweeping through her and stealing her breath. It peaked a moment before Stephen's body stiffened.

"Oh, *fuck!*" he breathed into her ear. A tremor passed through him, then another as a loud growl came from his throat. His arms encircled her tightly. He lowered them to the bed, his cock still inside her.

"God, that was incredible," he said.

"Yes, it was."

"I need a minute to . . . make sure my legs will work."

"I'm in no hurry for you to move."

Several moments passed before Stephen lifted his head and smiled at her. "Are you thirsty?" he asked before kissing her forehead.

"Some water would be nice."

"Okay." This time he kissed her lips. "Be right back."

She propped up on one elbow so she could watch him walk out of her room. He had such an incredible body. The longing to be in his arms again, to feel his hard cock thrusting into her pussy, had made it impossible for her to say good-bye, to tell him they had to end their relationship before it got too serious.

It was already much more serious than she'd imagined it would be.

With a heavy sigh, Julia fell back on the bed. She couldn't be falling in love so soon, especially not with an adrenaline junky. She couldn't stand to go through that pain again. And there would be pain. Maybe not tomorrow, maybe not for weeks to come, but eventually Stephen would do something to hurt himself.

Or someone else.

9
_____

The first sign of daylight barely penetrated Stephen's brain when he heard the beeper go off from his belt. He listened closely, waiting to be sure he'd actually heard it or if he'd only dreamed it.

Three beeps. A house fire.

The normal burst of adrenaline hit him, having him ready to jump out of bed and rush off to fight the fire. He couldn't do that with Julia wrapped around him.

"Hey." He kissed her forehead, trying to wake her gently. "Julia, I have to go."

She stirred against him, made a noise in her throat. "Hmmm."

"Move, darlin'. I have to go to a fire."

The three beeps sounded again. He had no choice but to push her away from him so he could rise. He rounded the bed, found his jeans and pressed the button to silence the beeper.

"There's a fire?" she asked, lifting her head from the pillow.

"Yeah, a house fire," he said as he jerked on his clothes. "I gotta get to the fire hall."

He sat on the edge of the bed to tie his shoes. Julia scooted closer to him and touched his back. "Call me later and let me know you're okay."

It pleased him to know she worried about him. "Will do." Clasping her nape, he gave her a quick kiss. "Bye."

He ran out of the house and took off in his Mustang. He could see the black smoke rising in the distance, showing him the exact location of the fire. He made a quick call to his fire chief to let him know he'd be at the fire hall in five minutes. The fire truck was about to pull out of the hall, so Clay gave Stephen the address and told him to meet the crew there.

Great idea, since getting to the house would be quicker than driving into town. Stephen hit his gas pedal and inched up the speedometer.

Dolly took Sundays off from Boot Scootin', so it surprised Julia when Dolly invited her to go to the bar with her. "Aren't you off today?"

"Supposedly, but I have some paperwork I want to finish. It'll be quiet there since it's Mother's Day. The nicer restaurants in town fill up, so my business dips. That's okay. It makes today a good day to work in my office." She sipped from her glass of tea. "Did you talk to Cathy?"

Julia nodded. "First thing this morning. We talked for almost an hour." Her throat still felt tight from that conversation. It had been really hard not to cry while on the phone with her mother.

"I'll be leaving in about half an hour," Dolly said. "Why don't you come with me? I still haven't fixed you one of my famous cheeseburgers."

Julia laughed. "You're determined to put weight on me."

"No, I just want to make sure you're eating enough."

She placed one hand over her stomach. "I feel as if all I've done the last few days is eat."

"Don't worry. Sex burns a lot of calories."

The impish grin on Dolly's lips made Julia laugh again. She shook one finger at the older woman. "You are bad."

"It's more fun to be bad than good." Dolly took the last sip of her tea. "So everything is okay with you and Stephen?"

The knowing look in Dolly's eyes made Julia hesitate before she answered. "Sure. Why do you ask?"

"I don't know. You seem . . ." She tilted her head to the side. "Down this morning."

Not ready to talk about her conflicted feelings for Stephen until she sorted them out, Julia forced a smile. "I'm fine. Just a little tired. I'm sure one of your cheeseburgers will perk me up."

Her cell phone rang. She looked at the display to see Stephen's face. Her heart skittered in her chest, both from pleasure and anxiety. "Hello?"

"Hey," he said, an obvious smile in his voice. "Fire's out, everyone is safe. There's quite a bit of damage to the house, so I don't know if it can be saved or not."

"But everyone is safe, so that's what counts."

"You bet." She heard something bang in the background, like a locker or cabinet door closing. "Some of the guys are going over to Boot Scootin' to shoot pool. Want to go with me?"

"Actually, I'm on my way there. Dolly invited me to try one of her cheeseburgers."

"My mouth is already watering for one. I'll see you there in . . . oh, probably an hour."

"Okay. See you then. Bye."

She pressed a button to end the call. "Stephen and some of the other firefighters are going to Boot Scootin'."

"Good. Then we can get the firsthand scoop on the fire." She stood and picked up their empty tea glasses. "Do you want to ride with me or take your own car? I probably won't stay much past three."

"I'll ride with you."

* * *

Julia felt a little guilty ordering her cheeseburger before Stephen arrived, but her growling stomach overrode her guilt. She'd taken two bites of the delicious sandwich when the door opened. Five men entered, Stephen in the rear. He zeroed in on her right away. With a sexy smile on his face, he strode toward her while the rest of the men walked to the pool room.

"Hi." He slid onto the stool next to her and looked at her plate. "I see you didn't wait for me."

The humor shining in his eyes proved he wasn't angry, yet Julia apologized anyway. "Sorry. I was hungry."

"I forgive you." Snatching one of her French fries, he popped it into his mouth. "Come to the back room with me and watch us play pool."

"Okay."

He picked up her plate and glass of Coke before she could and carried it to the table they'd sat at Thursday. After she took her chair, he leaned over and gave her a slow kiss. "Mmm, that's better than any cheeseburger."

He looked at her as if he wanted to drag her to a storage closet and fuck her until she couldn't walk. Julia didn't think she'd stop him if he tried it.

"I'm not waiting for Monica to make the rounds. I'll order at the bar." He took another of her fries. "Be right back."

Apparently the other four guys had the same idea, for they all descended on Mel to turn in their food and drink orders. "I think Stephen should buy for all of us," she heard Quade say. "He still has money left over from winning his race."

"Yeah," Manny agreed. "Besides, he's the hero today."

"Cut it out, guys," Stephen said with a frown. "I'm not a hero."

"You saved a life." Wes slapped Stephen on the shoulder. "I'd say that makes you a hero."

Stephen glanced her direction, an uncomfortable expression

on his face. He obviously didn't want the guys mentioning whatever happened today.

Quade turned and looked directly at her. "You should've seen him, Julia. He jumped through a window to save an elderly woman."

"Off the ladder." Tate made a diving arc with his arm. "Five feet away from the window. He crashed right through it. Flames shot up everywhere. Man, it was something."

"The next thing we knew," Wes said, "he came out of the house carrying the woman in his arms. Michaela was there from the newspaper. I won't be surprised if that's the picture on the front page of the paper Wednesday."

The more the guys talked, the more uncomfortable Stephen seemed to become. The few bites of cheeseburger Julia had eaten congealed in her stomach. He'd jumped from a ladder, which meant he had to be at least two stories in the air. He didn't wait until the ladder was safely positioned against the house, but pulled a daredevil stunt instead of following protocol.

She couldn't go through this again. No matter how much she cared for Stephen, she couldn't continue to date him.

He must have sensed her anxiety for he came over to the table, slid into the chair opposite her. "Hey, you okay? You look pale."

Her throat felt so tight, she could barely speak any words. "You *jumped* from the ladder and *crashed* through a *window?*"

"Yeah. Look, the guys are making a bigger deal out of it than it was."

Unable to consider eating any more, Julia pushed her plate aside. "I can't do this, Stephen. I can't be involved with an adrenaline junky."

His eyebrows drew together in a scowl. "What are you talking about?"

"You! With your motorcycle racing and your jumping through windows and all the other dangerous sports you do. I went through that with my boyfriend in California. I can't do it again."

His scowl faded, replaced by a look of alarm. "I don't know what happened with you and that guy in California, but—"

"I'll tell you *exactly* what happened, Stephen. Cole's carelessness caused him to crash his motorcycle with me on the back of it."

All the color drained from Stephen's face. "No," he said weakly.

"He pleaded with me for weeks to ride with him. He swore he'd be careful. So I finally gave in, even though I didn't want to.

"Cole wasn't capable of being careful. He zipped in and out of traffic, despite me asking him over and over to stop. I guess my complaining finally angered him because he looked at me over his shoulder and yelled at me to chill. A pickup pulled into our lane while he was distracted. He swerved to miss it and lost control. We slid for several yards.

"I was in the hospital for four days. My knee was so messed up, I couldn't walk on it for weeks. It still gives me trouble if I stand too long."

"Julia, I would never do anything to hurt you."

"That's exactly what Cole said."

Thinking back to the accident made her food roil in her stomach. Afraid she would be sick, she dashed toward Dolly's office and her private bathroom.

Stephen ran after Julia, but he wasn't quick enough to catch her before she slammed the door to Dolly's bathroom. Dolly whirled around in her chair, her eyes wide, and stared at Stephen.

"What happened?" Dolly demanded.

"She's upset."

Stephen could hear retching from the room. He rubbed the center of his chest, which had tightened from what she'd told him about her accident. Dolly stood, walked over to the bathroom door, and knocked softly. "Julia? May I come in?"

"No." Julia's voice sounded weak, but he still made out her negative response.

"Do you need help, sweetie?"

"No."

The toilet flushed, water ran, then the door slowly opened. Julia stood in the doorway, her face pale and her eyes dull. Stephen stepped forward to take her in his arms. One sharp look from her stopped him.

"Dolly, may I borrow your car?" Julia asked, her voice still weak. "I don't feel well."

"Of course."

"I'll take you home, Julia," Stephen said. He had to talk to her, in private. It couldn't be over between them before their relationship barely started.

Dolly looked from Julia to him and back again. He could almost see the wheels turning in her mind. "Actually, sweetie, it's a good idea for Stephen to take you home. I have a couple of errands to run in a bit."

Bless you, Dolly. Stephen slipped his arm around Julia's waist. He felt her body stiffen, but refused to release her. "I'll take you right now. Dolly, will you stop my lunch order?"

"Of course." She gave Julia a quick hug. "Do you have your house key?"

"No, I didn't bring my purse."

Dolly reached into her desk drawer, removed a key ring, and pressed it into Julia's hand. "Here's a spare key to the back door. Feel better. I'll see you later."

Stephen led Julia through the bar, glaring at the guys who looked as if they might approach or ask questions. By the time they made it to his Mustang, she walked on her own without his help. He opened the passenger door and let her slide onto the seat.

Once behind the wheel, he glanced her way, but she had her attention focused out the side window. She swiped at her eye, as if wiping away a tear. He wanted to touch her so badly, he ached all the way through his body.

"Julia, you said you can't be involved with me. We're *already* involved." Unable to resist a connection, he laid his hand on her arm. "I care very much about you."

She moved her arm away from his hand. It hurt that she didn't want his touch.

He refrained from speaking the next four minutes as he drove to Dolly's house. He felt as if he'd gone down for the third time without a life preserver anywhere around.

Julia had come to mean so much to him in a short amount of time. He couldn't lose her.

He parked in the driveway behind her car. "May I come in with you?"

She hesitated so long, he expected her to say no. Finally, she nodded.

Stephen followed her to the back door and into the kitchen. "I need something to drink," she said after laying the key ring on the counter. "Would you like something?"

"Sure. Whatever you're having."

He sat at the table and watched her prepare two glasses of Pepsi over ice. His stomach rumbled . . . not from hunger, but from dread of what she would say.

After setting one glass in front of him, she sat on the chair opposite him. She took a healthy gulp of her drink before wrapping both hands around her glass and staring down into the dark liquid for several moments. "Were you hurt?"

"When I went through the window?"

She nodded.

"No. I tucked and rolled. I may have a bruise on my hip or thigh tomorrow from how I landed, but I'm fine."

"Good." She ran her hands up and down the sweating glass.

"Maybe you think I'm being unfair to you," she said softly. "And maybe I am." She lifted her gaze to his. Tears swam in her cornflower-blue eyes. "But I watched Cole do things several times that could've taken his life. Then when the accident happened, I knew I couldn't be with him—or anyone like him—anymore. I won't go through that kind of pain again."

"Julia, I'm not Cole. I would never hurt you."

"Perhaps not intentionally. But I care about you, too, Stephen, and I don't want anything to happen to you."

"Nothing is going to happen to me."

"You don't know that!" She blinked away the tears, ran one hand through her hair. "What happens when jumping through a window into a fire or racing motorcycles isn't enough to give you the high you crave?"

"You make me sound as if I don't give a shit about protecting my life. I don't have a death wish."

"I didn't say you do."

"Didn't you?" A bit of anger crept into his apprehension at what he perceived as her demanding something from him she shouldn't. "You said I'm going to hurt myself if I don't stop what you consider my dangerous ways. You're going to break up with me if I don't change."

Tears filled her eyes again. "Yes, I am," she said in a choked whisper.

"You aren't being fair, Julia. We met four days ago. Yes, I care about you, but you can't ask me to change who I am after only four days. You have to give us more time to get to know each other."

"Don't you see, Stephen? I can't give us any more time unless you *do* change."

He stared at her as his heart crumbled. He'd finally met the woman who could be "the one" and she wouldn't even give them a chance because of something that happened to her in a previous relationship. Part of him understood her fear, yet a bigger part of him knew she had no right to try to change him. "I guess we have nothing else to talk about."

"I guess we don't."

Stephen continued to look at her, memorizing every one of her features for the upcoming nights when he'd ache for her. He'd still see her around town. A person couldn't help bumping into people he knew in a town as small as Lanville. He'd simply have to turn the other way to avoid her and wanting something that would never be.

He slowly pushed back his chair and stood. "Good-bye, Julia."

Without a backward glance, Stephen crossed the floor and walked out the back door.

10

Julia stopped running the vacuum in the library when the young woman from the *Lanville Journal* brought in this week's edition. She wanted to see the issue out of curiosity for the kind of newspaper Lanville produced, but also to see if Stephen appeared on the front page.

Not only did the photo of Stephen's rescue make the front page of the newspaper, it took up almost the entire area above the fold with the headline, DARING RESCUE SAVES WOMAN. Julia stared at it as her heart turned over in her chest. She couldn't see his face clearly because of the faceplate he wore, but she knew it was Stephen who carried the elderly woman close to his chest.

A hero, just like Manny had said.

She carefully replaced the newspaper on the stack at the check-in counter. These issues were for The Inn's guests, so she didn't feel right about taking one. She'd buy one on her way home tonight. Although she and Stephen no longer dated, she wanted to keep his picture. She only had the one picture of him that she'd snapped with her cell phone. This would make two.

Two pictures to remind her of their time together . . . a time she'd cut short out of fear, both for him and herself.

She missed him. Ever since he'd walked out of Dolly's kitchen three days ago, he'd rarely left her thoughts. She didn't think it possible to care so deeply about someone after a few days of knowing him, but she did. What she felt for Stephen could easily turn into love with a little nurturing.

She'd put an end to the possibility before it got the chance to start.

A prickling along the back of her neck had her straightening. Slowly, she turned her head to the right. Stephen stood three feet behind her.

Her heart took off at a gallop. He looked amazing in his brown McGettis Roofing polo shirt and faded jeans. Three days' worth of stubble covered his cheeks and chin. He carried a clipboard in his hand, the same one she'd seen him with at Dolly's house. That must mean he had work in the area.

She couldn't tell a thing from his blank expression. Julia had to swallow before she could speak. "Hi."

"Alaina called and asked me to stop by this afternoon."

Straight to the point and all business. Julia didn't know why she expected him to be any different after the way she'd demanded he change his life for her after knowing each other only four days. "She isn't here. She went to the post office, but I expect her back soon."

"Okay if I wait for her?"

"Sure." She motioned toward the room off the foyer. "You can wait in the library."

He nodded once to acknowledge her comment, then turned and walked away.

Just like Sunday.

Julia pressed a hand to the center of her chest. Her throat tightened, tears formed in her eyes. She should follow Stephen into the library, tell him she didn't mean to hurt him, tell him she wanted him in her life. Cowardice and fear kept her from doing it.

"You should talk to him, Julia," Kelcey said from behind her.

Julia turned to see her boss standing at the check-in counter, her eyes full of sympathy.

"I'm sorry. I didn't mean to eavesdrop, but I was in the next room when Stephen came in."

Julia blinked to hold back tears. "You know about what happened between us?"

Kelcey nodded. "There aren't many secrets in a small town." She rounded the counter, walked up to Julia. "Something happened to me when I was young that made me leery of ever trusting a man, especially a man like Dax Coleman." She released a small laugh. "He was such a tomcat, flitting from woman to woman without any intention of settling down. I couldn't trust a man like that."

She took Julia's hands, gently squeezed them. "But I *did* trust him and now I'm the happiest I've ever been in my life. He still flirts outrageously. That's part of him. He doesn't know how to be any other way. But I know it's all for play and in the evening, he comes home to me and only me. I have no doubt about that." She squeezed Julia's hands again. "Every moment in his arms is worth the pain I went through in my past. I can't imagine my life without him."

Although her time with Stephen had been brief, Julia could honestly say she'd been very happy with him, too. That didn't stop her fear. "He does such dangerous things. How can I live with the thought that I could lose him at any time?"

"Julia, *none* of us are guaranteed a long life. Stephen is more likely to fall off a roof while doing his regular job than wreck his motorcycle."

She couldn't help sputtering out a humorless laugh. "Great. Now I'll worry about him roofing, too."

Kelcey grinned, then turned serious again. "He's on a roof

almost every day. He races his motorcycle once a month. Figure out the odds and you'll see I'm right."

Kelcey's words gave Julia a lot to think about. Nothing would be settled, though, until she talked to Stephen. "Could I take my break now and talk to him?"

"Of course. Take all the time you need."

Julia turned and walked toward the library. As she got closer to the room, she heard voices. She stepped through the doorway to see Stephen speaking with Alaina. She must have come in the back door since Julia hadn't seen her come in the front.

The owner of The Inn smiled at her. "Are we in your way, Julia? We can go back to the office to talk."

"No, that's okay. I'm finished in here." She shifted her attention to Stephen. He still wore that blank expression. "Could I talk to you when you're finished with Alaina?"

"I have another appointment."

"Oh." It hurt that he didn't want to talk to her, but his refusal didn't surprise her.

"I could come by Dolly's house after work."

All the sadness drained out of her body, to be replaced with hope. "That would be great. Thanks."

Julia left Alaina and Stephen alone to conduct their business. She didn't know how the evening would end, but she prayed she and Stephen could work out their differences and be together.

Stephen wiped his palms on his thighs before he rang the doorbell to Dolly's house. He hadn't decided yet if he was an optimist or a fool to think he and Julia could start over.

She answered the door wearing a V-necked, pale blue T-shirt and denim shorts. His gaze swept down her legs to her bare feet. Pink nail polish covered her toenails.

He wanted to nibble on every toe.

"Hi," she said softly. She opened the door wider. "Come in."

The scent of cheese and spices wafted toward him when he stepped over the threshold. "Something smells good."

"Dolly made a Mexican chicken casserole before she left." She shut the door behind him. "It's in the oven."

"Dolly isn't here?"

Julia shook her head. "She went out to dinner with friends. She told me she wouldn't be home until late."

So they had the house to themselves. They could talk as long as necessary without interruption. Again, emotions battled inside Stephen . . . a mixture of hope and apprehension.

"I need to check on the casserole," Julia said. "Be right back."

Stephen waited five seconds before he followed Julia to the kitchen. He watched her open the oven door, bend over to peer at the bubbling casserole. Her shorts tightened across her ass, making him long to peel them off to get to the sleek flesh they hid.

Before they made love again—*if* they made love again—they had to talk first, settle things between them.

Taking a chance she'd want his touch, he walked up behind her as she shut the oven door and slipped his arms around her waist. "I've missed you," he whispered into her ear.

She laid her hands over the top of his. "I've missed you, too."

"Can we start over?"

Turning in his arms, she touched his chest and looked up at him with pleading eyes. "Can we?"

"I'm willing to try if you are."

She ran her hands up his chest, over his shoulders. "I'm still scared."

"I've been thinking about that a lot the last three days. It's natural to be afraid of something you don't know. Maybe you wouldn't be so scared if you went with me and experienced the things I do."

Her eyes widened in disbelief. "You mean race motorcycles?"

"Not race them, but you could watch and see all the precautions we take. We aren't reckless, Julia. None of us want to get hurt, or hurt anyone else in the race. And maybe eventually you can find the courage to ride with me. I promise no zipping in and out of traffic."

"Maybe."

He slid his hands up and down her back. "I'm going white-water rafting in Colorado in July. Go with me."

"I've never done anything like that."

"You can participate or just watch. It's up to you."

"I have a brand-new job, Stephen. I don't know if I could get any time off this quickly."

"Okay. I understand that." He slid his hands down to her hips. "What do you think about skydiving?"

"That people are insane to jump out of a perfectly good airplane with nothing but some cloth to keep them from splattering all over the ground."

Stephen threw back his head and laughed out loud. "Don't hold back, darlin'. Tell me how you really feel."

"You do that, too?"

He nodded. "I'm going this weekend. Come with me."

She covered her face with her hands. "Arrrggghhh! You aren't making this easy."

"Probably not." Clasping her wrists, he pulled her hands away from her face. "I live an active lifestyle, Julia. That doesn't make me an adrenaline junky. It makes me . . . adventurous." He kissed both her palms. "I'm willing to compromise. I can give up some of the more . . . physical things I do, but you have to participate or at least watch before I give up anything. Deal?"

Her gaze traveled all over his face. Stephen braced himself for her refusal. Then a soft smile turned up her lips. "Deal."

He kissed her, gently, sweetly. Soon, he needed more than

gentle and sweet. He needed her naked beneath him as fast as possible. The way she clung to his neck as they kissed proved she had a similar thought.

He moved his lips to the sensitive area beneath her ear. "How long does that casserole have to cook?"

She sighed when he nipped the pulse in her neck. "About twenty minutes."

"Plenty of time for a quickie."

Stephen bent over and pulled her across his shoulder. Julia squealed. "What are you doing!"

"Demonstrating a proper fireman's hold."

Laughing, she gripped his belt as he started toward her bedroom. "If you drop me, you're in big trouble."

"I have no intention of dropping you, darlin'. I'm going to hold on to you for a long, long time."

Smolder

1

Marcus Holt leaned on the fender of his pickup and took a long pull from his can of beer. The sun had set a few minutes ago, which meant the fireworks show would start soon.

He wouldn't be here if the Fourth of July barbecue and fireworks hadn't been sponsored by the Lanville Volunteer Fire Department. He'd avoided the downtown parade this morning, not interested in being around so many people, but couldn't avoid something in which he played such a huge part. As one of the three fire department captains, he felt he had to at least make an appearance. He planned to escape as soon as the show ended.

Some of his firemen buddies apparently had other ideas.

Nick Fallon and Stephen McGettis wandered over to him and took their places on either side of him. Beer cans in hand, they leaned against his pickup and crossed their ankles.

"Nice night," Nick said.

"Too hot," Marcus replied with a frown.

"It's July in Texas," Stephen said after taking a sip of his beer. "It's supposed to be hot."

Nick turned his head toward Marcus. "The breeze helps."

"The breeze is hot, too." Marcus released a heavy sigh. "Why are y'all bugging me?"

Stephen nudged Marcus in the ribs. "We couldn't let you watch the fireworks all alone."

"Shouldn't you be with Julia?" Marcus looked at Nick. "And you're a newlywed. Where's Keely?"

"Both our ladies are helping with the food." Nick turned his billed cap backward on his head. "Looks like you're stuck with us."

"Yippee."

Stephen leaned forward to look at Nick. "He's grouchy tonight."

"Yeah, even more than usual."

Marcus had had enough. He wanted to be alone, not in the middle of a "bro" sandwich. "Okay, what the fuck do y'all want?"

"We know what today is, Marcus," Stephen said, all traces of humor gone from his voice. He laid his hand on Marcus's shoulder. "We just want you to know we're here if you need us."

Marcus's throat tightened and his eyes burned. He wouldn't fall apart. Not in front of his friends. Tears could come later when he sat alone in his house, not out in public. He gave a quick nod to let them know he understood.

Stephen squeezed Marcus's shoulder. "I want another helping of Mrs. Hurley's peach cobbler. How about you?"

A hint of a smile worked its way to Marcus's lips. "She does make the best peach cobbler in town."

"That she does." Stephen jerked his head toward the fire hall, where all the food had been set up on tables outside the large building. "C'mon. I'll buy you another beer."

Despite the horrible memories of this day and what happened five years ago, his friends made him feel better. A real smile turned up his lips. "You're on."

* * *

"Hey, Marcus." Paige Denslow smiled at him with a "come hither" bat of her eyelashes. "What can I do for you?"

Marcus ignored Nick's snicker at the double entendre. Paige had made it very clear she wanted to date him. At six years his junior, he didn't consider them close enough in age to have anything in common. Except for maybe sex. He had no doubt she would be willing to share his bed. If Marcus felt any desire for her at all, he'd take her up on her numerous offers. The fact that a gorgeous, well-built woman with long blond hair and hazel eyes didn't turn him on meant some parts of his brain didn't fire the way they should.

"Any more of Mrs. Hurley's peach cobbler?" he finally asked her.

"Sure. She brought two huge pans of it." Her gaze passed to Stephen and Nick. "Y'all want some, too?"

"Yeah," Nick said, his stare fastened on Keely standing next to Paige. "And a kiss from my wife."

A lovely blush spread over Keely's cheeks. She leaned over the table and met Nick halfway for a gentle kiss. They'd married one month ago today and still had that newlywed air around them. A yearning clutched Marcus's heart, the desire to have the same kind of happiness.

He'd been in love and happy once . . . until his wife left him.

Pushing aside thoughts of Rayna, Marcus accepted the paper bowl of cobbler from Paige. She gave him another smile. "Enjoy."

Marcus returned her smile. "Thanks." Even though he didn't desire her, he could still be friendly. It made working together on the volunteer fire department much easier.

He turned away from the lovely blonde and found Stephen talking to Julia Woods next to the ice chests of drinks. Two large glass jars with slits in the lids sat in front of her, each bearing a label that read *Water or Cokes $1.00, Beer $2.00*. The honor system had worked well for drinks for years. The fire department threw barbecues and fish fries several times a year as fund-raisers. People often paid more than requested for the food and drinks to help out a service everyone in Lanville appreciated.

As a captain with access to the accounting records, he knew exactly how finances stood for the department. Whatever they took in from tonight would go toward the new tanker-truck fund. What they already had, plus what they'd make on the firefighters calendar that would come out in September, should push them over the top so they could order their truck.

Thank God he'd managed to avoid posing for the calendar. His fire chief's girlfriend, Maysen Halliday, had even begged him, but he'd refused. He'd help however he could to raise money for his department, but he'd drawn the line at posing shirtless with some of the other firefighters. Luckily, with twenty-four men and three women in the department, Maysen had had plenty of others to photograph.

Stephen slipped a five-dollar bill into one of the jars and took two cans of beer from a cooler. After kissing Julia's cheek, he turned toward Marcus and held out one of the cans to him. "Let's find a place to enjoy the fireworks."

Marcus swallowed his last bite of cobbler and accepted the can. He appreciated his friends' caring, but he believed a fireworks show should be enjoyed with a loved one. "Thanks, man, but watch it with Julia." Nick walked up to them, so Marcus turned to him. "And you watch with Keely. I was down for a bit, but I'm fine now."

Stephen didn't look convinced. "You sure?"

"Yeah, I'm sure." He tossed his bowl and plastic spoon into a nearby trash can. "Go be with your ladies."

Before either Nick or Stephen responded, the pagers attached to all three men's belts gave off loud beeps. Marcus unclipped his and looked at it. "Two beeps. Grass fire."

All around the trio, other firefighters' pagers sounded with the same alarm. Being the closest to the fire hall's entrance, Marcus shouted out, "Let's go!" and ran into the building.

Clay Spencer, their fire chief, stood inside the door. Marcus waved for the firefighters to be quiet so the chief could speak. "Grass fire on County Road 2221. Bad one. It's heading toward Parker Place. Move it!"

Marcus went into automatic mode, the way he always did when a fire broke out. Nothing mattered except taming the conflagration, hopefully before it destroyed much property.

Or took a life.

"Holy shit," Quade Easton muttered as he slowed the pickup several yards from the fire line.

"I second that," Marcus said. The blaze had definitely gotten out of control. Flames as far as he could see burned acres of dry brush and trees. With the drought that all of Texas experienced now, the flames had plenty of fuel. They shot several feet into the air in a wicked dance on their way to nearby houses.

Wasting no time, he exited the pickup with Quade and headed toward the rest of Lanville's crew. Fire departments from several of the nearby towns had already been called to help. Marcus knew the Lanville firefighters would need the extra help as there seemed to be three distinct blazes going in three different directions.

"Power and gas are off," Clay said loud enough to be heard over the commotion behind him. "Everyone's been evacuated from the houses. We're fighting three fires. You"—his arm swept a group of a third of Lanville's firefighters—"to the main brush blaze. You"—he pointed to the next group—"come with me to the secondary brush blaze heading toward the houses. And you"—he turned to the remaining group—"you're working the houses. Move, move!"

Marcus couldn't help taking a moment to glance over the nearby houses. His ex-wife's grandmother, Grace, lived in one of them. Right now, with all the commotion and the smoke making it difficult to see, he couldn't tell which one belonged to her.

Pushing aside thoughts of the elderly woman he adored, Marcus led his six firefighters toward the houses. Two of the new homes were completely engulfed with no chance of saving them. The roof of the third house burned, but not badly enough yet so it couldn't be stopped. Acting on instinct and experience, he helped Quade connect the hose to the fire hydrant and aimed the powerful spray toward the structure.

Nick raced up to him, an ax lying over his shoulder. "Anyone inside?" he yelled to be heard through the built-in microphone in his mask over the roar of the water.

"Not supposed to be," Marcus said.

Nick looked toward the house, a concerned expression on his face. "I think this is Grace Simpson's house."

Fear skittered down Marcus's spine. He knew Grace got around fine on her own, yet also knew she had a heart condition. He had no idea if her caretaker, Mattie, had gotten her out of the house safely.

He had to know for sure.

"Nick, with me. We're going in."

Two other firemen aimed the hose through a window as Marcus and Nick entered the front door. "Left first," Marcus said.

"Roger that."

Marcus led the way through the smoky living room. "Is anyone here?" he called out as loud as he could. No one in the dining room, or the kitchen. He assumed the bedrooms occupied the other side of the house.

He and Nick made their way down the hall, searching every room. The ceiling above him burned, so the fire made it through the roof at least in part of the house. Showers of sparks fell on him and he knew they had to get out of the house soon.

"All clear," Nick said. "We'd better get out of here."

He didn't have to say that twice. Marcus took a step toward Nick, intending to follow him out of the house, when a crack sounded overhead. A huge part of the ceiling collapsed, right over Nick.

"Look out!"

Marcus lunged toward Nick and pushed him backward. Nick fell against a wall as the burning debris came down on top of Marcus. His left arm twisted beneath him when he hit the floor. He cried out in pain and instinctively curled into a ball to protect himself from the flames.

"Man down!" he heard Nick yell over the microphone.

Marcus batted at the burning chunks of wood while trying to protect his wrist. Only a few moments passed before other firefighters were by his side, knocking away the remnants from the ceiling. Someone grabbed him beneath his arms and tugged. He pressed his lips tightly together as the movement jarred his arm and pain shot through his wrist.

"I've got you, buddy," Stephen said. "Hold on."

Once clear of the debris, Nick lifted Marcus's legs behind the knees. Marcus clutched his left wrist with his right hand while his friends carried him from the burning house all the way to one of their ambulances, despite his protest that he could walk.

Clay rushed up to the ambulance as Marcus sat inside the door. "You okay?" he asked.

"Yeah. Bummed up my wrist a bit."

Starla Harkins, one of their EMTs, helped Marcus remove his turnout coat. Stocky and tough with short dark hair, she looked like she'd just as soon break his arm as repair it. Her gentle touch while she checked his wrist didn't fit at all with her appearance.

"I don't think it's broken, Marcus, but we're taking you to the hospital to get it checked."

"I don't need to go to the hospital," Marcus said, frowning. "Just slap a bandage around it and I'll get back to the fire."

"You aren't going anywhere except to the hospital." Clay's firm voice clearly implied there would be no argument. "You know the rules, Marcus."

"Chief, I'm fine. I can still work the hose."

Ignoring his protest, Clay spoke to Starla. "Get him out of here."

"Yes, sir."

"Clay—"

"Nick, Stephen, back to the fire."

The two men hurried off while Marcus still sputtered in protest. Clay finally held up a hand to silence him.

"Enough! More fire departments are on the way. We'll handle it, Marcus. You get that wrist taken care of."

Blowing out a sigh, Marcus nodded. Starla stayed by his side while he climbed into the ambulance and sat on the gurney. "Ronnie driving?" he asked her, referring to another of the EMTs.

She nodded. "He's talking to the hospital now and letting the ER know we're on the way."

"Shit," he muttered.

Starla grinned, which transformed her face from rough to friendly. "Don't worry, macho man. You'll be back to swinging your hose before you know it."

He could take her statement two ways, and he knew that's exactly how Starla meant it. He laughed along with her.

"Lie back," she said, pressing on his shoulders. "I'm going to put an ice pack on your wrist and check your vitals."

Marcus did as she said. He closed his eyes and shifted until he found a comfortable spot on the gurney for the short ride to the hospital.

2

Rayna Holt brushed back the soft white hair from her grandmother's face. She'd cried all her tears on the flight from San Francisco to Dallas–Fort Worth, so now her eyes remained dry. She didn't want Nana to wake up and see her granddaughter upset.

Rayna silently kicked herself for not insisting her grandmother move to San Francisco to live with her. Despite having heart problems, Nana always said no when Rayna mentioned it, saying she'd lived in Lanville her entire life and had no plans to ever move away. She visited Rayna often and always enjoyed seeing the city's sites, but no place would be home except Lanville.

Rayna's only other option had been to hire a live-in caretaker. Although Nana got around fine on her own, Rayna knew the day would come when her seventy-nine-year-old grandmother would need help taking care of herself. So she'd bought a house for Nana in a brand-new housing development, one with wide doorways and lots of open space so she could move around easily. After balking about the expense, Nana had finally relented and accepted Rayna's gift. Once settled in the house, her grandmother had told Rayna how much she loved it.

Rayna glanced around the hospital room, noting the pale yellow walls and white trim. Soothing. She'd never been inside the hospital. Nana's health had generally been good until a few years ago, when her heart problems intensified. There'd never been a reason for Rayna to see the inside of a hospital room in Lanville.

There hadn't been a reason for her to see anything in Texas, period. The painful memories made it impossible for her to come here to visit her grandmother. Since Nana loved to fly, it had been easier for Rayna to make the arrangements for Nana to visit her.

"What are you doing here?"

Turning her attention back to her grandmother, Rayna saw Nana's smoky blue eyes open and alert. She smiled. "Hey, Nana."

Nana didn't return her smile. "Rayna, what are you doing here?"

"I came to see you. I was worried about you."

"*Pffft*. All this commotion about a little shortness of breath."

"Nana, you had an exacerbation of congestive heart failure. That's serious."

"Yeah, yeah, whatever." Frowning, she looked around as if she'd lost something. "How do I raise this damn bed so we can talk?"

Rayna pressed the button to lift the head of the bed. Once Nana gave her okay to the position, Rayna adjusted the pillows behind her grandmother's back and head.

"Don't fuss over me, child."

"Don't give me a hard time," Rayna snapped.

Nana's sour expression vanished, to be replaced by a grin that lit up her entire face. "I knew that would piss you off."

Rayna laughed, which she thought a miracle since a few minutes ago she'd been so worried about the woman she loved more than anyone in the world.

"How long do I have to be in this place?" Nana asked as she smoothed the covers around her hips.

"At least a couple of days. Maybe three. I spoke to the nurse on duty. Your doctor wants to run some tests."

"Tests, schmests. A waste of my money and his time. I'm fine."

Rayna picked up Nana's hand and clasped it between both of hers. She looked at the pale skin and light blue veins so close to the surface. "For my peace of mind, let your doctor run the tests, okay? I want to be sure you're all right."

Nana studied her with that shrewd blue gaze that had always made Rayna believe her grandmother could see right inside her brain. "Who told you I was in the hospital? Mattie?"

Rayna nodded. "She called me this morning. I took the first plane I could get."

"I told her not to bother you."

"And I told her I wanted to be kept up-to-date on how you're doing. She did exactly what she should've done."

Nana's eyes turned soft, sympathetic. "I know how hard it must be for you to have come here." She squeezed Rayna's hand. "You haven't been back to Texas since you moved to California."

No, and she wouldn't be here now if she hadn't been so worried about her grandmother. Pushing aside her discomfort, she smiled at Nana. "I'm the worrier, not you."

A gentle knock sounded on the door. Rayna looked over her shoulder to see Mattie's face in the open doorway. "Could I talk to you, Rayna?"

"What is it?" Nana asked, anxiety evident in her voice. "If it's about me, tell me, Mattie."

Mattie smiled, but Rayna thought it looked forced. "It isn't about you, Grace. I just want to talk to Rayna a minute."

Rayna kissed her grandmother's cheek. "I'll be right back."

Once outside the room, Rayna followed Mattie a few yards down the hall. "What's up?"

The concern in Mattie's eyes made her look older than her twenty-six years, and made Rayna's stomach churn. "There's a fire at Parker Place."

Now her stomach roiled along with churning. Her grandmother and Mattie lived in the Parker Place housing development.

Mattie grabbed Rayna's hands. "Grace's house is okay. The roof and outside kitchen wall caught fire, but the house is still standing. It's mostly smoke and water damage, although the roof and that wall will have to be repaired. There are holes in both."

Rayna released the air in her lungs in a long *whoosh*. "Repairs can be done. I'm thankful her house wasn't destroyed. Were any of the houses badly burned?"

Mattie nodded. "Three have been completely destroyed, three others have major damage. The fire is still burning, but it's a lot smaller than it was. Some of the neighboring fire departments are helping. I heard that some of our firefighters were hurt."

"Seriously?"

"Enough to bring them here to the hospital."

Hearing that some of the local heroes had been hurt made Rayna want to hunt down a set of scrubs to wear and jump in to help.

"I'm going back to Parker Place and see how things are going," Mattie said. "Clay said I could go in the house and get some personal items once the fire is completely out."

"Clay?"

"Clay Spencer. He's our fire chief."

The mention of Mattie's personal items clicked in Rayna's brain. "Do you have a place to stay tonight? I have a room at The Inn on Crystal Creek. You can stay with me."

Mattie smiled. "Thanks, but I'm going to my sister and brother-in-law's house for a couple of nights." Her smile faded. "I don't know where Grace will go when she gets out of the hospital. I have no idea how long it will take to repair her house."

Rayna hadn't planned to stay any longer than it took for her to be sure her grandmother would be all right. With the fire causing damage to Nana's house, she might have to extend her visit. "I'll take care of getting Nana settled. She'll be here for at least two more days. That'll give me time to make a plan."

"Okay." Mattie glanced at her watch. "It's almost midnight. I'm going back out to check on the fire department's progress."

"Call me and let me know."

"Will do."

Mattie turned as if to walk away, then faced Rayna again. "You should call Coleman Construction for the repairs. They're the best. They do a great job and won't cheat you with inflated prices like some companies would do in a disaster."

"Coleman Construction. They're here in Lanville?"

Mattie nodded. "I can get the phone number for you."

"I'll find it. Thanks, Mattie."

Rayna returned to her grandmother's room to find Nana fast asleep, a contented, peaceful look on her face. She reached to press the button to lower the bed's head, but stopped. Worried the movement might wake Nana, Rayna left the bed in the current position. She gently tugged up the sheet and light blanket to her grandmother's neck, kissed her forehead, and left the room.

Rayna followed the signs to the emergency room's exit, where she'd parked her rental car. Several men and women milled around in the ER waiting area. None of them appeared hurt, so they must be waiting for loved ones who were receiving treatment.

The double doors to the ER swung open as she walked by them. She automatically turned her head that direction. The sight of a man walking toward her stopped her in mid step. She locked gazes with the last person in the world she expected to see.

Her ex-husband, Marcus.

If Marcus hadn't known for sure that he'd received no head injury, he would swear hallucinations plagued him. Rayna stood in his path, no more than five feet from him.

He quickly glanced over her slim but shapely body. She wore a simple green blouse, brown slacks, and brown flats. Her straight, red hair brushed her shoulders. Her hazel eyes appeared huge. She had to be as shocked to see him as he was to see her.

So many emotions swirled through him at the sight of her—love, passion, anger, sadness, confusion, disappointment, pain—all caused by the lovely woman standing before him. Some feelings came from the past, some from the present. They all mixed together until he had trouble separating them.

He didn't know whether to speak or ignore her. He settled on dipping his head once to acknowledge he'd seen her. She blinked a couple of times, then did the same.

Rye Coleman stepped closer to him. "Hey, Marcus, you okay?"

Tearing his gaze away from Rayna, Marcus nodded at his boss. "Yeah, just banged up my wrist a bit." He cradled his left arm in his right hand. An Ace bandage wrapped around his left wrist. "I have to keep it iced and elevated for a couple of days."

"You're lucky it isn't worse." Dax, Rye's brother, squeezed Marcus's shoulder. "We're glad you're okay."

"Thanks." He looked from one brother to the other, but

could still see Rayna from the corner of his eye. "Have you been out there?" he asked Rye.

Rye nodded. "We've already talked to a lot of people about repairs. Griff is at the office now, manning the phones. Even this late at night, it's been crazy."

"I'll bet." Coleman Construction stayed busy year round. As foreman, that meant Marcus stayed busy, too. He wouldn't let a sprained wrist keep him from working. He lifted his left arm a bit higher. "This won't stop me. No break, just a bad sprain. I can still order everyone around like I usually do."

"Which is exactly what a foreman is supposed to do." Rye smiled. "I know you can still bid jobs. Just don't push it and pick up something heavy until that wrist is healed."

Movement to his left had Marcus looking that direction. He watched Rayna walk through the waiting room and out the exit door.

Dax's gaze followed Marcus's. "Pretty lady. Do you know her?"

"Yeah. She's my ex-wife."

"Dayum. And you let her go?"

"I didn't have a choice, Dax. She left me after . . ." Marcus's voice trailed off, not wanting to say the words aloud why Rayna had decided to end their marriage.

Marcus could see in Dax's eyes the moment the lightbulb went off in his head. "Oh, shit. This is July fourth. God, man, I'm sorry."

"Technically, it's now the fifth, but thanks." Before Dax could say anything else, Marcus turned to Rye. "What time should I be at the office tomorrow?"

Rye gestured toward Marcus's arm. "You said you're supposed to ice and elevate your wrist for a couple of days."

"I can do that and still work." The expression on Rye's face told Marcus that his boss was about to argue. Marcus quickly continued before Rye could. "I need to work, Rye. It helps me forget . . . things."

Rye ran a finger over his moustache. "You promise to take breaks?"

"I promise."

"Okay. Be there at eight. I'm sure you'll have a shitload of work to do."

"A shitload of work is exactly what I want."

Marcus. Here. Rayna couldn't believe her ex-husband lived in Lanville. But then, she shouldn't be surprised. They had visited Nana here many times during their marriage and he'd often commented on how much he liked the small town. They'd lived in Irving, right in the middle of the Dallas–Fort Worth Metroplex, so visiting Nana had been like a vacation from the traffic and noise of the large cities. The hustle and bustle hadn't bothered Rayna, yet Marcus preferred a quieter lifestyle.

His new lifestyle must include being a part of the volunteer fire department. She wondered if his toned, muscled body came from fighting fires. He'd always had a killer body, but now she'd describe him as buff. His golden brown hair had swirled over his ears and covered his nape, much longer than he used to wear it. His T-shirt and firefighter pants had been covered in dirt and smoke, but didn't detract from his incredible good looks.

Her throat tightened as she started her rental car and headed for the bed-and-breakfast where she would stay for the next few days. Seeing Marcus brought back so many memories, both bad and good. She had been ridiculously in love with him. Walking down the aisle toward him on their wedding day had been the happiest moment of her life. She'd thought they'd be together forever.

Fate had other ideas. Just when they should have been the happiest, their joy had been snatched away from them on July fourth five years ago.

Rayna blinked back the tears before they had the chance to fall. Their divorce could have been prevented if only she'd had more courage. Facing the pain, the heartache . . . she hadn't been able to do it. Seeing Marcus every day, blaming him for that pain and heartache, had slowly drained away any small amount of good left in her life. Her only choice had been a fresh start in a new city, a new state.

Away from the man she'd loved with all her heart and soul.

At least she wouldn't have to see him again while she remained in Lanville. She would be busy with her grandmother's house repairs and getting Nana settled again. She figured it would take only a few days for that to happen. Then she'd go back to her life in San Francisco.

Once again, she would run away and not look back.

3

"These are the calls that came in last night." Griff Coleman handed a legal pad to Marcus that contained a list of twelve names and telephone numbers, along with the damages to each of those twelve names' homes. "The last two are minor smoke and water damage. I already have a call in to the company we use in Fort Worth for fire and flood cleanup. Luckily, we haven't had to use them much in the last few years. The rest of the houses on this list will need a lot more."

Marcus scanned the list. The three houses that had been completely destroyed sat at the top of the list. Nothing could be done on those until the owners decided if they wanted their homes replaced as they had been originally built or if they wanted something different. The remaining nine listed damages from half the house burned to replacing a few roof shingles.

He looked a second time, but didn't see Grace Simpson's name. "Mattie didn't call about Grace's house?"

"No, not yet. The damage there wasn't too extensive. Maybe Mattie decided to wait until this morning to call about repairs after she talks to Ms. Grace. Rye told me Ms. Grace had a mild heart episode and is in the hospital for some tests."

Marcus's entire body tensed to discover Grace was in the hospital. "Is she okay?"

"Yeah. Rye said he talked to Mattie while we were waiting to find out about you. Something about an exacerbation of a heart something." Griff shrugged. "That's all I know."

Rayna's grandmother being in the hospital had to be the reason he'd seen Rayna there last night. Grace's condition must be more serious than anyone thought or Rayna wouldn't have flown here from San Francisco. When she left Texas, she'd vowed never to come back to the state.

He made a mental note to visit Grace later today, after he figured out his schedule for calling the people on this list.

The other part of Griff's comment didn't make sense. The whole cciling in Grace's home collapsed on top of him. It had to have more than minor damage. "Wait. Wasn't it Grace's house that Nick and I went into last night?"

Griff shook his head. "No, her house is across the street from that one. The fire damage wasn't as bad on her side."

Relief swept through him that Grace's home had been spared. "I guess I got turned around in the smoke. I thought her house had a lot more damage."

"She was lucky. As were a lot of the folks in Parker Place. The remaining eight homes in the development didn't receive any damage at all." Griff glanced at his watch. "Speaking of Parker Place, I'm on my way there to help with the cleanup. Emma put out the word for help in preparing food for the workers. The kitchen at Café Crystal is full of volunteers. All the restaurants are chipping in to help."

"I'll go out there after I finish these phone calls—"

"You'll do no such thing," Griff said with a frown. "You'll stay here and ice your wrist. No lifting anything heavier than an ink pen. Got it?"

"I want to help, Griff."

Griff tapped the legal pad in Marcus's hand. "You're helping by taking care of the people on that list. That's your main job now."

"Yeah, okay." Marcus knew helping people repair their homes had to be the highest priority. Still, he wished he could help physically at the site of the fire.

"Coffee's fresh and Dax bought donuts before he went to Parker Place." Griff picked up his cell phone from the desk, clipped it to his belt. "Make the appointments for whenever it's convenient for these people." He tapped the pad again. "Rye, Dax, and I will arrange our schedules to fit theirs. I've already talked to James Parker about postponing construction of the house we're building now in Parker Place. He agreed without hesitation. Once we finish the repairs, we'll start working on the new houses again."

Hearing James hadn't hesitated to put the new houses on hold didn't surprise Marcus. A truly good guy, James had moved to Lanville a year and a half ago and soon fell in love with Teanna Caldwell, who helped run the local pharmacy. After James and Teanna married, they'd financed the new housing addition named Parker Place. Thirty-five homes would eventually fill the development . . . some rentals, some that people could buy. Coleman Construction had the contract to build all of them.

"Some of these people might not want to wait for us," Marcus said as he studied the list. "They might hire another construction firm."

"True, and that's their choice if they want to do that. I don't think they will, since they've already called us."

"Y'all will have to hire more workers so we can take care of everyone without them waiting too long."

"Mom will be in later to take care of placing ads for more help. You're in charge of the hiring."

Marcus blinked. "I am?"

Griff nodded. "Rye, Dax, and I talked about it this morning before they took off. We decided it's time to give you more . . . managerial duties since you're our foreman. Plus a few days here in the office will give your wrist time to heal the way it should. More duties mean more pay. You'll see a raise in Friday's paycheck."

Completely surprised by Griff's statement, Marcus didn't know what to say. Even a small raise meant he could afford to finish the remodeling on his house quicker than he originally planned. He would enjoy walking through his home and seeing all the rooms finished and decorated. "I . . . Thanks, Griff."

"Don't thank me yet. You don't know how hard we're going to work you."

"I'm ready."

"Good." He glanced around the office, as if making sure he hadn't forgotten anything. "I'm heading out. Call my cell if you need me."

"Okay." Marcus held out his hand to shake. "Thanks again, Griff."

Smiling, Griff accepted Marcus's hand. "You're welcome."

Once Griff left, Marcus wandered to the break room and helped himself to an apple fritter and a large mug of coffee. He devoured a third of the fritter on his way back to the office. Laying it on a napkin on the desk, he wiped his hands on his jeans and sat down, prepared to begin making phone calls.

Before he had the chance to punch in the numbers of the first customer, the front door opened. He lifted his head to greet whoever walked in. The greeting died in his throat when he saw Rayna.

Her eyes widened the way they had at the hospital last night. Slowly, Marcus rose from his chair. He watched her close the door and take a few steps into the room. She'd come into the place where he worked. He couldn't avoid speaking to her. "Hey, Rayna."

"Marcus." Her voice sounded hoarse, raspy. It reminded him of the way she'd said his name while on the brink of orgasm.

Don't go there, buddy. That part of your life is gone.

"You work here?" she asked after clearing her throat. She must have heard the huskiness in her voice, too.

He nodded. "I'm the foreman."

"Oh."

While she glanced around the spacious, airy office, Marcus took the opportunity to let his gaze wander over her. She wore a simple olive green T-shirt, faded jeans, and white running shoes today. Ivory combs held her hair behind her ears. She looked every bit as stunning in the everyday clothes as she had last night in the silk blouse and creased slacks.

He didn't know what to do, what to say. For someone who had no trouble talking to anyone, his tongue seemed glued to the roof of his mouth. All the confusing feelings he'd experienced last night came barreling back to swamp him . . . feelings he didn't know how to handle.

He had to push everything aside and be professional in order to get through the reason for her visit. "I assume you're here about Grace's house."

His statement seemed to shake her from her shock. "Yes. It suffered some damage from the fire last night. Mattie told me I should contact Coleman Construction."

Marcus smiled at the thought of the young, cute brunette with the freckles scattered over her face. "Mattie's a good kid. She takes great care of Grace."

"Twenty-six is hardly a kid, Marcus."

"Anyone younger than thirty is a kid to me."

Her lips quirked in what Marcus could call a small smile, if he used his imagination. "You're only thirty-three."

"Some days I feel older than that. I guess that happens to

everyone." He motioned toward one of the two chairs before the desk. "Sit down. Let's talk about Grace's house."

She peered into his mug before she sat. "Do you have any more of that coffee?"

"Sure. I'll get you some."

He found another ceramic mug in the break room's cabinet and filled it with the hot brew. After splashing a generous amount of creamer in it, he peered into the cardboard box of donuts. Locating a chocolate-covered old-fashioned, he laid it on a napkin and headed back to the office.

"Here you go." He set the mug and napkin on the desk in front of her.

Rayna stared at the donut and coffee for a long moment before looking back at him with a deer-in-the-headlights expression. "You remember how I fix my coffee and the type of donut I like?"

Marcus shrugged. "I remember a lot of things."

Including one Sunday morning when he'd gone out early to pick up muffins and donuts. He'd brought them to Rayna in bed and proceeded to place pieces of a chocolate old-fashioned donut on her nude body. Starting at her neck, he'd eaten the pieces as he made his way down her silky flesh. After he finished the last crumb that he'd placed at the top of her pubic hair, he'd feasted on her pussy until she'd cried out from her climax.

She looked at the donut, then back at him. He thought he saw lust flash through her eyes as if she, too, thought of that morning. Or perhaps he imagined he saw lust. Maybe deep inside, he wanted her to remember the amazing sex life they'd shared and hurt the way he had at the loss of something so extraordinary.

He didn't imagine the way her hands trembled when she picked up the mug and sipped her coffee.

"It's good. You always did make great coffee."

"Thanks, but Griff made the pot."

"Griff?"

"One of the triplets who owns Coleman Construction."

She smiled for real this time, making her hazel eyes sparkle. "Triplets? Really?"

"Yep. You may have seen two of the brothers last night with me at the hospital. Rye and Dax."

"I thought those guys looked a lot alike." She pinched off a bite of her donut, popped it into her mouth. "They have interesting names."

"They're great guys and terrific bosses."

She glanced at his wrist. "Are you okay?"

"Sure. Just a mild sprain. No big deal."

Marcus couldn't believe he sat here and carried on a normal conversation with his ex-wife. She'd trampled all over his heart when she'd left him five years ago. Anger had consumed him for months that she could've thrown away their love when they needed each other the most.

He supposed time really did make things better.

Although he'd never forget the pain and heartache, he could look at Rayna now and remember the good between them instead of concentrating on the bad. He had no choice. If he kept concentrating on the bad, it would eat him up from the inside out.

He realized several moments had passed without either of them saying anything. He drew the legal pad closer to him, flipped it to a clean page, and picked up a pen. "Do you know about the damages at Grace's house?"

"I went out there before I came here and looked around. There's a lot of water everywhere. The roof and kitchen wall were burned enough that there are small holes in both."

"I have other customers to contact about their repairs and I have to set up appointments with everyone at their homes. That'll take me most of the morning. I could meet you at Grace's house this afternoon. How about three-thirty?"

"Whatever works for you. I'm going to the hospital to visit Nana as soon as I leave here. Other than that, my schedule is open."

"Tell her I'll get over there to see her after lunch, okay?"

Her eyebrows shot up in obvious astonishment at his request. "Do you see her often?"

"All the time. I visit with her at least once every couple of weeks." He tilted his head when her expression didn't change. "That surprises you?"

"Well, yes. I didn't know you'd stayed close with her. She doesn't mention you to me."

"She doesn't mention you to me either. It's probably better that way."

"I guess." Rayna cleared her throat, set her mug on the desk. "I'll go so you can get back to work. I'll see you at three-thirty."

He noticed she didn't look him in the eyes again as she wrapped the rest of her donut in the napkin. She held it in both hands as if it was something precious.

A few years ago, Marcus would have done almost anything to hurt Rayna as much as she'd hurt him. Seeing her looking so dejected made him long to make her feel better. He followed her to the door, put his hand over hers on the door handle before she could press it down.

"Would you rather work with someone else?" he asked, his voice gentle. "I can have one of the Colemans meet you at Grace's house. Or you can hire a different company."

"No," she said, staring at his hand on top of hers, "I don't want to hire a different company. I know Nana would want me to hire Coleman Construction. I think the more important question is . . ." She looked into his eyes. They stood close enough for him to see the gold ring that circled her hazel irises. "Can *you* work with *me*?"

4

Rayna held her breath while waiting for Marcus's answer. He'd been incredibly nice to her, much nicer than she deserved. If he'd pushed her out the door without a word spoken, she wouldn't have blamed him.

"I'm a representative of Coleman Construction," Marcus said. "If you hire the company for Grace's repairs, I won't have any problem working with you."

Disappointment flashed through her when he removed his hand from on top of hers. Since he had been nothing but professional with her, Rayna decided she had to be the same way. "I'm definitely hiring Coleman Construction. I'll meet you at Nana's house at three-thirty."

"I'll be there."

She opened the door and stepped out into the warm, humid morning. She'd never cared for the humidity in the summer when she lived in Texas, but it hadn't made her feel as if she'd been hit in the face with a wet wash cloth the way it did today. Her five years in the cool San Francisco summers had spoiled her.

A shopping spree for tank tops might have to be added to

her to-do list today. That would mean a trip out of town since Lanville didn't have any clothing stores. Or at least there hadn't been any here five years ago. She knew little about the town now.

Perhaps a trip around the square should be added to her to-do list, too. Or she could ask Mattie or Nana.

Rayna glanced at her watch. 8:40. Nana should be awake and ready for a visit by now.

She munched on her donut on the drive to the hospital. She remembered so many occasions when Marcus had bought her a chocolate old-fashioned. Their favorite donut shop had been located only four blocks from their house in Irving, so he'd gone there often. Probably more often than he should have, considering she'd never been able to resist them . . . especially when he incorporated one into their sex play.

One Sunday morning, he'd let her sleep in since she didn't have a shift at the hospital. She'd awakened to the wonderful smell of fresh coffee, and to his lips moving down her spine. He'd dropped soft kisses all the way to her cleft before she rolled over. He sat on his knees, completely naked, holding up one of her favorite donuts. When she started to sit up to take it from him, he'd gently pressed between her breasts to keep her lying flat. Then he'd torn the donut into small pieces and scattered them down her torso.

Rayna remembered the way he'd plucked up the bits of pastry with his lips before licking the spot clean with his tongue. He'd moved slowly down her body . . . much slower than she would've liked. By the time he'd eaten the last bite of donut, she'd been ready to push him to his back and ravish him.

He'd stopped all her thoughts of ravishment when he'd lain between her legs and started licking her pussy.

His mouth on her had always shot up her desire in a matter of seconds. That time had been no different. He'd barely touched her clit with the tip of his tongue when the orgasm had roared through her, heating her blood, melting her bones, dissolving her muscles. She'd been too weak to do anything but lie there and attempt to catch her breath while he kissed his way back up her body. When he reached her mouth, he'd kissed her to breath-lessness again as he plunged his cock into her channel. Another climax had rocked her at the same time she felt Marcus tense from his release.

Desire had always smoldered just beneath the surface. A single look from Marcus and her body began to ready itself for his possession. His lovemaking had ranged from sweet and loving to take-her-against-the-wall rough.

She'd loved every moment of it.

Rayna waved one hand before her face as she pulled into a parking space at the hospital, trying to cool herself from the heat of her memories. Her nipples beaded in her bra, her clit gently pulsed. Sex had never been a problem between her and Marcus. It had been hot and romantic and completely satisfying.

And very much missed.

The past couldn't be changed, no matter how much she wished it so. Pushing aside the memories, Rayna opened the car door and stepped from the cool interior back into the humid air. She walked briskly to the entrance doors, eager to be inside the air-conditioning once again.

She gave a small smile to the people she passed in the hall-ways on her way to Nana's room. All returned her smile, some said a greeting. She didn't recognize anyone, but it had been five years since she'd been in Lanville. Her visits then consisted of mostly visiting with Nana at her house, perhaps going out to lunch or dinner. She hadn't taken the time or opportunity to meet people.

It would be the same this time. As soon as she knew Nana's situation had stabilized, she'd go back to her home and job in San Francisco.

Smiling broadly, she pushed open Nana's door. Her smile faded when she saw the empty bed.

A noise from the bathroom drew Rayna's attention. She walked toward the room as a nurse came out carrying a small vase of colorful flowers. The nurse stopped when she saw Rayna, her eyes widening in obvious surprise. Then she smiled. "Hello."

"Hello. Where is my grandmother?"

"Ms. Grace is your grandmother?"

Rayna nodded.

The nurse's smile turned tender. "She's such a sweet lady. Everyone in town loves her." She lifted the vase a few inches higher. "The latest from one of her friends. I was giving it a drink. Now I just have to find a place to put it."

Her comment made Rayna glance around the room. Vases holding flowers or plants covered every available space. A bouquet of colorful balloons was tied to the footboard of Nana's bed. A small cart held at least a dozen cards. "Wow. None of this was here last night."

"It's been coming all morning. I expect more this afternoon. I may have to bring in another rolling cart."

She grinned, which Rayna couldn't help but return. "I'm Rayna."

"Tracy."

Rayna guessed Tracy to be around fifty from the streaks of gray in her dark hair and the laugh lines at the corners of her eyes. Rayna recognized kindness and caring in the nurse's pale blue eyes. "It's nice to meet you."

"You, too." Tracy rearranged a few vases on the windowsill and made a place for the new addition. "Your grandmother is having some tests done now. I don't expect her back for a couple of hours."

"Oh." That meant changing the schedule she'd worked out for today so she could come back later. "I have some other things to do. Will you tell her I was here and I'll be back before lunch?"

Tracy smiled again. "Of course."

Rayna started to leave, but remembered her ex-husband's request. "Also, Marcus Holt wanted me to tell Nana that he'll stop by after lunch to visit with her."

"Ms. Grace will like that. She adores Marcus." Tracy shook her head. "He's such a nice man. It's a shame about his marriage break—" She stopped and a mortified look passed over her face, as if she knew she'd said more than she should have. "Uh, I mean . . ."

Rayna took pity on the woman who apparently tried to claw her way out of the hole she'd dug. "It's okay, Tracy. I agree with you. Marcus *is* a nice man."

Tracy slipped her hands into the pockets of her scrubs top, obviously still uncomfortable about her slip. "Well, I'd better check on my other patients. I'll give Ms. Grace your message."

"Thank you."

She stepped to the side so Tracy could pass her. When Tracy came even with her, Rayna touched her arm. "Is there a women's clothing store in town? I'd like to buy some cooler tops."

The question seemed to relax the nurse. "Yes. Janelle's is on Olive Street on the north side of the square. She has a lot of really cute clothes."

"Thank you again."

Rayna headed for the exit. She decided to go shopping now, then come back to visit with Nana before lunch. After that, she'd finish her errands before she met Marcus at Nana's house.

It surprised and pleased Rayna to find such a wonderful selection of clothing at Janelle's. She spent the next two hours browsing and trying on over a dozen items. She settled on three tank tops, two short-sleeved blouses, two pairs of capris, a flowing skirt in a colorful flowered pattern, and a pair of slingback sandals.

Rayna made a very good salary as a floor supervisor at the hospital, but the cost of living in San Francisco could not be described as cheap. She'd managed to put aside a nice nest egg since she rarely spent money on herself. It felt good to let go and shop for pleasure.

Humming to herself, she pressed the button on her key fob to open the trunk. Her stomach had been growling at her for the last fifteen minutes. A visit to Nana came next on her to-do list, then lunch.

A vehicle stopped beside her car. A sliver of fear sliced through her, until she remembered she stood on a street in Lanville, not San Francisco. She looked to her left to see Marcus leaning his head out the window of a black pickup with a magnetic Coleman Construction sign on the door.

"Did you buy out the store?" he asked with laughter shining in his eyes.

She couldn't help but smile. She felt too good not to. "Not quite, but I made a good dent." She placed her sacks inside the trunk and closed the lid. "Nana was in the middle of tests when I went to the hospital earlier, so I decided to go shopping until she was back in her room. I'm on my way there now to see her."

"I just came from there. She's asleep. Tracy, her nurse, said the tests wore Grace out."

"Oh." She didn't want to wake her, especially when she obviously needed the rest. "I guess I could have an early lunch and go see her later."

"Sounds like a plan to me." He rested his elbow on the window's opening. "I had to be in Parker Place, so I looked at Grace's house. I only saw the outside, but the damage isn't too severe. I had a couple of our guys put plywood over the hole in the kitchen wall."

"Thank you. I didn't think about that. Do you think looting will be a problem?"

"No. Brad—our sheriff—told me two deputies will be out there all the time to make sure no one is there who shouldn't be. It's Lanville, Rayna. Sure, we have theft sometimes, but it's usually people from out of town. Crime here is almost nonexistent."

She'd heard the same thing from her grandmother many times. Nana never thought about locking her doors when she went out because she didn't worry about anyone going in her house who shouldn't be there. Luckily, Mattie took care of the locks and other security. It might be Lanville, but Rayna didn't want to take any chances with her grandmother's safety.

"Have you talked to Grace's insurance agent yet?" Marcus asked.

"I left a message for her to call me back this afternoon."

"My one o'clock appointment rescheduled to later today. Want to have lunch and go to Grace's house early?"

Lunch with Marcus would *not* be a good idea. She didn't want to spend any more time than necessary with him. Seeing him stirred up too many memories.

As if he sensed her hesitation, he raised his hand, palm toward her. "Strictly a business lunch, I swear. I made some notes while at your grandmother's house. We could go over them while we eat."

A business lunch would be all right. No talk of their past, no mention of anything personal. She could do that. "Okay. That sounds good."

Marcus smiled. "Great. I was thinking of a hamburger. The Purple Onion specializes in them and has about twenty different kinds on their menu. Will that work for you?"

At the mention of a hamburger, her stomach growled. "That sounds great. Is it far?"

"On the corner of Elm and Main. Do you want to ride with me?"

That would be way too much closeness. "I'll follow you so I'll have my car."

Rayna pulled away from the curb, did a U-turn, and followed Marcus past the courthouse. He turned left on Main Street, then right on Elm Street and into a parking lot at the back of the restaurant. He found two spots together beneath a large elm tree. Rayna smiled at the memory of finding a shaded place to park in the summer. It didn't matter if she had to walk farther to get to wherever she needed to go, as long as she could park her vehicle beneath a tree to help combat the brutal Texas heat.

By the time she slid her cell phone into an inside pocket of her purse and slipped the purse's strap over her shoulder, Marcus was there to open her door. He'd always had impeccable manners. He held out his hand. She laid her hand in his and allowed him to help her from the car, but released it as soon as she stood. Holding his hand any longer would be too much of a temptation to keep touching him.

Rayna would have to describe the inside of The Purple Onion as eclectic. A mixture of paintings, pictures, and paraphernalia hung on the wooden walls. Flowers sat on tables in pretty glass vases or old-fashioned Mason jars. A piece of plastic covered each table, protecting the photos of people, animals, and clip art. It looked as if the owner told children to have fun decorating and they had.

She loved it.

A young woman who didn't appear to be more than twenty greeted them with a smile. "Hi, Marcus. Table for two?"

"Hi, Jami. Yeah, near the windows if possible."

"Sure." She grabbed two menus from the holder at the side of the hostess stand. "Follow me."

He placed his hand on the small of Rayna's back, the way he always had when they'd walked together. It threw her back in time to all the occasions when his hands had coasted over her skin . . . sometimes in passion, sometimes in a simple caress, sometimes in awe of the differences in her body and his.

The short trip to their table meant he soon moved his hand. Rayna didn't want to acknowledge the disappointment she felt at the loss of his touch.

"Can I get y'all something to drink?" Jami asked as she handed menus to each of them.

Marcus looked at her. "Rayna?"

The natural light shining through the large plate window highlighted the lines at the corners of Marcus's eyes, lines that hadn't been there five years ago. His face had matured since the last time she'd seen him. He'd been a man at twenty-eight, yet now he appeared more . . . seasoned. Experienced. Wiser.

Muscular.

Sexier.

She stopped herself from clearing her throat. "Iced tea please."

"Regular, peach, or black mango?" Jami asked.

"I'll be adventurous and try the black mango."

"You'll like it. It's really good." The waitress turned to Marcus. "Regular for you?"

"Guess I'm too predictable, huh?"

"In some things." Jami smiled. "Be right back with your drinks."

Marcus watched her walk away, a small smile on his lips. "She was just a gawky teenager a couple of years ago. Working here has helped her grow up and not be so shy."

It surprised Rayna when a spear of jealousy hit her stomach, until she realized Marcus didn't look at Jami the way a man who wants a woman does, but as a big brother.

Or a father.

Stop thinking like that, Rayna, she scolded herself. *You can't let memories intrude on a business lunch.*

She opened her menu to see a selection of at least twenty-five different types of hamburgers. Marcus hadn't exaggerated about the variety. She had no idea how she could pick only one when they all sounded so good. Marcus laid his menu on the edge of the table without opening it. "You already know what you want?" she asked.

Marcus nodded. "Chophouse Burger. It's huge and delicious." He leaned forward and tapped a selection on her open menu. "As much as you love mushrooms, you'll like the 'Shroom Swiss Burger." He pointed to another selection. "Don't try the Burnin' Love Burger. It'll be too spicy for you."

First the chocolate old-fashioned donut, and now this. Rayna stared at him, amazed again that he still knew what she liked to eat, or not eat. "You remember I like mushrooms and don't like spicy food?"

He lowered his eyelids to half-mast, which gave him that sexy, bedroom look that had always turned her bones to mush. "I told you this morning I remember a lot of things." His gaze briefly dipped to her breasts. "I remember *everything* about you, Rayna."

5

Marcus watched Rayna's eyes turn liquid and dreamy, the way they had so often when he took her in his arms. The hard nipples showing through her T-shirt proved her thoughts traveled along the same path as his—right into their bedroom. Or living room. Or backyard. Or any of the other dozens of places where they'd made love.

Knowing how mortified she would be if she knew how her eyes gave away her thoughts, he pulled his clipboard over in front of him. "We'll talk about the repairs to Grace's house after we order."

His statement seemed to snap her back to the present. "Right. Okay. Well, I'll take your advice and try the 'Shroom Swiss Burger. Is it huge like the Chophouse?"

"There are two sizes—the regular, which is a third of a pound of meat, and one for the smaller appetite, which is about a fifth of a pound."

"I'll take the smaller one."

"It comes with fries, but you can substitute onion rings. They make the rings fresh from sweet purple onions. There will also be a slice of purple onion on your plate with your burger, unless you specify that you don't want it."

The corners of her mouth tilted up. "Hence the name of the restaurant."

Marcus grinned. "You got it."

She bit her bottom lip, which she'd always done while trying to make a decision. "I haven't had fresh onion rings in forever."

"Then it's time you had them again."

Jami returned with their teas. Before Rayna could say anything, Marcus placed their orders, substituting rings for the fries and including the slice of purple onion on their plates.

"You realize we won't be able to get within twenty feet of each other with our onion breath," Rayna said once Jami left.

Marcus shrugged. "If we're both eating onions, it won't matter." He flipped to the page on his legal pad where he'd made notes about Grace's house. "Part of the roof will definitely have to be replaced, and the kitchen wall that was damaged. I peeked through the hole, but couldn't see enough to know if there's extensive damage in any other rooms besides the kitchen. I can tell you more once we go inside after lunch."

"I hate that this happened. Nana's house is only three months old."

"All the houses in Parker Place are no more than eight months old."

Rayna took a sip of her tea through the straw. "Does anyone know how the fire started?"

"Our fire marshal is still investigating, but I heard a rumor that it was three teenagers setting off fireworks in the undeveloped field. Fireworks have been banned in the county because of our drought. The fire department put on the show last night. We hired a professional company and the fireworks were all shot out over the river to reduce the chance of an accident."

"Any idea which three teenagers?"

"Yeah, but I'm not naming names until I know for sure."

"I hope they're punished."

"Trust me, our sheriff will make sure they're punished. Instead of partying all summer, they'll be on cleanup detail at Parker Place."

"Good. That's what they deserve for being so irresponsible."

He looked around their table to be sure no one sat close enough to hear him. Although people began to file into the restaurant for the lunch rush, no one sat directly next to them yet. "One of the kids is the high school principal's son."

Rayna's eyes widened. "Seriously?"

"Again, that's the rumor. And if it's true, that kid is in trouble big time. His dad is great with the students and they like him, but he doesn't believe in letting the kids get away with pranks and mischief."

"I think I like him."

The corners of her eyes crinkled with her smile. She wore her hair to her shoulders now instead of flowing to her midback. Marcus could see subtle signs of aging on Rayna's face, but all those signs only made her more lovely. He'd still describe her body as slim, yet her breasts seemed fuller, her hips a bit rounder.

She still stole his breath whenever he looked at her.

After taking a gulp of his tea to turn off those kinds of thoughts, he turned back to the legal pad. It gave him the excuse not to look at her for a few moments. "After we go through the inside of Grace's house, I'll give you an estimate of the cost of repairs. Does Grace have a local insurance agent?"

Rayna nodded. "Her insurance is with The Marilyn Peters Agency."

Marcus had worked with Marilyn Peters many times and her agency had always been fair. "Marilyn's good. Is she the one you're talking to at three?"

"Either her or one of her agents."

Jami returned with their plates of food. Marcus grinned when Rayna's eyes widened.

"This is the *small* burger?"

"Compared to mine, yes."

"It's a good thing your one o'clock appointment rescheduled. It'll take me most of the afternoon to eat this."

Marcus chuckled before he added the slice of purple onion to his burger and took a bite. He watched her as he chewed. She stared at her slice, as if debating whether or not to add it to her burger. He could almost see her mental shrug before she lifted the bun, slid the onion on top of the melted Swiss, and took a bite of her sandwich. She closed her eyes in pleasure.

"Oh, that's good."

"Told you you'd like it." He squirted a healthy amount of ketchup on his plate. "I remember another time when you enjoyed mushrooms."

Rayna quickly looked around them while she wiped her hands on a napkin. "Shhhh!"

"What? I didn't say what kind of mushrooms you ate."

"*We* ate. And *you* were the one who got them."

"Actually, Lee Wilkerson was the one who got them and shared with me." Marcus shook his head. "They popped up by the football field after three days of rain. Can you imagine that?"

"I imagined a lot of things after eating that Salisbury steak you made. You neglected to tell me those were psilocybin mushrooms in the gravy until after I'd already eaten it."

"You were high for six hours."

"At least."

He grinned when a smile tugged at her lips. "You have to admit it was fun. Colors were brighter, food tasted better—"

"Sex was hotter."

Her eyes widened and she pressed her lips together a moment, obviously wishing she could take back what she'd said. "Sorry," she muttered.

"*I'm* not. The sex *was* hotter that night. You were insatiable."

"I think we both were."

They'd only been married three months at the time of the mushrooms incident, so they still had a lot to learn about what pleased the other sexually. Rayna had been a passionate lover from the first time they'd ever made love, yet Marcus had always felt she held a piece of herself back, almost as if she didn't want him to think badly of her if she let go and became even more passionate with him. After eating the magic mushrooms, all her walls collapsed. He'd lost count of the number of orgasms she'd had that night. Hell, he'd lost track of how many orgasms *he'd* had.

Walking the next day hadn't been easy. But worth every moment of discomfort.

After that, she never held back in the bedroom. He couldn't think of strong enough adjectives to describe how amazing they had been together.

To erase the uncomfortable vibes he could feel coming from her, he returned to the subject of Grace's house. "I visited with Grace about a month ago. She told me she loved her house, but wished she had a few more plugs in certain spots. Coleman Construction can add those for her when the repairs are done. No extra charge. It'll be my gift to her."

He could see by the softening in her eyes how much his offer pleased her. "Thank you. That's very generous."

"It's easy to be generous with Grace. She's a great lady."

"Yes, she is."

Rayna swished her straw through her tea. The sound of the ice tinkling against the glass reminded Marcus of the wind chimes they'd had on the patio of their house in Irving. When she left him, she'd taken nothing except her clothes and personal items. He'd packed up everything in the house that reminded him of her, but hadn't been able to throw away anything. He'd ended up renting a storage locker until he'd moved to Lanville. Once settled in his house, he'd built a large shed in the backyard and moved all the plastic storage tubs into it.

It had taken him three years to unpack the chimes and hang them on the back porch of his house. The rest of the items she'd left remained in the shed. He kept telling himself someday he'd go through all those plastic tubs and have a yard sale, or just toss everything. If Rayna had left the items, that had to mean she didn't want them. Not even the photographs.

No sense in going there. She obviously didn't love me as much as I loved her or she wouldn't have walked out on me when I needed her the most. There's no going back from that kind of pain.

"Look around while we do the walk-through at Grace's house," Marcus suggested to get his mind off the past and back on the reason why he and Rayna sat here together. "If you see anything else you want done, I'll make a note of it."

"Mattie should be there, too, since she lives with Nana. She'll know more about what Nana might want than I would. This will be the first time I've seen her house."

"She told me you bought it for her. How did you buy something as permanent as a house without even looking at it?"

"It was Nana's decision since she'd be living there. I just supplied the financing."

He swirled an onion ring through the puddle of ketchup on his plate. "You must have a well-paying job to pay cash for a house."

"I'm a floor supervisor at my hospital. I earn a nice salary." She shrugged one shoulder. "It took me almost three years to save enough money, but houses are a lot less expensive in

Lanville than in San Francisco. I was able to pay for half up front and I'm making payments. It's worth it for Nana to be comfortable. I didn't like her living alone so far out of town." She shook her head. "She fought me about the new house for weeks. That woman defines stubborn."

Marcus chuckled. "I'll agree with that."

"She finally gave in and let me buy the house. She has plenty of money to pay her bills, groceries, and Mattie's salary, so I don't have to help her with any of that. I'm so thankful Nana agreed to my suggestion of a live-in caretaker. She could pick who would help her, but I insisted she not live alone anymore. Mattie has been wonderful. Nana adores her."

"I'm surprised she didn't move in with you in San Francisco."

"I asked her to, several times. She always said Lanville was home and that's where she wanted to stay. She loves it here."

"I do, too. It's a great place to live. It's growing, but still has the small-town flavor and friendliness."

He could see the indecision in her eyes, as if she wanted to say something but didn't know if she should. "What?"

"When did you move here?"

Marcus took the last bite of his burger, washed it down with a sip of tea. "Two months after our divorce was final."

"Oh."

She looked down at the remaining onion ring on her plate. Anger slowly built in his chest while he waited for the question that didn't come. "Aren't you going to ask?"

"Ask what?" she said without lifting her gaze.

"You know damn well what. I can't believe you haven't even—"

"I'm going to visit Nana." Rayna pushed aside her plate and picked up her purse from the chair beside her. "I'll meet you at her house at three-thirty."

"Rayna—"

She threw up a hand, palm toward him. "Don't." She hurried away before he could say anything else, almost knocking Jami down in her haste to get out of the restaurant.

Jami came over to the table with two pitchers of tea. "She's in a hurry."

"Yeah."

Setting down one pitcher, she picked up Marcus's glass and refilled it. "I heard a rumor she's your ex-wife."

One thing not so great about a small town—the gossip. "Yeah."

"You still care about her." She uttered a statement, not a question.

Marcus lifted his gaze to Jami's face. "No. That ended a long time ago."

The waitress tilted her head to the side and openly studied his eyes. "I don't think so."

He released a humorless laugh at the serious tone of her voice. "You're too young to think you know everything."

"Feelings have a nasty way of sneaking up on you whether you want them to or not."

He opened his mouth to comment, but she continued before he could. "I know what you're going to say. I'm only twenty-one, I couldn't possibly know that much about feelings or even life in general. I know what's it's like to be hurt so badly you can't even breathe. So don't tell me I'm too young."

A deep blush rushed to her cheeks. "Sorry," she muttered. "I didn't mean to . . ." She cleared her throat, straightened her shoulders. "Would you like dessert? We have fresh key lime pie today."

"No, thanks," Marcus said softly.

Jami nodded once. "I'll get your check."

He watched the young woman walk away. He couldn't help

wondering what had happened in Jami's life that hurt her so much.

Blowing out a breath, Marcus removed his wallet from his back pocket, withdrew his credit card to pay the bill. He had too many other things to think about without adding Jami to the list.

Like getting through the next few days with his ex-wife.

6

Despite the hot summer day, cold sweat covered Rayna's skin. She'd barely made it out of the restaurant on her shaky legs. She thought she had prepared herself for whatever questions Marcus might ask.

She apparently hadn't prepared herself enough.

It took several minutes of sitting in her car in the hospital parking lot before Rayna felt strong enough to visit with her grandmother. She'd managed to hold back the tears, so at least her eyes and nose wouldn't be red. Nana could always tell when she'd been crying with only one look at her rosy nose.

She checked her reflection one more time in the rearview mirror before getting out of the car. The slap of heat and humidity helped bring her back to the present. She pushed aside all thoughts of her lunch with Marcus and concentrated solely on her grandmother.

Rayna found Nana sitting up in bed, watching her favorite soap opera on television. It pleased her to see her grandmother seeming so refreshed. "Hi."

Nana looked her way and smiled. "I was beginning to wonder if you'd forgotten about me."

"Never." She kissed her grandmother's cheek, then sat in the chair next to the bed. "How are you feeling?"

Nana pushed the Mute button to silence the squabble between the two characters on TV. "I feel fine. A little tired, but fine. When can I go home? Or do I have a house to go home to?"

Gossip traveled fast in a small town, and even faster in a hospital. "You know about the fire?"

Nana nodded. "Mattie told me there was some damage to my house. How bad is it?"

"I haven't been there yet. I have an appointment at three-thirty to look at it with Marcus."

Nana's white eyebrows rose and a pleased glimmer filled her eyes. "With Marcus, huh?"

"Get that gleam out of your eyes, Nana. My meeting with Marcus is strictly business."

"It could be more."

The hopeful tone to Nana's voice sent a shaft of pain into Rayna's heart. She knew how much her grandmother loved Marcus, and how much it hurt her when Rayna left him. "No, Nana, it can't. Marcus and I have been divorced for four years. There's no going back."

"*Pffft*. Until you're dead and buried, there's always a chance of righting a wrong." She held out her hand, palm up, until Rayna laid her hand on top. Nana squeezed it gently. "You and Marcus belong together. You have since you were teenagers necking in my driveway."

Heat rushed to Rayna's cheeks. She had no idea her grandmother knew about that. "Nana!"

"What, you think I'm an idiot? I knew exactly what went on when Marcus brought you home from a date. It doesn't take thirty minutes to say good night." The sparkle of laughter filled her eyes. She squeezed Rayna's hand again. "You were always an intelligent girl. I knew when you and Marcus went beyond kisses, y'all would be careful."

"We didn't . . . go beyond kisses until his first year in college."

"And you were always careful, so I didn't worry. Your parents—rest their souls—raised you with manners and morals, something a lot of young people don't have these days. When you came to live with me after they died, you were already a well-mannered, courteous young lady."

"I was only fourteen, hardly a lady."

"You were already a young lady at fourteen," she said with the don't-argue-with-me tone that Rayna had learned years ago.

Leaning her head back against her pillow, Nana looked at the ceiling. "I remember how you would pick up a bug or spider on a piece of paper and take it outside because you couldn't stand to kill it." She rolled her head toward Rayna and smiled. "It didn't surprise me at all when you told me you wanted to be a nurse." Her smile faded. "There's so much goodness in you, Rayna. I don't understand why you broke up your marriage."

"I *told* you why, Nana."

Nana waved her free hand in the air as if to erase Rayna's words. "I know what you told me, but it never made sense to me. A couple is supposed to lean on each other through hard times, not break up."

"I couldn't," Rayna whispered around the lump in her throat.

"You didn't *want* to. There's a huge difference. You blamed Marcus for something that wasn't his fault."

Any minute, Rayna would burst into tears. To keep that from happening, she changed the subject. "How about if we talk about you? I'll know after I see your house if you can move back into it while the repairs are being done. If not, we'll talk about what to do. You may have to stay in one of the motels for a while."

The shrewd look in her grandmother's eyes proved she knew exactly what Rayna had done. Rayna expected Nana to continue talking about Marcus. She surprised Rayna by responding to her suggestion instead. "Well, that wouldn't be so bad. I'd have housekeeping service every day."

"You have that anyway with Mattie."

"Yes, I do." A soft smile touched Nana's lips. "She's such a sweet girl. If I can't have you living with me, I'm glad to have Mattie."

Rayna recognized the guilt trip her grandmother attempted to start. "Nana," she said with a hint of sternness in her voice.

"Come home, Rayna. I have two extra bedrooms in my house, so there's plenty of room for you. I'll even give you the master bedroom and I'll move into a smaller one. I don't need all that room anyway."

"Lanville was never my home."

"Texas was. You were born here and this is where you belong."

"And how am I supposed to make a living in Lanville?"

"You can give up that stressful supervisor's job in San Francisco and go back to nursing. I'll bet with your experience, you could get a job here in a second."

Rayna took her grandmother's hand in both of hers. "I know what you're doing and it isn't going to work. I'm not getting back together with Marcus."

Nana's eyes narrowed, her lips thinned in a scowl. "You always were stubborn."

"I wonder where I got that?"

Nana sighed heavily. "Probably from me."

Grinning, Rayna leaned over and kissed her grandmother's cheek again. "I have a couple of things to do before I meet Marcus at your house, and I don't want to tire you out. I'll be back around five or so, okay?"

She nodded. "I wouldn't mind a nap. Take your time. If you decide to have supper with Marcus, that would be okay."

"Good-bye, Nana."

One more kiss on her grandmother's soft, wrinkled cheek and Rayna left the room. Once in the hallway, she leaned against the wall and cradled her nape in her hands. A headache marched through her temples and up into the top of her head. Her grandmother had mentioned her stressful job. That stress didn't compare to what she experienced now being so close to her ex-husband.

A glance at her watch showed her she had over an hour before her appointment with Marcus. That gave her enough time to finish the things she needed to do for Nana before she headed for her grandmother's house.

The black Coleman Construction pickup parked in front of Nana's house proved Marcus had already arrived. Closing her eyes, Rayna took a couple of deep breaths. She could do this. She could get through this meeting with Marcus for Nana's sake. Then she'd never have to see him again.

She tugged the strap of her purse over her shoulder and exited her car. The sight of Nana's trampled flower beds almost made her cry. She knew how much her grandmother loved flowers. Nana wouldn't be able to work in her flower beds for a while, not until she could get back to her normal routine.

The thought that she could extend her stay and help her grandmother get her house back to normal flittered through Rayna's mind. She just as quickly told herself no. Staying in Lanville any longer might mean running into Marcus numerous times. She couldn't handle that.

She heard a man's voice as she walked through the front door. Not recognizing it, she moved toward it to the kitchen. A tall, broad-shouldered man with dark hair to his shoulders stood with his back to her, a cell phone at his ear.

"I want *good* men, Mom," he said into the phone, "ones who are experienced in construction. I don't mind training some, but we have a lot of work to do and I need men who know what they're doing. . . . Yeah, in all the surrounding counties and the *Star-Telegram*. . . . Good idea. It wouldn't hurt to hit the Dallas papers, too. . . . I have three more appointments, then I'll be back there. Should be around six, six-thirty. . . . You're the best. Bye."

He pressed a button to end his call and turned around. A startled look crossed his face when he saw her. It quickly morphed into a smile. "Hi."

"Hi." Rayna knew she'd never met him, yet he looked familiar. She would remember a man so incredibly handsome. "Who are you and why are you in my grandmother's house?"

His smile widened. "I'm Rye Coleman. My brothers and I own Coleman Construction. Marcus asked me to fill in for him."

His mention of Marcus shook her memory to where she'd seen Rye Coleman. He and another man who greatly favored him had been at the hospital last night with Marcus. He'd told her his injury was no big deal, but maybe it was more serious than anyone originally surmised. A chill went down her spine at the thought of Marcus being hurt. "Is he okay?"

"Oh, yes, he's fine. He told me something came up. He said he didn't want to reschedule your appointment because he didn't want Ms. Grace to have to wait for her house repairs. I got the house key from Mattie." His voice softened. "He cares a great deal for your grandmother."

"She cares about him, too." Not sure what to say, she shifted the strap of her purse on her shoulder to stall a few moments. "So, what's first?"

He picked up an aluminum forms holder with a clipboard on top from the kitchen counter. "I made a list of the repairs that will have to be done and the approximate cost. I'll give you a more detailed listing for you to show your insurance agent, but this should be enough for you to get an idea of what needs to be done."

Rayna looked around the room. She could clearly see the smoke and water damage, and the boarded-up hole in the roof, but hadn't noticed anything amiss when she walked through the living room. "Is the damage mostly in here?"

Rye nodded. "Yes, but there's also some damage in the hall and one of the bedrooms. I can walk you through the rooms and show you everything, if you'd like."

"Yes, please."

It didn't take long for Rayna to realize Rye Coleman knew exactly what needed to be repaired in Nana's house, how long it would take, and how much it would cost. He obviously had a lot of experience at his job. She didn't hesitate to say yes when he asked her if she still wanted Coleman Construction to do the repairs on her grandmother's house.

"Can Nana move back in here when she gets out of the hospital?"

Concern flashed through Rye's eyes. "I wouldn't recommend it until we get the smoke damage cleaned up and the hole in the roof repaired. There will be a lot of sawdust flying around. That wouldn't be good for Ms. Grace to breathe."

"I have a room at The Inn on Crystal Creek. She can stay with me."

"How do you like your room?"

"It's beautiful. The entire inn is magnificent."

A pleased smile brightened his eyes. "Thank you. My brothers and I did the restoration for my wife. She's the owner."

"Alaina is your wife?"

Rye nodded.

"She's lovely. And very nice."

"I agree." He tore off the top copy of the NCR form and handed it to Rayna. "Here's your estimate. Marcus told me he offered to take care of some minor things for Ms. Grace, too, as a gift to her. If you'll make a list of those, I'll add them to the work order."

"I know she wants more electrical outlets, but I'm not sure where. Other than that, I don't know what she might need."

"I'm putting this house at the top of our repair list. If you can check with your grandmother and let me know in the next day or two, that would be great. We'll start the repairs Friday."

"So soon? That's wonderful."

"We'll move as fast as we can, but still do a good job. I promise you that." He handed her a business card. "My cell number is the best way to reach me, or you can leave a message at the office."

She looked at the white card with the bold black lettering. Definitely masculine. "I thought I'd be working directly with Marcus."

The smile on Rye's face slipped a bit. "I'm taking this job over for him, so you'll contact me."

"Is he avoiding me, Mr. Coleman?"

"Rye, please." He rubbed his thick mustache with one finger. She could tell by his hesitation that he didn't want to answer her question. "I think it would be best for everyone if you worked with me on the repairs."

With the way she'd run from Marcus at lunch, Rayna couldn't blame him for avoiding her. She nodded. "Thank you for your time, Mist . . . Rye."

"You're welcome. Don't hesitate to call me if you have any questions or need anything else."

"I won't."

She walked with him to the front door. Once he opened it, he looked at her over his shoulder. "How long do you plan to be in Lanville?"

"Only until my grandmother is settled back in her house. You said the repairs would take a couple of weeks, right?"

"Two probably, three at the most. Coleman Construction

will do most of the repairs, but we hire subcontractors for some of the work, so it depends on their schedules, too."

Rayna hoped the work could be completed in two weeks. She didn't want to stay in Lanville any longer. "Thank you again, Rye."

He dipped his head in acknowledgement of her thanks. Her cell phone rang as she shut the door. The phone number of Nana's insurance agent appeared in the window. Perfect timing. Rayna answered the call while she walked back to the kitchen to get the estimate she'd left on the table.

A slow stroll through Nana's house made Rayna smile. She recognized many of the pictures and mementoes that had been in Nana's old house where Rayna lived from age fourteen to eighteen, when she left to attend college. The extra-wide hallway contained bookshelves down the entire length. Books filled the shelves, along with knickknacks, framed photos, photo albums, and what Nana called her "special jars." Whenever a special occasion happened in her life, she put something in a jar to help her remember it. A paper tag tied to the top contained the date and place in Nana's handwriting that coincided with whatever she placed in the jar.

Rayna smiled when she saw the jar holding the five seashells she'd picked up on the Gulf Coast the first time Nana took her there. It had been only three weeks after Rayna's parents were killed, a time when she didn't think she'd ever smile again. Nana had made sure she not only smiled, but laughed out loud while the two of them walked the beach at Corpus Christi.

More jars held the blue ribbon Rayna had won at the Lanville County Fair for her oatmeal chocolate chip cookies, the tassel from her high school graduation mortar board, a copy of her first paycheck when she worked at Boot Scootin' the summer before she left for college.

A small mesh bag filled with bird seed and tied with a pale blue ribbon from her wedding.

Rayna touched the tag on the top. She'd been so happy on that day, sure that she and Marcus would spend the rest of their lives together. That's exactly what should have happened, what *would* have happened, if she hadn't destroyed their relationship.

Her throat tightened, burned. She stared at that little mesh bag and thought of the vows she'd made on her wedding day, vows she had broken because it had been easier to leave her husband than face her pain.

The overwhelming need to see Marcus and apologize for hurting him couldn't be denied. On trembling legs, she walked to her grandmother's bedroom and located Nana's address book in the small desk beneath the window. She found Marcus's address at the top of the H section. She entered it into her cell phone and quickly got directions.

Ten minutes later, Rayna parked before an older house in the center of a large grouping of oak trees. The house badly needed a coat of paint. She couldn't help but smile at that realization. Marcus made his living building new homes and repairing older ones, yet his own house needed some TLC.

The sun played peekaboo through the darkening clouds as she climbed the steps to the porch. The forecast called for rain by sunset. Rayna hoped the forecasters got it right. A shower might help cool the temperature down to a tolerable level.

She took a deep breath and rang the doorbell. Long moments passed with no response. She assumed Marcus was home because she saw the Coleman Construction pickup in his driveway. She started to press the doorbell again when the door opened.

Marcus stood before her, wearing nothing but a pair of low-slung jeans. Water droplets clung to his shoulders and arms, wet hair framed his face. She'd obviously caught him in the shower.

"Rayna," he said, surprise evident in his voice. "What are you doing here?"

"I wanted to . . ."

Her voice trailed off as her gaze slid across his chest to the tattoo over his left pec. Bold, dark letters in an old-fashioned font formed an arc over his heart.

DEREK

The name of their lost son.

Her body began to shake. Her throat tightened again, this time so she could barely breathe. She reached out slowly, touched the letters with trembling fingertips. Covering her lips with her other hand, she swallowed again and again to try and fight back tears. It didn't work. Tears filled her eyes, flowed down her cheeks.

"I'm sorry, Marcus," she whispered in a tortured voice. "I'm so sorry."

7

Marcus reached out to grab Rayna when her knees buckled. Wrapping his arms around her, he pulled her over the threshold and kicked the door shut with his foot. She clung to his neck and cried—deep, hard sobs that shook her body and broke his heart.

"Shh, it's okay. Don't cry, Rayna."

"I'm so sorry," she said again. "I'm so, so sorry."

Instead of her tears slowing, they flowed even faster. No matter how tightly he held her, he couldn't keep her body from quivering.

"Rayna, stop crying. Please."

"I c-c-can't!"

Afraid she'd make herself sick, he thought about what he could do to help her. He used to be able to stop her tears when they were together. They weren't together any longer, but perhaps what he used to do would still work.

He fisted a handful of her hair, pulled her head from his shoulder, and covered her lips with his.

Her body jerked as if he'd shocked her. Then, with a soft

moan, she relaxed against him. Her arms tightened around his neck, her mouth softened beneath his. What started out as a kiss to halt her crying soon turned into lust.

A jolt passed through his body. He didn't understand how one kiss with his ex-wife could affect him so strongly, yet it did. Perhaps because it had been much too long since he'd held a woman against him, had her hands run over him in passion. His dick lengthened, thickened, in preparation to take her.

Something that couldn't happen.

Marcus ended the kiss. He stared into hazel eyes that remained wet from Rayna's tears. She stared right back at him, her lips parted, her breathing sounding harsh and labored.

He should release her. He should step back and not touch her again.

Apparently, she disagreed with what he should do. She grabbed the back of his head and urged him into another kiss.

Instinct, memories, hormones—whatever—took over for Marcus. The taste he remembered flowed past his lips and over his tongue. He tightened his arms around Rayna until their bodies touched in as many places as possible. Holding her ass with one hand, he urged her closer until her belly cushioned his cock.

When she wrapped one leg around his thigh and hunched her mound against him, Marcus lost all ability to think. Gripping her ass tighter, he backed her the few steps to the front door. He hooked her legs over his arms and lifted her until he could press his hard cock to the warm place between her thighs.

Rayna moaned again. She kissed him with passion, with hunger, her tongue swiping across his lips before venturing into his mouth. Marcus copied her actions, licking her lips, nipping at them, darting his tongue into her mouth to tangle with hers. The entire time they kissed, he pumped his fly into her pussy, creating friction against her clit.

Marcus moved his mouth to her jaw, her neck. He bit the

pounding pulse in her throat. Rayna gripped his hair, holding him in place at her neck. She'd always loved a lot of attention to her neck and throat, attention Marcus had gladly given her. He sucked the tender flesh between his lips, bit again, soothed the bite with his tongue. The entire time he teased her throat, he ground his denim-covered cock against her clit.

He heard the hitch in her breath, felt the pounding of her heart. Recognizing the signals of her approaching climax, he covered her mouth with his again and swallowed her cries as she came.

The kiss went from full-on ravishing to the gentlest of caresses as he allowed her body to float back from the heavens. Once her breathing sounded softer, he lifted his mouth from hers. That slumberous, amazing-orgasm light shone in her eyes. But he also knew one climax wouldn't be enough for Rayna. She'd always demanded more from him and he'd been only too happy to do whatever she needed to come over and over again.

"You aren't through," he said in a statement, not a question.

She shook her head.

"Do you want more?"

Instead of answering with words, she tunneled her hands into his hair again and kissed him with hunger. Marcus clamped her legs tighter to hold her firmly against him. Without breaking their kiss, he walked toward his bedroom.

Marcus saw no reason to make the bed in the morning when he'd crawl right back into it that night. The lady who cleaned for him came on Thursday, so he'd slept on his sheets for almost a week. A thought flittered through his mind that he wished the sheets could be clean and fresh for Rayna.

The way she kissed him, though, clearly told him whether or not he made his bed wouldn't cross her mind.

He tumbled them to the mattress, putting out one hand so he wouldn't land too hard on top of her. Her legs immediately encircled his waist, her arms went around his neck. She obviously had no intention of letting him go anytime soon.

That worked for him.

Although he loved kissing Rayna, Marcus needed more. He wanted to run his hands all over her, reacquaint himself with her curves and hollows. He wanted to suck her nipples, lick her tummy, taste the cream trickling from her pussy.

After one more long, passionate kiss, Marcus rose to his knees between her legs. "Hands beside your head," he ordered softly.

She did as he said, laying her hands palms up.

"Leave them there."

A nod proved she would obey his command. Marcus pushed up her T-shirt to above her breasts. Lace and satin in the palest of blue covered mounds the size of apples. He swallowed when he saw the front closure. His hands trembled. He flexed his fingers to get them to cooperate the way they should, then released the hook and drew apart the cups. Dark coral nipples stood up from the center of the areolae. Tiny bumps scattered across the colored circles proved desire still coursed through her body.

"God," he muttered.

Gently, almost reverently, Marcus cradled her breasts, pushed them together. He watched his thumbs as he brushed them over the firm tips. A smile played over his lips when her nipples hardened even more.

He glanced at Rayna's face. She lay with her lips parted, her hands clutching the pillow beneath her head. Her gaze traveled from his face to his hands and back to his face.

"Your nipples were always sensitive," he said, his voice low and raspy. "Are they still?"

"Yes," she said in a bare whisper.

He continued to thumb the crests while he kneaded her

breasts. "I remember a few times I made you come by sucking your nipples."

"Yes, you did."

"Think I could do that again?"

"Maybe. But . . ." Her voice trailed off.

"But what?"

She lifted her hips from the bed, pointedly looked at the bulge behind his fly. "I want your cock inside me."

His dick jumped, as if it agreed with her sexy request. He'd love nothing more than to bury his hard flesh inside her wet sheath. First, he had other things he wanted to do to her.

He tugged her into a sitting position long enough to remove her T-shirt and bra. Once she reclined with her hands by her head again, he unfastened her jeans. Panties, jeans, and shoes came off together. He dropped them over the edge of the bed, not caring where they landed. He only cared about giving as much pleasure as possible to the beautiful woman lying before him.

He rested his clenched fists on his thighs, let his gaze slowly travel over her body. He'd noticed in the hospital waiting room that her body remained slim, but her breasts seemed fuller and her hips wider. Now, with her lying nude before him, he could see he'd been correct in his assessment of her yesterday.

Some things had remained the same, others had changed. Her ivory skin continued to be unmarred by freckles that sometimes happened with redheads. The evidence of her natural red hair spread across her mound in a neatly trimmed patch. She used to shave her pussy, but no longer.

Reaching out one finger, he fluffed the red curls. "When did you stop shaving?"

"A couple of years ago."

He looked into her eyes. "I like this better."

He leaned over and kissed the spot he'd touched with his finger. Running his hands along her sides, he moved up her body, dropping kisses along the way. One nipple received a gentle kiss before he drew it into his mouth to suckle. He lavished attention on it for several moments before repeating the process on her other nipple. He stopped when he felt Rayna's hands in his hair. Taking her wrists, he pressed her hands beside her head again.

"You weren't supposed to move these."

"I want to touch you."

"Not until I'm through touching you."

The wrinkling of her forehead told him she didn't like his take-charge attitude. She'd gone along with it for a while, but she must have tired of obeying him. He fought back a smile when she released a huff of air. "You aren't being fair."

"You'll think I'm very fair when I make you come another three or four times."

Her eyes widened. "Three or four?" she squeaked.

"At least."

"Marcus, you—"

He cut off her words with a kiss. His mouth slanted across hers, parting her lips with his tongue. She arched beneath him, pressed her pussy against his fly, her breasts against his chest. The proof that she wanted him as much as he wanted her caused his blood to flow faster, his blood pressure to rise higher. He could reach between them, unfasten his jeans, and be inside her in seconds.

To keep from doing that, Marcus tore his mouth from hers and retraced the journey he'd made along her body. He showered more attention on her breasts, kneading and squeezing one while sucking the nipple of the other. The scent of her arousal wafted between them, urging him to continue down her body to the satiny flesh between her thighs.

He covered her mound with kisses as he pushed her legs farther apart. Sliding down on the bed, he stretched out on his stomach. His kisses moved to the inside of her silky thighs. With only the light from the living room filtering across the bed, he couldn't see her pussy as clearly as he'd like, but he could feel.

And taste.

One swipe of his tongue had her quivering and him groaning. Spreading her labia with his thumbs, he licked the full length of the feminine lips again. She tasted a little salty, a little sweet, a little tangy.

Delicious.

Marcus slid his hands beneath her ass to bring her pretty cunt closer to his mouth. He flashed his tongue across her clit, darted it into her channel, tickled her clit again. The bundle of nerves hardened, grew, beneath his tongue. Cream oozed from her sheath. He lapped it up as quickly as it formed, letting it flow over his tongue and down his throat.

She moved her hands into his hair again. This time, he didn't reprimand her. He wanted her touch as much as she wanted to touch him. Holding hunks of his hair, she guided his mouth directly over her clit.

"Suck it," she whispered.

Only too happy to obey her, he settled his mouth over her clit and sucked. Rayna drew in a sharp breath, tugged hard on his hair. He winced at the bite of pain, yet didn't stop. He had no intention of stopping until she'd come again.

It didn't take long. Mere moments later, Rayna's body tensed, then bucked as she released a long moan. Marcus pushed two fingers inside her. Her internal walls milked them through her climax.

No longer able to wait one more second to be inside her, Marcus lifted his groin enough to release his cock from his jeans. Crawling up her body, he entered her with one fast thrust.

It was like coming home.

He kissed her while beginning a slow, gentle pumping. Slow must not have worked for Rayna, for she rested her ankles on his thighs and dug her fingernails into his ass. This bite of pain he liked. It urged him to move faster, pump harder. Marcus did both as he kissed her again.

He wanted to draw out the lovemaking and make it last, but being inside Rayna felt too good. Her slick pussy clamped his cock every time he started to withdraw, almost as if it didn't want to release him. He didn't know whether he should speed up or slow down.

Rayna made the decision for him when she lifted her hips off the bed. "Faster, Marcus."

He once again slipped his hands beneath her ass and gripped it so he could pump quicker. She slid her fingernails up and down his back. . . . not scratching, but in a sensual caress.

Burying his face against her neck, he pressed kisses along her jaw, her neck, her shoulder. "Come with me, Rayna," he growled in her ear. "I want to feel your pussy grip my dick when you come."

He'd barely said the words when she arched beneath him. "Marcus!"

Wrapping her tightly in his arms, he let the little ripples inside her sheath drive him over the edge, too.

8

It amazed Rayna that she could think at all when her body felt like one big overcooked noodle. She could barely keep her arms around Marcus's neck, her legs around his waist. Somewhere she found the strength, for she didn't want to let him go yet.

He must have felt the same way, for he didn't move either. He lay with his face against her neck, one hand beneath her butt, the other hand resting on her breast. Every few seconds, his thumb brushed across her nipple. That's the only part of his body that moved.

She didn't plan this. When she came to check on her grandmother, she had no intention of seeing Marcus. She didn't know he lived in Lanville, or worked for Coleman Construction, or that she would run into him at the hospital.

He lifted his head and looked at her face. The dimness in the room kept her from seeing his expression clearly. "Is something wrong?" she asked.

"Yeah." He shifted his hips, proving that just because he'd climaxed didn't mean his cock had softened. "I'm not through either."

He shifted again, driving his cock farther inside her. This time, Rayna planned to be in charge.

"Your jeans are rubbing my legs."

"I can fix that." He slowly withdrew from her. Rayna pressed her lips together to keep from moaning at the pleasure of his hard flesh dragging across sensitive tissue. She watched him lie on his back, push his jeans down his legs, and toss them on the floor. He started to roll back on top of her. A hand on his chest stopped him.

"What's wrong?" he asked.

"It's my turn to play with you."

He didn't move for a few moments, then relaxed on his back. "Go for it."

He lay before her like a smorgasbord of tasty treats. She didn't know where to start. Reacquainting herself with his new body would be a good place. He'd matured in the five years since she'd been with him—his shoulders wider, his muscles more defined. She'd always thought of his body as husky, but the physical work he did in construction had definitely sculpted all the planes and hollows into a work of art.

Propping up on her elbow, she trailed her other hand over his shoulders, across his chest, down his torso. She stopped at his waist and repeated her journey back to his shoulders. She liked the tickle of his chest hair beneath her palm. She'd always enjoyed playing with the light sprinkling that grew across his chest before tapering to his navel. From there, it widened, thickened, to form a nest for his cock.

His shaft jumped when she let her fingertips trail from head to balls. She would swear it had increased in size, just like the rest of his body. His breathing grew more labored as she circled his balls with her forefinger. She moved her fingertip back up to the head, circled it once, twice, three times.

Seeing Marcus grip the sheet beneath him sent power surging through her body. She liked knowing she could affect him so strongly.

Rayna moved between his legs on her knees. Starting at his shoulders, she dragged both hands down his torso, letting her fingernails lightly scratch him. She didn't keep them long due to her job, but had enough length so he would feel them on his skin. He hissed in a long breath when her nails skated over his nipples. Enjoying his response, she scratched his nipples again, a bit harder this time.

"Damn, Rayna," he said in a choked voice.

"You don't like this?" she asked before she leaned over and licked each firm nub.

"You know I do."

Yes, she did. She remembered how much he loved for her to touch him . . . everywhere.

She licked each nipple again as she palmed his cock. Damp from her juices, it slid easily across her hand. Holding her prize, she slithered down his body, making sure her nipples slid over his skin on her journey. She placed his cock between her breasts, then plumped them around the hard column.

Marcus whimpered.

It had been years since she'd had a man's cock between her breasts—or a man's cock anywhere, for that matter—so it took her a few moments to establish a comfortable rhythm. He laid his hands over hers and pressed her breasts tighter against his shaft. Each time he pumped, pre-cum oozed from the slit. Rayna lapped up each drop. The salty flavor made her long for more of his taste.

Suddenly, Marcus stopped pumping. His abrupt action froze her in place. "What's wrong?"

"I was about to come."

Her pussy clenched at the thought of his cum shooting all over her breasts. "I want you to."

"Not this way. Inside you."

Wanting to feel him thrusting into her sheath again over-ruled her desire for him to come on her breasts. Rayna rose to her knees, then straddled his hips. Gripping the base of his cock, she started to lower herself to take him.

"Wait." Marcus grabbed her hips before she could sink onto his cock. "I'm still too close to coming. Let me take care of you first." He patted his mouth with one finger. "Right here."

She'd be an idiot to refuse his suggestion. Rayna waited until Marcus pulled the pillow from beneath his head and tossed it aside, then moved up his body. He palmed her ass, guided her pussy to his mouth. She held tightly to the headboard and waited for the brush of his tongue.

It came as a bare flick to her clit. Rayna closed her eyes, let her head fall back to better enjoy the sensation. After two intense orgasms, his tongue shouldn't feel so good. She shouldn't want him as much as she did, yet years without sex had left her ravenous.

Marcus flicked her clit again, a bit harder this time. The tip of his tongue circled the sensitive nub, laved up and down the feminine lips, licked her clit again. He'd always known where to touch her, and how, to give her the most pleasure. The years apart hadn't changed that. Of course, he'd probably made love to dozens of women since they'd divorced, so he'd had lots of practice. Just because she'd been celibate didn't mean Marcus hadn't had lovers.

It hurt to think of Marcus with another woman . . . touching her, kissing her, licking her pussy the way he now licked Rayna's.

A fingertip brushed her anus, bringing her back to the present and the wicked things Marcus did with his tongue. Soon any thoughts of other women in his bed disappeared as she concentrated on the feelings roaring through her body. He pushed one finger into her ass, pumped it in and out while he continued to lick, stroke, suck.

Rayna tightened her hold on the headboard. She moved her hips back and forth, dragging her pussy across Marcus's mouth and chin. The bit of stubble caused a delicious friction across the swollen, wet tissues.

"Oh, *God!*"

The climax rushed through her body from her toes, to the top of her head, and out to her limbs. She would've melted on top of Marcus if he hadn't gripped her butt so firmly. He slowly pulled his finger from her ass, helped her to move backward until she once more straddled his hips. This time, he didn't stop her when she lowered herself onto his cock.

He grasped her hips, pulled her down as he thrust up. "Ride me, Rayna."

She wondered if she'd have the strength to breathe, much less ride. The feel of him surging inside her gave her a boost of energy. Rayna placed her hands on Marcus's chest for support and began to move.

The sound of flesh slapping flesh and heavy breathing filled the room. So did the scent of sex. Rayna's breasts bounced with every movement, which must have pleased Marcus because he stared directly at them. Rayna cradled them in her palms, caressed the nipples with her thumbs. He went back and forth from looking at her breasts to gazing into her eyes.

"I love to watch you touch yourself," he whispered.

"I remember. I love watching you touch yourself, too."

They'd often indulged in a mutual masturbation session, which led to a fast and furious fucking session. It had always amazed Rayna how quickly Marcus recuperated after a climax. His cock barely softened before he would be ready to go again.

Just like tonight.

Marcus slid his hands beneath hers and caressed her breasts. A gentle squeeze, a harder kneading, a pluck of her nipples. Everything he did sent a pleasant zing directly to her clit.

"Faster, Rayna. Ride me faster."

Once more placing her hands on his chest to brace herself, she increased the speed of her movements. Marcus continued caressing her breasts, plucking her nipples ... driving up her desire until it couldn't possibly go any higher.

Then ...

A flash of heat. A blast of pleasure. A gasp of breath as the climax galloped through her body.

Digging her fingernails into Marcus's chest, she hung her head while little pulses continued to burst. She kept her elbows locked, not wanting to collapse until Marcus came, too.

A few more thrusts and his body jerked beneath hers. He grabbed her ass, arched his hips, and released a long groan.

Knowing he'd reached a climax drained the last of the strength from Rayna's arms. She stopped trying to hold herself upright and melted on top of Marcus's chest.

For a few moments, she only heard her shattered breathing and his heart pounding beneath her ear. When both of those had calmed, she could hear drops pattering against the window. "It's raining."

"Has been for about five minutes." His hands made a slow sweep up and down her back. "Guess you were too busy having orgasms to notice."

She smiled at the humor in his voice. "Guess so." Her smiled faded as quickly as it had formed. "It's ... been a long time for me."

"Me, too," he said softly.

"No secret girlfriend stashed somewhere?"

"No girlfriend. You?"

"No, I don't have a girlfriend either."

She giggled when he swatted her butt. She'd asked the question partly in jest, but mostly because she wanted to know if he had someone special in his life. "Has there been a girlfriend?"

He swept his hands up and down her back again. "No."

"Lover?"

"No."

She tilted her head so she could see his face. "Not ever?"

"No."

She couldn't believe a man as sexy and virile as Marcus would've stayed celibate for five years. "You haven't been with a woman since we separated?"

He touched her hair, let his fingers sift through the strands. "You're the only lover I've ever had, Rayna." He tunneled beneath her hair and cradled her nape. "Can you say the same thing?"

"Yes," she whispered. "There's never been a man in my bed but you."

"Why not?"

"I never . . . met anyone I wanted to share that kind of intimacy with."

He didn't ask anything else. Rayna wished more light shone into the room so she could see his expression clearly. She touched his cheek, ran her fingers over his soft lips. He held her wrist when her fingers glided across his mouth, keeping her hand in place. He kissed each fingertip and the center of her palm.

Tenderness welled up inside her, mixed with a reawakening of desire. She leaned forward until her lips met his.

Marcus flipped their positions so he lay on top of her. His cock, still inside her, began to harden again. He didn't deepen their kiss, but left it soft and gentle and loving.

Tears filled Rayna's eyes at the show of affection. She kept her eyes closed, yet some drops escaped to run down her temples. She reached for Marcus's hands, intertwined their fingers when he began to slowly pump. He didn't increase the speed of his thrusts, but kept them slow and easy.

Another climax overtook her . . . not a big bang like the others of this evening, but a gentle wash of sensation. Marcus groaned, softer this time, as if he'd experienced the same kind of gradual climb to the heavens.

She didn't know how long they lay entwined together before Marcus finally moved to his back and gathered her close to his side. Rayna slipped one leg between his and rested her hand over the name of their son. With a sigh, she closed her eyes and let the sound of the rain lull her to sleep.

9

Marcus lifted the lid on the heavy skillet and stirred the fried potatoes. He'd heard the shower start a few minutes ago, which meant Rayna would soon wander into the kitchen in search of food. She'd always been ravenous first thing in the morning, especially after a night of sex.

They'd definitely had a night of sex.

His feelings were all jumbled this morning. What he and Rayna shared last night had been wicked hot, yet tender. It had felt so right to hold her, taste her, fuck her. Yet he knew it never should have happened. He'd kissed her only to stop her crying, not as a prelude to lovemaking. As soon as Grace got out of the hospital and settled in her home again, Rayna would leave. Last night's explosive sex would soon be another memory for him, just like all the other memories of his time with Rayna.

He flipped the ham slices in the other skillet before he removed a carton of eggs from the refrigerator. Rayna had sometimes wanted her eggs over easy, sometimes scrambled. He'd have to wait and ask her which type she preferred today.

"Something smells wonderful."

Marcus looked up and almost swallowed his tongue. Rayna walked toward him wearing one of his green T-shirts. From the gentle sway of her breasts, she obviously hadn't bothered putting on her bra after her shower. She'd pulled her hair into a ponytail high on the back of her head. With her face free of makeup, she looked much younger than thirty-two.

"I'm starving," she said as she slipped onto one of the chairs at the island.

"Me, too. Neither of us ate supper last night."

"No, we didn't."

She didn't say it, but he could tell by the slumberous look in her eyes that she remembered exactly why they hadn't bothered with food last night. They'd been too busy satisfying another type of hunger.

Bracing on her forearms, she leaned forward to peer into both skillets. "Ham and fried potatoes?"

Her position pushed up her breasts. The loose fit of his shirt made the neckline gap, letting him see the top of her breasts and a hint of cleavage. He had to swallow before he could speak again. "Yep. Bread is ready for the toaster and I'll start the eggs as soon as the ham is done. Over easy or scrambled?"

"Over easy, please."

"You got it." He hitched a thumb toward the refrigerator. "There's OJ and grape juice in the fridge. I have one of those one-cup-at-a-time coffeemakers, so I can make you a cup of coffee in a couple of minutes."

"I'll have juice for now."

He'd already set the two spots at the island with plates, silverware, and juice glasses. He watched her walk to the refrigerator. His T-shirt hit right below her ass, giving him an unobstructed view of her toned, shapely legs. He wondered if she still walked every day.

She looked at him over her shoulder after she'd opened the refrigerator. "Do you want juice?"

"Yeah."

"Which kind?"

"Whichever kind you're having."

She brought the bottle of grape juice to the island. After pouring some into each glass, she replaced it in the refrigerator and returned to her stool. He continued his cooking, even though he sensed she had many questions she wanted to ask. Perhaps she didn't know if she should—or had the right to—ask him anything.

Marcus transferred the potatoes and ham to a platter, pressed the button on the toaster to lower the bread, and began to cook the eggs. He hadn't bothered to put on a shirt with his jeans and could feel her watching him. Lifting his gaze a moment, he caught her staring at his tattoo. Unsure if she wanted to talk about their son yet, he decided to wait for her to start that conversation.

She picked up her fork, speared a piece of potato from the platter. Her eyes rolled in pleasure as she chewed. "You haven't lost your talent in the kitchen."

"Thanks."

"I cook on the weekends, but I usually make do with a sandwich or soup or takeout during the week. I'm usually too exhausted after work to consider cooking."

"Sounds like you have a stressful job."

"At times. It's more the commute that gets to me than the job. I wish I lived closer to the hospital, but there's nothing in that area I can afford. All the houses and apartments in that part of town start in the high six-figure range. I make a good salary, but not *that* good."

"Do you have a house or apartment?"

"An apartment. It's a little smaller than I'd like, but nice. If I look out my bathroom window in a certain spot, I can see a little sliver of the bay." She held up her thumb and forefinger, less than an inch apart. "About that much."

He chuckled when she grinned. Picking up her plate, he placed two perfectly browned eggs on it. The toast popped up behind him. After quickly buttering it, he laid a slice on each of their plates before dishing up his eggs. Grabbing his cup of cooling coffee, he sat on the chair next to her. "Dig in."

"You don't have to tell me twice."

He chuckled again when Rayna attacked her food. She'd taken two bites of everything before she spoke once more. "This is amazing, Marcus."

"You're just hungry."

"I am, but it's still amazing." She took a sip of her juice, her gaze focused on the window over the sink. "I've missed your cooking."

He'd waited for her to talk about something personal and now she had. No mention of Derek yet, but he wondered if her statement might be a start to complete honesty between them. "I've missed cooking for more than just me."

"You don't ever . . . entertain?"

"Rayna, I told you last night I haven't been with any other women."

She looked back at him. "I know you said that, but that doesn't mean you haven't dated. Right?"

He scooped up a dollop of egg on his toast. "Yeah, I've dated."

"But no lovers?"

"No." He gazed directly into her eyes. "You were never attracted to any of the guys you met in San Francisco?"

"I was *attracted* to some of them, enough to go on more than one date. But I didn't want to sleep with any of them."

"Why not?"

She shrugged one shoulder as she speared another bite of ham. "No chemistry, I guess."

"That was never a problem for us."

"No, it wasn't. I fell for you the first time I saw you."

"So why did you keep saying no to anything but kissing?"

Her mouth dropped open. "I was fourteen!"

"I was fifteen with raging hormones. I had to walk around with a book in front of my fly whenever you were around."

He laughed when she swatted his arm. "Typical male, always thinking with his cock."

"Hey, at fifteen a guy's brain is nowhere near his head. At least not the one on his shoulders."

Rayna shook her head before she began to eat again. Marcus polished off everything on his plate and went back for seconds of the potatoes and ham. He saw her studying the walls, cabinets, island. "Something wrong?"

"When I got here last night, my first thought was that you need to paint your house." Her gaze swept the room again, came back to him. "The inside is beautiful."

"Thanks. I'm still working on it. There are two small bedrooms at the back of the house. And I do mean small. I'm going to add on to both of them. Once that's done, I'll paint the outside."

"I love your master bath. I could've stood under those six shower heads all day."

He wished he'd seen her in his shower with the water running down her skin. He'd done that many times throughout their relationship, which had usually ended up with Rayna plastered against the shower wall while he fucked her.

Pushing those memories from his mind, he drained his coffee cup. "I added on to it and the master bedroom. This house was built in the sixties, so didn't have large closets like today's houses do. I added a walk-in closet when I remodeled the bedroom. I'll do that with the other two bedrooms, too."

"So you plan to stay in Lanville?"

Marcus nodded. "It's a great place to live. I'll have my house finished soon, I have a job I enjoy, and lots of friends. I see no reason to go anywhere else."

He watched her push the last piece of potato around on her plate. "You like it in San Francisco?"

She shrugged. "I wish some things could be different, but I imagine most people can say that about where they live."

Not looking at him, she laid her fork on her plate, clasped her hands together in her lap. Marcus could tell by the way she straightened her shoulders that she had something on her mind. He remained silent and waited for her to speak.

"Is he here?" she asked, her voice soft and full of pain.

Again he waited, this time for her to look at him, but she didn't. "Yes, he's here. I had him moved the first anniversary of his death. That's also when I got the tattoo."

Her chest rose and fell with a deep breath before she finally looked at him. Tears glistened in her eyes. "You must think I'm the worst mother ever for not asking about him as soon as I saw you."

For years, he'd thought her a horrible mother for never visiting Derek's grave after the funeral. She'd left Texas barely a month after their son's death and had never returned. She hadn't taken any pictures of Derek, any mementoes of his short five years on Earth. He'd never been able to understand how a mother could completely forget her child.

"Yeah, I thought that at first. You didn't even take any pictures of him when you left, Rayna."

"I had pictures on my cell phone and digital camera. I still have those. I don't look at them every day because . . ." A tear slipped from her eye to flow down her cheek. "It hurts too much. But a day doesn't go by that I don't think of him and miss him."

Marcus had to hold her, to offer her whatever comfort he could. Slipping from his stool, he stood between her legs and wrapped his arms around her. She laid her cheek against the name of their son. Tears continued to seep from her eyes, wetting his chest.

He didn't know how much time passed before he realized

she no longer cried. Her arms remained around his waist, her cheek pressed to his chest, but didn't feel her tears on his skin. He *did* feel her soft breasts against his stomach. Her warm breath ruffled his chest hair.

Marcus cradled her nape with one hand, let his other hand slide down her back. He burrowed beneath the hem of his T-shirt to find nothing but bare skin. Not only had Rayna failed to put on her bra, she hadn't bothered with panties either.

She tilted her head back, parted her lips in silent invitation. He should resist. Making love with Rayna again would accomplish nothing other than a few minutes of pleasure.

His cell phone rang from across the kitchen where he'd left it. He didn't know anyone who would call him at seven in the morning, unless it was someone from work. He gave her nape a gentle squeeze before he released her. "I'd better get that."

The disappointment on her face almost made him change his mind. She released him and straightened in her chair. "Sure."

Griff's number appeared on the screen. Marcus pressed the button to accept the call. "Mornin', Griff."

"Hey, Marcus, sorry to call so early. Rye came down with some kind of stomach bug. He was sick most of the night. Any chance you could take over his appointments today?"

"No problem."

"Thanks. Normally Dax and I would divide them up, but there are so many because of the fire damage—"

"Say no more. I just finished breakfast. I'll get dressed and meet you at the office in about half an hour."

"See you then."

He ended the call and turned to face Rayna. He saw her carrying their dishes toward the sink. "I'll clean up for you," she said, setting their plates on the counter.

"You don't have to do that, Rayna."

"I don't mind." She smiled at him over her shoulder. "I know you have to go. It won't take me long to do the dishes."

The tip of her nose remained red from her recent crying. He used to tease her about being related to Rudolph the Red-Nosed Reindeer.

He wouldn't tease her today.

He walked over to her and lifted her chin. "I'm sorry we didn't get more time to talk."

"I can come back tonight. If you want."

Her eyes told him she very much wanted to come back and talk. Perhaps that would be a good idea. Maybe they could finally settle everything between them. "On one condition."

Worry filled her eyes. "Condition?"

"Yeah. Will you make that teriyaki pork that I like so much?"

The worry disappeared, to be replaced by joy. "I can do that."

"I'll get you a house key. I have an extra one in my bedroom. Come back whenever you want to. I usually get home between five-thirty and six."

"And you like to shower before you eat. So I'll figure supper for six-thirty."

Marcus smiled. "Perfect."

Rayna peeked around the edge of the door, not wanting to bother her grandmother if she slept. She needn't have worried. Nana sat up in bed, her eyes bright, her cheeks rosy. The picture of good health.

"Hi," she said, entering the room.

Nana's face lit up with a smile. "Hi."

Rayna sat in the chair next to the bed. "I'm sorry I didn't call you last night. I hope you didn't worry about me."

"I didn't worry at all. I knew Marcus would take care of you." She arched one white eyebrow. "He *did* take care of you, right?"

He certainly did. Not willing to tell her grandmother about the incredible lovemaking she'd shared with Marcus, she quickly changed the subject. "I met Rye Coleman yesterday afternoon at your house. He said Coleman Construction will start on the repairs Friday. It'll take two to three weeks. He suggested all the flying dust wouldn't be good for you, so you can't move back in until the repairs are finished."

"That's fine. My friend Bella Olinghouse offered me one of her guest rooms for as long as I need it. Mattie, too. Bella probably has ten extra bedrooms, so there's plenty of space for us. You, too, if you want to stay there instead of at The Inn." She tilted her head and a sly look filled her eyes. "Or are you planning on staying with someone else?"

"I can't stay here for three weeks, Nana," Rayna said, ignoring her grandmother's question. "I thought about staying until your house repairs are done because I figured you'd move into my room at the B-and-B. Now that I know you can stay with a friend, I'll go back home."

"A friend isn't family, Rayna." She took one of Rayna's hands in both of hers. "I lost my daughter. I lost my sister and brother. You're the only family I have left. Please don't go yet."

It broke Rayna's heart to see tears filling Nana's eyes. She placed her other hand on top of their clasped ones. "I'll be here through Friday, at least. After that . . . We'll discuss what I'll do once you're out of the hospital. Okay?"

"Okay." She released Rayna's hand, straightened the sheet over her lap. "Now, tell me about your evening with Marcus."

"What makes you think I was with Marcus?"

She gave Rayna that I'm-not-stupid look. "He's the only person who could've kept you from coming to see me like you said you would. What happened?"

Knowing her grandmother wouldn't give up until she knew the truth, Rayna sat back in her chair. "I went to his house to talk to him. I was crying and he kissed me to stop my crying and . . . We didn't do very much talking. But I'm going to cook supper for him tonight and this time we *will* talk."

"Maybe about getting back together?" she asked with hope in her voice.

"I don't think that's possible, Nana. We've been apart for too long. Our lives have gone in completely different directions. But I'd like to leave Lanville knowing we settled some things between us."

"Talking is the first step, Rayna. That first step could be the start of an incredible journey."

10

Walking into his home to the smell of supper cooking was something Marcus hadn't experienced in five years. It sent him back in time to the days when Rayna's work schedule allowed her to be home in time to prepare supper. That hadn't happened often since her nursing schedule varied so much. They'd both appreciated the time when they could share a meal together.

He found her in the kitchen, removing cookies from a cookie sheet onto a piece of waxed paper. She wore an open, short-sleeved, blue blouse over a white tank, and a full skirt with brightly colored flowers splashed all over it. Combs held back her hair over her ears, gold hoops hung from her earlobes. He couldn't see her feet from where he stood, but he'd bet money she wore the little strappy sandals she always preferred.

His heart swelled in his chest at the sight of her. This is what he wanted—to share his life again. He'd been so lonely the last five years without Rayna. He wanted to marry again, have another child. He wouldn't hesitate to get involved with a woman if he could find the right one.

She must have sensed his presence for she looked up from the cookies. A welcoming smile spread across her mouth. "Hi."

"Hi." He stepped up to the island and peered at the round disks. "Oatmeal?"

Rayna nodded. "Do you still like oatmeal cookies?"

"Who doesn't?" He picked up one and tore it in two halves. A generous amount of raisins and chopped pecans were scattered throughout the soft treat. He popped one of the halves into his mouth, then had to quickly move it around since it hadn't had the chance to cool yet. "Hot."

"You'd be hot, too, if you'd just come out of a three-hundred-and-fifty-degree oven." She slapped at his hand when he reached for another cookie. "Supper before dessert."

"I've always thought that a silly rule." He ate the other half and grabbed another cookie before she could hit him again. "I'm gonna shower. Back in a bit."

He returned to the kitchen a few minutes later, wearing faded jeans and one of his Dallas Cowboys T-shirts. Not seeing Rayna, he followed the sound of clinking silverware to the dining room. He rarely used this room, preferring to eat at the island, or on the couch in front of the TV during football season. Leaning against the archway, he watched her arrange wineglasses by each plate. He didn't know where the snowy white tablecloth came from because he didn't have any nice linens. A bachelor who never entertained didn't need that kind of foo-foo stuff.

When she struck a match to light the two tall tapers in the center of the table, he had to speak. "Looks nice."

She smiled at him over her shoulder. "Thank you."

"Very . . . romantic."

Her smile faded as she shook out the match's flame. "It's too much?" She turned to face him, her hands clasped before her. "I

188 / *Lynn LaFleur*

borrowed the tablecloth, napkins, and candleholders from Nana's house. I wanted the table to look nice for you."

"Did you hear me complain?" He ran one finger down her cheek. "I appreciate the effort you went to."

Her shoulders relaxed and he could hear the relief in her voice when she spoke next. "It wasn't any effort. I think food tastes better by candlelight." She smiled again. "Are you hungry?"

"Starving."

"Come help me get everything."

Marcus sat down across from Rayna a few minutes later. Not only had she cooked the teriyaki pork he liked so much, but had also prepared wild rice, broccoli, and crusty rolls. A nice Pinot Noir complemented the meal perfectly.

He moaned at the first bite of pork. "Wow, this is good."

She gave him a pleased smile. "I'm glad you like it."

"I always did." He cut another bite of the tender meat with his fork. "Do you make this very often?"

"Actually, this is the first time I've made it since we sep—" She froze while reaching for her wineglass. Her gaze flew to his, mortification evident in her eyes.

Marcus finished the sentence for her. "Since we separated."

Rayna nodded. "I guess I'd made it so often, the recipe was burned into my brain."

"Lucky for me."

His playful teasing seemed to relax her again. She scooped up a forkful of wild rice. He enjoyed watching her eat, enjoyed the way she savored every bite. She'd never dieted. With her naturally slim build, she'd never had to.

"Do you still walk every day?"

"Not outside. I do my walking up and down hospital corridors. My job is supposed to be mostly supervisory, but I'm always needed somewhere to help or answer questions or check on supplies."

She'd never been a sitter, so walking hospital corridors would be an ideal job for her. "And you love that."

"I do. I like it when I get out of my office and back out into the nursing world."

"Why did you take that job?"

"Advancement. More money." She shrugged one shoulder. "I thought I'd enjoy it more than I do. I mean, I *do* like it, but not as much as being with patients."

"So go back to nursing. You shouldn't spend the rest of your life in a career that doesn't satisfy you."

"I make a really nice salary, Marcus. It would be hard to give that up, especially with the cost of living in San Francisco."

Marcus washed down his last bite of broccoli with a sip of wine. "You don't have to stay in San Francisco."

She laid her fork on her half-empty plate. "Do you have a suggestion as to where I could go?"

He could see eagerness in her eyes, and hope. She wanted him to ask her to move to Lanville. He didn't know if he could do that. She'd torn out his heart when she left him. The fact that she'd blamed him for the death of their son couldn't be pushed under the rug and forgotten. Something that cruel, that hurtful, stuck with a man for a long, long time.

"You kept saying you were sorry last night," he said, changing the subject instead of answering her question. "Sorry for what?"

"For hurting you. For leaving you. For breaking the vows I'd made to you on our wedding day." She picked up her wineglass, stared into the dark liquid. "I stayed at Nana's house for a couple of hours after Rye Coleman left. I spent a long time looking at her special jars."

"The ones on the hallway shelves?"

Rayna nodded. "When I saw the one holding the little mesh bag of bird seed from our wedding, I . . . lost it. It hit me then how wrong I'd been to blame you for Derek's death."

"Why *did* you blame me?" he asked softly. "You knew it wasn't my fault."

Regret and sadness filled her eyes. "I know that now," she said in barely a whisper. She set her glass on the table without drinking any wine. "But at the time, I was in so much pain, I had to lash out at someone. Unfortunately, you were the closest one available."

Marcus laid his napkin next to his empty plate. "Cindy had taken Derek for ice cream, something she'd done every time she stayed with him. Yet you said it was my fault Derek died, that I'd picked Cindy for our babysitter. You said I should've found someone older than seventeen, with more experience behind the wheel of a car. Cindy was a careful driver. If you were going to blame anyone, you should've blamed the drunk driver who'd done too much Fourth of July celebrating and plowed into the side of her car."

"I know that. I know Cindy's parents lost their child, too. But I couldn't think logically then, Marcus." She splayed one hand over her chest while tears filled her eyes. "I was in so much pain, I couldn't think at all."

"I lost my son, too, Rayna. Didn't you think I was hurting right along with you?"

"No, I didn't. I didn't think anyone could hurt as much as a mother who'd lost her child." She reached across the table, covered his hand with hers. "I'm so sorry, Marcus. I can't put into words how sorry I am for hurting you, for pushing you away, for . . . everything."

Rayna waited for Marcus to turn his hand over and link their fingers together. When he pulled his hand from beneath hers instead, she wanted to curl into a little ball and cry the rest of the night.

What did I expect? That he'd drop to one knee and swear his

*love to me? I destroyed him five years ago. It takes more than a
night of sex and a special dinner to get over something like that.*

Slowly, she moved her hand back to the side of her plate.
"The cookies are to snack on whenever you want one. I made
lemon mousse for dessert."

"I'm pretty full right now. Maybe later."

"Oh, sure. It's in the refrigerator whenever you want it."

Not knowing what else to say, Rayna stood, picked up her
plate and wineglass, and headed for the kitchen. She heard Marcus's chair slide across the wooden floor and knew he'd be right
behind her. She kept swallowing to try and dislodge the lump
in her throat. Later, she could give into her tears, but not in
front of Marcus.

"Everything was delicious, Rayna," he said as he set his plate
on the counter next to hers.

"Thank you. I'd forgotten how good the teriyaki pork is. I'll
have to make it for myself sometime."

"It's a great midnight snack."

No mention of her ever making it for him again. It shouldn't
hurt her so much. She'd come to Lanville to be with her grandmother, not reunite with Marcus. But being with him again reminded her of how very good they'd been together, and how
very much she'd loved him.

Not past tense. I still love him.

More time in Lanville would only make her want what she
couldn't have—a second chance with Marcus. She'd pick up
Nana at the hospital tomorrow morning, take her to her
friend's house, then go back to San Francisco on Friday.

"I cleaned as I cooked, so there isn't much else to do. I think
I'll go say good night to Nana before I head to The Inn."

She thought she saw disappointment in his eyes, but decided
she'd imagined it since she wanted so much to stay with him.
"Tell her good night for me, too."

"I will."

He followed her to the front door. "Thank you again for fixing supper. It was nice to have a home-cooked meal I didn't make myself."

"I'm glad you enjoyed it." She reached into the pocket of her skirt, drew out his house key. "Here's your key."

Their fingers brushed as he took it from her. Rayna felt that simple touch sweep through her entire body. She prayed he'd take her in his arms, ask her to stay. She longed to feel his body against hers one more time.

"Thanks." He took the key, slid it into his jeans pocket. "Take care of yourself, Rayna."

"You, too," she whispered.

Somehow, she made it out the door and onto the porch. She held the handrail going down the three steps, worried her legs would collapse and she'd fall in front of him. Tiny raindrops began to fall as she started toward her car parked in the driveway.

"Rayna!"

She turned at the sound of Marcus's voice to see him running toward her. She didn't have time to do more than inhale before he grabbed her, held her tightly against him.

"Don't leave," he pleaded into her ear. "Stay with me. Please."

"Marcus—"

His lips cut off her words. Moaning softly, Rayna wrapped her arms around his neck and held him while he kissed her. All the pain, all the loneliness of the last few years seemed to flow out of her body, leaving nothing but her love for him.

"I'm so sorry, Marcus," she whispered once he ended their kiss. "I wish I could take back all the pain I caused you."

"I know you do." He cradled her face in his hands. "Think we can start over?"

"Only if you can forgive me."

His gaze passed over her face. "I do. I forgive you. I want a second chance with you." He kissed her again. "I love you, Rayna. I love you."

Tears of joy filled her eyes at his beautiful words. She wrapped her arms around his neck again, held him as tightly as he held her. "I love you, too."

The clouds opened up as he kissed her. Warm rain quickly drenched them. Rayna didn't care. She'd stand in the rain all night if it meant being in Marcus's arms.

"It's raining," he said against her lips.

"I know."

"We're getting wet." He pulled back enough to look into her eyes. "Are you getting wet anywhere else?"

The light spilling through the open front door let her see the hungry look on his face. If her pussy wasn't already dampening from his kiss, that look would make it wet in seconds. She nodded.

He scooped her up in his arms and walked toward the house. After kicking the door shut behind them, he carried her to the couch and sat down with her in his arms. "The bed is too far away."

Rayna agreed with that. She shifted so she could straddle his lap, feel the delicious hard bulge of his cock between her legs. Feeling it through wet denim wasn't enough. She needed skin against skin.

She rose from his lap long enough to slip off her panties. She tackled the fastening of his jeans next. It delighted her to discover he'd gone commando. She slid her hand into the opening of his jeans, pulled out his hard shaft. Lifting her skirt, she straddled his lap again, ready to impale herself.

Marcus gripped her hips to stop her movement. "Wait."

Wait? He didn't actually tell her to wait. "What?"

"We didn't use any precautions last night."

Rayna didn't understand what he meant. "Precautions?"

"Birth control. I didn't even think about using a condom."

Neither had Rayna. She and Marcus hadn't used condoms since the early days of their marriage while experimenting with different kinds of birth control. It had been completely natural for her to take him inside her body without anything to separate them. "I didn't think of that either." Still gripping his hard cock, she gave it a gentle squeeze. "Do you want to stop?"

Marcus groaned. "Hell, no, but I don't have any condoms."

Rayna did a fast calculation of her cycle. "It should be safe, Marcus. I don't think I can get pregnant now."

"You don't *think*, or you know for sure?"

"Anything is possible, but I'm pretty sure it's safe now." She squeezed his cock again. "Please. I don't want to stop."

"I don't want to stop either."

Rayna lowered her hips and took his shaft inside her. Marcus moaned at the same time she did. Rayna rested her forehead against his. She wanted to savor this time together, joined as one, before they rushed toward climaxes. "You feel so good inside me."

"It's where I'm supposed to be." His hands slid down to her ass, grasped it through her skirt. "Move for me, sweetheart."

He tunneled his fingers into her hair, brought her mouth to his for a fierce kiss. Lips slid across lips, tongues collided, breaths meshed. Rayna slowly lifted her hips and lowered them again, easing only the head inside her at first, then more of his cock with every movement. Marcus gripped her ass tighter, raised his hips to meet her each time she lowered hers. Holding to his shoulders for balance, she moved faster, took him deeper.

"You're so wet." Marcus slipped his hands beneath her skirt and held her bare hips. "And tight. God, so tight."

He pumped faster into her, his thrusts brushing against her clit exactly the way she needed. Rayna hadn't wanted to come so quickly, had wanted to feel Marcus inside her for a long time, but she couldn't stop the pleasure from overtaking her body. It rushed through her faster than a flash fire. She threw back her head, groaned deeply in her throat, and shot toward heaven.

Marcus held back his climax as long as he could. He couldn't delay it any longer when he felt Rayna's internal walls pulsing around his dick during her orgasm. Lifting his hips, he buried his cock as deep inside her as possible and followed her into bliss.

She wilted against him, her face against his neck. Her warm breath flowed over his skin each time she exhaled. Perhaps they should've talked first, made some decisions about what they would do before they'd made love again, but he didn't regret this. He could never regret something that felt so right.

He had the love of his life in his arms again, right where she should be.

"I'm sorry, Marcus." She sat back, rested her hands on his chest. "I regret so many things. Hurting you, never visiting my son's grave after the funeral, letting his death destroy our marriage." Her eyes filled with tears. "I never should have left you."

"Hey." Cradling her face in his hands, he gave her a soft, loving kiss. "It's in the past. We're starting over, right?"

She nodded. A tear slid down her cheek. He wiped it away with his thumb.

"I want to visit Derek."

Her comment surprised him, so much he didn't know how to respond.

She smoothed his T-shirt over his chest. "Did you get a headstone?"

"Yes," he said around the lump in his throat. "I think you'll approve."

"I'm sure it's perfect." She looked into his eyes. "I have to go back to San Francisco and give notice at my job and apartment. Or maybe not my apartment. One of the nurses—who's also a friend—is living with her parents while she looks for a place that she can afford. I know she likes my apartment. She might even be willing to buy some of my furniture." Her gaze traveled around the room. "I like that you kept some of the pieces we bought together."

"I kept everything you left, Rayna. It's all packed in plastic tubs in the storage shed out back."

"It is?" she asked, disbelief in her tone.

Marcus shrugged. "I couldn't make myself throw away anything. Maybe I thought—hoped—you'd come back someday."

She rested her forehead against his again. "I'm back. And I promise I won't leave again. Even if I have to put up with the heat and humidity."

"We'll take a lot of cool showers together."

His kiss sealed her declaration and returned one of his own for another chance. They'd make it this time. He had no doubt about that.

He kissed her once, twice again. "So, what's your plan?"

"I'll pick up Nana tomorrow from the hospital and take her to her friend's house—"

"*We'll* pick up Nana tomorrow."

Rayna smiled. "*We'll* pick her up and get her settled. I'll make my flight reservation for Friday. As soon as I get back, I'll give notice at the hospital. It'll be at least two weeks, maybe three before I can move here."

"Once you know for sure when you're heading this way, I'll fly out there and we'll drive here together."

Her smiled widened. "I'd like that."

"Do you want to go back to nursing?"

She nodded. "Think I'd be able to get a job at the hospital?"

"With your talent and résumé, they'll hire you in a second."

An apprehensive look crossed her face. "Do you think we

should take it slow? I could live with Nana while we decide if things will really work for us this time."

Marcus had no doubt everything would work for them, but he understood her hesitation. Although he forgave her for leaving him, they had five years of pain to overcome. "If that's what you want, that's what we'll do."

Her pleased smile lit up her face. He couldn't resist giving her one more kiss before he slid his hands beneath her tank to the smooth skin of her back. They'd talk more, make additional plans, tomorrow. Now, they had other things to do. "Know what I want?"

"What?"

"Dessert. How about if I spread lemon mousse all over your body and lick it off? Then you can do the same to me."

He loved the slow, sexy smile that graced her lips. "Sounds like a great idea to me."

Spark

1

Talia King kept sneaking glances at Dylan Westfield whenever possible. He stood across the room with three other men on the Lanville Volunteer Fire Department. She kept wishing he would look at her, acknowledge her presence in the room. Then she wondered why she wished that since he only thought of her as a friend.

It sucked to be a friend.

Short of dancing in front of him naked, she'd done everything she could think of to get him to notice her as a woman. She doubted if even the dancing naked part would work. She'd be old and gray before he ever asked her for a date. The few times she'd asked him out, he'd always had an excuse as to why he couldn't go.

After almost two years of working with him on the fire department, she'd come to the conclusion that he'd never feel that energy, that spark, she felt whenever she came close to him.

Which also sucked.

Talia glanced at her watch. Their fire chief, Clay Spencer, would soon arrive at the fire hall with his girlfriend, Maysen

Halliday, and boxes of the firefighters' calendar Maysen had created for a fund-raiser. Talia thought her boss kind to let her take an extended break from the clothing store to come to the fire hall for the unveiling of the calendars. Of course, Janelle had made Talia promise to bring her one.

Curious at how the calendar turned out, Talia silently urged Clay and Maysen to get here for the big unveiling. The calendar had been Maysen's idea for a fund-raiser. She'd come to Lanville to do an article for her magazine, *Hot Shots,* about the Lanville firefighters, who had been voted the sexiest volunteer firefighters in Texas. She and Clay had fallen in love. She'd left the running of her magazine in Houston to her assistant and moved into Clay's house. No wedding bells yet, but Talia wouldn't be surprised if Clay popped the question at any time.

Lucky Maysen.

The man Talia loved didn't love her. Fine. She could think of dozens of things that would be worse. She'd pined after Dylan long enough. She dated occasionally, but had always compared the guy to Dylan. That wasn't fair to her date. She had to forget about anything developing between her and Dylan, move on with someone else.

That decision made, she turned her back on the four men and joined the conversation with Paige Denslow and Lucia Vega.

Talia had the sweetest ass Dylan had ever seen.

She stood across the room by the kitchen, talking to the other two female firefighters. Whoever had claimed women to be the weaker sex had never seen those three women fight a fire. No one on the fire department worked harder or longer than Talia, Paige, and Lucia.

No one on the fire department looked as good in a pair of jeans as Talia.

He ached for her. Ever since she'd moved to Lanville two

years ago and joined the volunteer fire department, he'd ached for her. It had taken willpower he didn't know he possessed to keep from asking her out. Then when *she'd* asked *him* out, he'd had to dig down deeper for even more willpower to say no.

He had no choice but to say no. He couldn't take the chance of hurting her.

"You know you're an idiot for not asking her out," Quade Easton said.

Dylan turned his head and looked at one of his fellow fire-fighters. He knew exactly who Quade meant, but pretended he didn't. "Who?"

Quade rolled his eyes. "Like you don't know I'm talking about Talia. Your tongue hangs out every time you get within fifty feet of her."

"Yeah," Stephen McGettis said from the other side of Dylan. "What's with that? Why don't you ask her out?"

"Or accept when she asks you out," Dusty McGettis said.

Quade looked at Dusty. "She's asked Dylan out?"

Dusty nodded. "I've heard her at least twice. Dylan said no both times."

"Not smart, man," Stephen said, playfully punching Dylan's upper arm. "Talia is hot."

"Hey, you aren't supposed to notice hot gals," Dylan said as he rubbed his abused arm. "You aren't supposed to look at any-one but Julia."

"I love Julia, but I'm not blind or dead." He glanced over his shoulder at the object of their conversation. "I can see where a man would want to wrap all that long, blond hair around his hands."

So could Dylan. He fantasized about doing that very thing almost daily. He dreamed of holding her, kissing her, sliding his hard cock into her sweet cunt. She would take him perfectly. He had no doubt about that.

Before his thoughts made his cock swell, he looked away from her. "Not gonna happen, guys."

A frown turned down Stephen's lips. "Why not?"

"It wouldn't work."

"I'm not suggesting you ask her to marry you, man. Just go out with her."

Dylan would like nothing better, but knew it could never be. Deciding it was time to change the subject, he turned toward Dusty. "How's the baby?"

Dusty's entire face lit up with his grin. "Great. Handsome as his daddy."

Stephen snorted. "Yeah, right. You mean handsome as his uncle."

"Just because R. J. has your middle name doesn't mean he got anything else from you."

"Maybe he inherited my daredevil spirit. It might be time for his first motorcycle ride."

A look of horror passed over Dusty's face. "He's only two months old! There's no way I'm letting you take him on your motorcycle."

"Gotta start 'em young." Stephen winked at Dylan and Quade. "Bet I can have him racing by the time he's five."

Dylan couldn't hold back his laughter any longer. Quade and Stephen soon joined him, until Stephen slapped Dusty's back. "Just pullin' your chain, cuz. I'd never do anything to hurt R. J. You know that."

"Yeah, I do. Geez, don't tease me like that." He placed one hand over his heart. "The protective instinct kicked in big time."

A twinge of envy settled beneath Dylan's heart at the thought of having a son or daughter of his own. Which would never happen. Dylan made sure of that by always using a condom whenever he had sex. Not that he had sex that often. His friends might think of him as Mr. Stud, but they'd laugh if they knew how long it'd been since he'd held a woman's naked body in his arms.

Too bad his dad had never possessed the protective instinct for his son. Life would've been so different if his father had cared for his son the way a father should.

Pushing aside those gloomy thoughts before they could overtake him, Dylan drained his cup of coffee. "You guys want a refill?"

Before any of them could answer, the outside door opened. Maysen walked in, followed closely by Clay pushing a hand-cart holding four cardboard boxes. Before anyone could rush forward to peek in one of the boxes, Clay held up a hand to stop them.

"Everyone will get calendars. We have enough here for each firefighter to get four. Whoever couldn't come today will gets theirs whenever they can pick them up. They'll be in my office." He parked the cart next to one of the long tables. When he looked out at the crowd, Dylan could tell by Clay's eyes that the next thing he had to say wouldn't be pleasant.

"I got off the phone a few minutes ago with Walt Kinney's attorney. Walt passed away about an hour ago in a Fort Worth hospital."

Murmurs and gasps of surprise came from everyone, including Dylan. Walt had been part of Lanville for years. He'd sit outside his gas station in nice weather and play checkers with some of his buddies. As a kid, Dylan had ridden his bicycle to Walt's gas station with his friends. Walt always had the coldest Cokes in town.

Clay had bought Walt's station last year to be part of the national Spencer's Station and Convenience Store chain. He'd renovated and added on to the old building. It now included a three-bay garage for car repairs, as well as a large, modern store and twelve gas pumps. Clay hadn't skimped on the best equipment, making it a pleasure for Dylan to work there as a mechanic. Some days, he changed the oil in only one car, but other days he stayed so busy, he barely had time for a bathroom break.

"Walt never married, never had any children," Clay continued. "His brother passed away several years ago, so he didn't have any family. He always supported the fire department and never passed up one of our fund-raisers." His gaze swept the room, touched each person. "His attorney didn't give me a specific amount over the phone—I have an appointment with him next week—but he did tell me Walt left a substantial amount to us. With the presales of the calendars and what we've already earned from other fund-raisers, we should have more than enough to buy our new tanker."

Applause erupted in the room. Dylan imagined everyone here felt the same as he—sad that Lanville had lost one of its oldest citizens, yet happy the fire department would be able to serve the people of Lanville County even better with new equipment thanks to Walt.

Dylan looked over at Talia in time to see her wipe tears from her cheeks. He wished he could hold her, comfort her. She'd loved Walt just like everyone else in this room.

"One more thing and then I'll unveil the calendars."

"*I'll* unveil the calendars," Maysen said.

Laughter flowed through the crowd. Dylan chuckled as Clay bowed to his lady. "I stand corrected. *Maysen* will unveil the calendars." He straightened, looked over the firefighters again. "I'm sure you're all familiar with the land behind Sonic. The attorney told me ten acres of it belonged to Walt. He also left that to the fire department."

"What does that mean, Chief?" Tate Coughlin, one of the captains, asked. "Are we going to build a new fire hall?"

Tate's question made everyone start talking at once. Clay raised his hands to request quiet. "I'll know more after I talk to the attorney. We need a bigger fire hall and bays for the equipment, especially if we acquire more, and there's no more room on this lot to expand. We won't have any more empty bays once we buy the new tanker. But it'll cost money to build a new fire hall."

"We've got lots of free labor right here," Dylan said.

Several heads nodded in agreement with Dylan's statement.

"Supplies won't be free. Even with the discount we get from the lumber stores, we're talking a lot of money." He raised his hands again when the murmurs started once more. "Let me see what the attorney says. He'll be in town Tuesday for the official reading of the will. Walt left some things to a few of his long-time friends here in Lanville. Once I know exactly how much money is involved, we can start planning the best way to use it, and the land."

Dylan saw more nods as the firefighters accepted what Clay said. A rush of excitement flowed through him at the thought of building a brand-new fire hall on that ten acres. Only a block from the main highway through Lanville, it would be more convenient than their current location three blocks from the downtown square. A faster response time of even a couple of minutes could mean the difference of the fire department saving a home, or fire destroying it.

"Okay, now we get to the other reason I called all of you here." Clay grinned. "The unveiling of the calendar. Maysen, I'm sure you have everyone's attention."

"Exactly as it should be."

Dylan laughed along with several of the other guys. Maysen and Clay fit perfectly together. He couldn't imagine either of them being with someone else.

With a few cuts of the box cutter in her hand, Maysen removed the top flaps of the first box. "I think Talia, Paige, and Lucia should get the first look." She gave them a come-here motion with her forefinger.

Dylan watched the three gals walk over to Maysen. Or

rather, he watched Talia. She wore a short-sleeved blouse in various shades of purple tucked into her jeans with a belt at her waist that looked like woven white rope. She must have come here directly from Janelle's, where she worked as a sales clerk. Talia wearing some of the clothes a woman could buy at the store had to be the best advertisement Janelle could get. With Talia's petite body and long, golden-blond hair, she looked good in anything she wore.

He'd bet she looked even better wearing nothing at all.

Paige released a loud wolf whistle when she picked up the first calendar. Grinning widely, she held it in front of her so everyone in the room could see it. Dylan groaned. His image, along with Shawn's, Jose's, Wes's, and Quade's, graced the cover of the calendar. They stood beside the ladder truck in full gear. Well, except for the fact that their turnout coats hung open over their bare chests.

Paige licked her finger, touched the picture, and released a hissing sound. "Hot stuff, guys!"

"You realize we'll be teased for weeks about this," Quade said to Dylan.

"More like months."

He looked at Talia flipping through the calendar. Something she saw made her stop. She stared at the item in her hands for several seconds before she looked at him. Her gaze swept his body from shoulders to thighs, then she returned her attention to the calendar.

Oh, shit. What did Maysen put in that damn thing?

"Okay, enough with the women getting first dibs." Dylan walked over to Talia. "It's time to share with us guys."

He stood close enough to smell the flowery scent of her perfume. Or maybe the scent came from her hair. He had to catch himself before he touched the blond waterfall that flowed halfway to her waist.

Remembering his reason for coming over here, he peered

over her shoulder. She had the calendar open to the center, where Maysen had put together a collage of pictures. He saw himself standing next to Stephen, both of them shirtless and leaning against the tanker, arms and ankles crossed. Even in turnout pants, the position of his feet emphasized the bulge at his crotch. He hadn't noticed that in the little thumbnail pictures Maysen had posted online.

All the firefighters had signed a waiver giving Maysen the right to choose the photos for the calendar. Nothing about the picture could be called obscene. He just didn't expect it to be quite so . . . sexy.

"It's a great picture of you and Stephen," Talia said, looking at him over her shoulder.

Talia's green eyes made him think of the first grass of spring . . . which led him to thinking of her lying nude on that green grass with her hair spread out around her head. She'd open her arms to him, welcome him inside her body . . .

"Clay and I want to celebrate the release of the calendar," Maysen said. Dylan forced his gaze away from Talia's eyes and back to his chief's girlfriend. "What do you say to a combination fish fry and barbecue Saturday night?"

Applause and whistles answered Maysen's question. She grinned. "Great! Now I need some volunteers to help put it together. Lucia," she said as she pointed to one of the female firefighters. "Nick, Stephen, Tate," she continued, moving around the room and pointing at each one. Her gaze landed on Dylan. She grinned again. "Dylan and Talia. Y'all get together and plan everything. Clay and I will take care of social media and making sure the information gets posted on the department's and newspaper's Web sites."

"Hey," Dylan protested playfully, "I thought you were going to ask for volunteers."

"I changed my mind. It's much easier to delegate than depend on people to raise their hands." She clapped once, as if to emphasize she'd ended the subject. "Okay, folks, come get your calendars."

Dylan had no desire to hang up a calendar of his buddies, so declined to take any. He saw Talia remove her four from the box and hug them to her chest. She'd probably give one to each of her two sisters and keep one for herself. Maybe she'd give one to her boss, Janelle. Then she'd be out of her free copies.

He lightly touched her bare arm. A spark shot through his hand and up his arm, directly to his heart. It happened every time he had the chance to touch her. "Hey, Talia, I'm not going to take any of my four. You can have them if you need more copies."

"You don't want at least one for a keepsake?"

"Nah. I see these guys naked all the time. I don't need a calendar to remind me they're all ugly."

He grinned when she laughed. "Then I'll take two of yours. That'll leave you two if you change your mind."

Tate approached them, laid a hand on Dylan's shoulder. "Y'all want to meet at Bunkhouse around six? I'll order the barbecue for Saturday and we can plan what else to do while we eat. Since it's fire department business, I can use our credit card to pay for supper."

"Works for me," Dylan said. "How about you, Talia?"

"I get off work at five-thirty, so I can be there by six." She glanced at her watch. "Speaking of work, I have to get back. See y'all later."

She grabbed two more calendars, said good-bye to the other gals, and scurried toward the exit. Dylan would see her again in only a few hours.

Yeah, well, a lot of good it'll do me to see her again. There can't be anything between us except friendship, no matter how much I love her.

2

Talia stepped through the entrance of Bunkhouse Barbecue ten minutes past six. A last-minute customer meant she couldn't close Janelle's until almost six o'clock. Since that customer spent almost two hundred dollars, and Talia earned an extra five percent commission on any sale over one hundred, she didn't mind staying late.

She saw the gang at a table for six in the corner on the left side of the restaurant. Lucia waved at her as she made her way toward them. Talia noticed they'd left an empty chair between Tate and Dylan. Talia had no choice but to take it.

"Hi, everybody. Sorry I'm late."

"No problem," Lucia said. "We haven't ordered or started the meeting yet."

Two half-full pitchers of beer sat in the center of the table. "Looks like someone ordered *something*."

"We couldn't wait for you for *everything*." Tate picked up one of the pitchers. "Want some?"

"Please."

She could feel Dylan looking at her as Tate filled her mug

with the cold brew. If she scooted her chair a few inches closer to his, their legs would touch.

Pushing that silly thought from her head, she took a sip of beer and licked the foam from her upper lip. Wondering if he still looked at her, she peeked at Dylan to see him staring at her mouth. His gaze slowly lifted to her eyes. Talia swallowed at the heat she saw in the blue irises.

"Lucia offered to take notes," Tate said, drawing Talia's attention to him. "How about if we order and then we'll start our business meeting?"

No one argued with him, so Tate motioned to the waitress. Talia would love to order the ribs, but they would be way too messy to eat in front of Dylan. When Lucia ordered them, Talia decided, what the hell. She didn't need to impress Dylan. He wouldn't care one way or the other if she dribbled barbecue sauce in her lap.

The guys at the table followed Lucia, too, meaning Talia probably wouldn't be the only one who wore barbecue sauce home on her clothes. She and Lucia decided to order different sides so they could share and have four choices to eat instead of only two. Talia already imagined the snack she'd enjoy while she watched one of the late-night talk shows.

Once everyone turned in their order, Tate pounded his hand on the table three times in lieu of a gavel. "Okay, meeting officially begins now. Saturday night will be a celebration of raising enough money for our new tanker."

Applause rounded the table, causing Tate to grin. "Yeah, I'm happy about that, too. So, this will be a freebie, not a fund-raiser." He looked at each person seated at the table. "How many usually come to the fund-raisers?"

"We plan for three hundred," Lucia said. "Sometimes there are more, sometimes less, but that seems to be a good number to use for buying food."

"But that's for a fund-raiser." Dylan said. "This is free. People love free, especially when it's food. Clay and Maysen plan to really promote the celebration. I think we need to plan for double what we usually do."

"That wouldn't be a bad idea," Talia said. "We can always split up the leftovers between the firefighters, if we have any leftovers. I'd rather have too much food than to run out and have anyone be disappointed."

Stephen nodded. "I agree with Talia. Since this is something the fire department is doing, we can't depend on people donating food like they do at the fund-raisers."

"Yeah, but I bet they will." Nick picked up his beer mug. "I wouldn't be surprised if half the people who show up bring some kind of food."

"Unless we tell them not to." Lucia jotted a note on her legal pad. "Maysen is posting the announcement online tomorrow. If we say that this is something the fire department wants to do to thank the community, no one would feel obligated to contribute."

Nick sipped his beer, returned his mug to the table. "You know Mrs. Hurley will bring her peach cobbler, whether it's a fund-raiser or free. For which I am very thankful. She makes the best peach cobbler I've ever tasted." He peered over his shoulder toward the kitchen. "Don't tell Judy I said that."

Talia chuckled. Larry's wife, Judy, made wonderful desserts, but no one could top Mrs. Hurley's peach cobbler. Many had tried, but all had failed. "What about this?" She leaned forward in her chair. "The announcement will state this is the fire department's way of thanking Lanville for the support. We'll supply all the meat, the bread, several side dishes, and iced tea, but if anyone wants to contribute something, it would be appreciated."

"I like it." Lucia jotted down another note. "We could sell beer, bottled water, and Cokes, like we do at fund-raisers. Maybe for half price."

"Good idea." Tate leaned back as the waitress set his plate of food in front of him. "I'll talk to Larry when I order the meat about buying some of Judy's cobblers and pies. Even if Mrs. Hurley brings her peach cobbler, we'll need more desserts."

"Not everyone will want beef or fish," Talia said. "Be sure and order some of Larry's turkey."

"Lucia, make a note—"

"Got it, Cap." Lucia grinned at him. "Didn't know I could read your mind, did you?"

"That's a scary thought."

"If we're going to have double the people," Stephen said, "we'll need more tables and chairs."

"I'll check with the churches about borrowing some. We've done that in the past, so it shouldn't be a problem." Lucia wrote that on her tablet. "What if the weather's crappy?"

Talia unfolded her napkin to remove her silverware. "I saw the weather this morning before I went to work. It's supposed to be dry and hot the whole weekend."

"How about if we park some of the equipment on the street?" Nick asked. "That would give us room inside the bays to set up four serving lines instead of two like we usually do."

"Ooh, I like that." Lucia continued to scribble on her paper. "Nick, do you think Keely will help us serve?"

"Sure. She'd be happy to."

"Doesn't she work at Boot Scootin' on Saturday night?"

"I'm sure Dolly will give her the night off to help the fire department."

Tate waited to speak again until everyone had been served. "We can still make plans, but I'm not waiting to eat."

Talia agreed with Tate. She picked up one of the thick beef ribs on her plate and took a huge bite. The barbecue sauce had just enough kick to have her reaching for her beer mug after she'd swallowed the meat.

"Too hot for you?" Dylan asked, the humor evident in his voice.

No way would she admit any weakness to Dylan. She lifted

her chin an inch. "It's perfect." To prove her point, she took another bite, followed by a bite of potato salad to cool a little of the burn.

"You have some sauce right here."

He touched the corner of her mouth with one finger. Talia automatically swiped her tongue there to lap up the sauce. She licked Dylan's finger instead.

She froze and so did he. She stared into his eyes, watching the heat slowly return. Or perhaps it had never left. She'd avoided gazing directly at him since she'd taken her first sip of beer. Now, she couldn't seem to look away from him.

Conversation continued among the other four people at the table. Talia paid no attention to it. She'd promised herself today that she'd forget all about Dylan, that she couldn't keep pining for a man who didn't want her. The yearning in his eyes not only said he wanted her, it screamed out his desire.

Sensation skittered down her spine. Her clit pulsed at the thought of all that heat wrapping around her, engulfing her. She imagined his lips and hands on hers while he lowered her to lie beneath him . . .

Talia cried out at the kick to her shin. "Hey!" She frowned at Lucia. "Why did you do that?"

"You aren't paying attention."

"Neither was Dylan," Stephen said with a grin. "He's too busy making goo-goo eyes at Talia."

Dylan tossed his wadded-up napkin at Stephen, who ducked to avoid it hitting him in the face. "Shut up, McGettis."

"Why don't y'all get a room and work out that built-up frustration?" Nick suggested with a waggle of his eyebrows.

"Why don't you mind your own business?" Dylan asked, frowning.

"Just trying to help, buddy."

Talia stared at her plate. Teasing didn't bother her. More often than not, she gave as good as she got. But Stephen's and

Nick's comments hit too close to home. She hated feeling all flustered and gooey around Dylan when no other man affected her the same way.

"Ignore them," Dylan said while he refilled her mug with beer. "They're idiots."

"Oh, I know that." Determined to stop the yearning for Dylan and treat him as a friend like the other men at this table, she let her gaze touch Nick and Stephen. "It would take more than some childish comments from these jerks to get to me."

Lucia grinned. " 'Atta girl."

Nick leaned past Lucia and peered at Stephen. "Do you believe she called us jerks?"

"I'm completely crushed that Talia could be so cruel to us."

"Trust me," Talia said, stabbing her fork into a piece of fried okra, "you don't know how cruel I can be."

"Sounds like a challenge to me, Stephen."

"I think you're right, Nick." Stephen's gaze swung to Dylan. "What do you think, Westfield?"

Dylan held up both hands, palms out. "I'm not getting involved in whatever y'all have planned. I've been on the receiving end of Talia holding a fire hose."

Stephen tapped his chin. "Fire hose. Hmmm."

Talia pointed her fork at him. "Don't even go there. I promise you'll regret it."

"A challenge." Grinning, Nick rubbed his hands together. "I do love a challenge."

"All right, children," Tate said, humor lacing his voice, "finish your supper. We still have work to do."

Happy to have given as good as she'd received from Nick and Stephen, she glanced at Dylan to see him grinning. He winked at her. Relieved some of the sexual tension had evaporated, she returned his grin.

She couldn't have Dylan the way she wanted him, but she could still have him as a friend. That meant a lot to her.

* * *

Dylan helped Marcus Holt unfold the legs of another table inside the empty bays. The ladder truck and other fire equipment had been moved to the grassy field across the street so they had the entire area to set up for tonight's celebration. Kirk and Kory Wilcox set chairs around the table as soon as Dylan and Marcus set it in place.

Glancing outside, Dylan saw Stephen and Dusty also setting up tables and chairs on the fire hall's lawn. There wouldn't be enough chairs to seat six hundred people if that many showed, but he knew from past fund-raisers that some people would bring their own folding chairs, or blankets and sit on the ground. The Rose River ambled past the fire hall's property, making a scenic and cool place to enjoy the evening.

Nick had been right about people donating food, even though they didn't have to. People had been dropping by all afternoon to leave items with the promise of coming back at six for the official start time of the serving lines. Emma Keeton, the chef at Café Crystal, had dropped off a huge platter of fried chicken barely an hour ago. Several of the firefighters decided they had to sample it, just to make sure it would be good enough to serve tonight.

It received a big thumbs-up from everyone.

"That's the last table," Marcus said. "Ready for a beer?"

"Past ready." He pushed his hair back from his forehead. "It's damned hot in here."

"It'd be hotter if we didn't have the big box fans to help move the air."

"True. But I'd like to skip over the rest of September and get right to October. I'm ready for fall."

"October will be here in two weeks. Don't wish your life away, Dylan. It passes quickly enough on its own."

Dylan followed his captain to the huge ice chests against the wall that held bottles of beer, water, and soft drinks. He accepted a beer from Marcus and gulped down half of it before he took a breath. "Oh, yeah, that's good."

Marcus closed the lid of the ice chest and sat on it. "Six hundred might be a conservative number for the people who plan to come tonight."

Dylan sat on another ice chest next to Marcus. "I hope so. We have enough food to feed almost the whole town."

"I hope there are enough parking spaces for everyone."

"A lot of folks will get their food to go."

"They still have to park to get in the serving lines."

"They'll find a place, even if they have to walk a block or two. Don't worry."

Marcus raised the bottle to his mouth for another drink, but stopped with it halfway there. A huge smile spread over his face. "There's my lady."

Dylan followed the direction of Marcus's gaze to see Rayna coming toward them with a large Crock-Pot in her hands. Marcus quickly set down his bottle and hurried to relieve her of the load. She smiled warmly at him and accepted his kiss before they walked into the building.

Dylan smiled. Marcus and Rayna had remarried last month in a simple ceremony in their backyard. He remembered the look of joy on their faces when the judge had declared them husband and wife. He also remembered how Marcus's eyes had filled with tears of delight when he'd announced to the department two weeks later that he and Rayna would be blessed with a baby in April, a result of their reunion in July after five years apart.

They'd lost their son in a tragic accident when Derek was only five years old. Renewed marriage vows and a baby on the way meant they had another shot at happiness. Dylan didn't doubt that Marcus and Rayna would make it this time.

A car pulled into the parking lot. Dylan watched Talia climb out of the small compact. His cock gave an interested twitch in his briefs at the sight of her in form-fitting denim capris and a sleeveless blouse tied at her waist. The color of the blouse reminded him of ripe raspberries.

He wondered if her nipples were the same color.

She motioned toward Stephen and Dusty before she popped the trunk lid of her car. They ambled over to help her remove more folding chairs. Dylan debated about offering his help, but decided he'd rather sit here and ogle Talia as long as he could.

"You guarding the beer?" Quade asked.

The sound of his friend's voice startled Dylan. He'd been so wrapped up in watching Talia, he hadn't heard Quade come up behind him. "Actually, I'm guarding the water." He jerked his head toward the ice chest where Marcus had sat. "Beer's in there."

Quade helped himself to a bottle, twisted off the cap, and took a long swallow before he sat on the chest. "Hot today."

"Yeah," Dylan said with his gaze on Talia.

"Supposed to cool off next week, back down to normal temps. We might even get some rain."

"Yeah."

"Well, since I've exhausted the weather topic, I'll ask why you're sitting in here staring at Talia instead of out there with her?"

Quade's question drew Dylan's attention away from the woman outside and to the man seated next to him. "Stephen and Dusty are helping her."

"That doesn't mean you couldn't help her, too."

Dylan drank the last of his beer and set his bottle on the cement floor. "I'm fine right here."

Quade blew out a breath. "I know how you feel about her, Dylan. You have to know she feels the same way about you. Why are you denying the happiness she can give you?"

Out of all his friends, only Quade knew about Dylan's past due to an evening of one too many beers and a loose tongue. Quade had always been easy to talk to, probably due to his job as a counselor at the high school.

But even Quade didn't know all the hell Dylan had gone through.

"It isn't that simple, Quade. You know that better than anyone."

"I know the past can fuck with your head if you let it. Don't let it, Dylan."

"Yeah, well, easier said than done."

"Why don't you talk to Talia, tell her—"

"No," Dylan said firmly. "That isn't an option."

"So what are you going to do? Pine after her your whole life? Never get married, never have a family?"

Sometimes Quade's questions really pissed Dylan off. "Look, I confided in you one night when I was really down. You don't have the right to keep throwing that back in my face."

"I wasn't aware I was throwing anything in your face." His voice softened. "I'm your friend, Dylan, and I care. I wish you'd let me help you."

"I'm not crawling on your therapist's couch and letting you inside my head."

"I've been inside your head. It's not a bad place. But it could be better with some help."

"Thanks, but no thanks."

Quade looked like he might argue, but then he nodded. "Okay. Let me know if you change your mind."

He slapped Dylan on the back, stood, and tossed his empty bottle into the glass recycling bin. Dylan watched his friend saunter outside and begin to help Stephen and Dusty set up the folding chairs Talia brought. She laughed at something one of the guys said. The musical sound carried across the breeze to his ears.

He clenched his hands around his empty bottle as thoughts of his past filtered through his mind.

Damn you, Dad. Damn you for making me just like you.

3

"I brought a present for us," Paige whispered into Talia's ear.

Talia picked up the empty bowl that had held Mrs. Hampton's amazing pasta salad and placed it on a tray with other dirty dishes. "What?"

Paige looked around the area. "Where are Lucia and Keely?"

"Lucia's in the kitchen washing dishes with Maysen and Clay. Keely is probably necking with Nick."

"Well, they're still newlyweds, so I can understand that." She pulled a tall paper sack from behind her back. "She'll just have to miss out on the present."

Paige lifted a bottle of sweet-tea vodka so Talia could see the label. Talia immediately flashed back to the last time she, Lucia, and Paige had indulged in that particular liquor. "Oh, no. I'm not doing shots of that stuff. It's dangerous."

"Oh, come on, Taly! It'll be fun. We only have a little bit more to clean up and then we're through with the celebration. Most of the people are gone. We can go across the street to the riverbank, watch the moon come up, and get plastered. We worked hard today. We deserve it."

They had worked really hard today, although Talia had loved every minute of it. They'd served close to seven hundred people, according to the count Keely kept of the paper plates she'd stacked on the tables. They'd run out of some of the side dishes that people donated, but still had plenty of leftovers of some of the other sides, plus lots of barbecue and turkey. Clay had passed the word that any of the firefighters who wanted to take home food could help themselves.

Paige made a good point. It had been weeks since Talia had just let go and had a good time with her girlfriends. "Okay. Sounds like a good plan to me."

Paige grinned. "All right! I'll put this in a safe place so one of the guys doesn't steal it, then help you finish here."

Shaking her head at her silly friend, Talia continued to pile dishes onto the tray. Once she had what she figured she could carry, she lifted the tray to her shoulder and headed for the kitchen.

She rounded the corner and stopped in her tracks. Clay held Maysen in a tight embrace. His hand slid up and down her back and over her butt while they kissed. No one else occupied the room, so Talia heard nothing but their deep breathing and an occasional moan.

Jealousy exploded inside her. She wanted to be the one in her lover's arms, feel his hands drift over her skin, taste his lips. She wanted to be the one who would accept him into her body later tonight, pleasure him as much as he would pleasure her.

To her mortification, tears flooded her eyes. She had to get out of here before she spoiled their private moment.

As quietly as possible, she set down the tray and backed out of the kitchen. Once back in the garage, she closed her eyes and leaned against the door. She hated the self-pity that clawed at her. She'd always been a positive person, one who looked on the bright side of things. Loving Dylan and his not loving her in return had turned her emotions upside down until she didn't recognize herself any longer.

Getting plastered tonight sounded better than when Paige first mentioned it.

Tears still blurred her vision, so Talia didn't see Quade until she bumped into him. He grabbed her upper arms to steady her.

"Whoa! Easy."

"Sorry," she muttered, not looking in his face. She didn't want him to see her crying.

"No problem. I love to have beautiful women bump into me." Still holding her arms, he leaned down, peered into her face. "You okay?"

"Sure," she managed to choke out.

"Now why don't I believe that?" He gave her arms a gentle squeeze. "What's wrong? Maybe I can help."

She lifted her gaze to look at Quade's handsome face. One look at his six-foot-three, two-hundred-pound-plus body, and a person thought linebacker. Buff and incredibly strong with long black hair, he had the appearance of a badass biker. Instead, he had the kindest, most gentle nature of any man she'd ever known.

Why can't I love you instead of Dylan?

More tears flooded her eyes as she gently touched his cheek. "You can't. But thank you for offering."

"Are you sure? I'm a great listener."

"I know you are. And you're a good friend."

He drew her into his arms for a comfort hug. Talia wrapped her arms around his waist, laid her cheek on his chest. Quade stood a foot taller than she, but she felt safe in his arms, not overpowered. It was like hugging a big teddy bear. Granted, a teddy bear with nice, solid muscles, but still a teddy bear.

"Am I interrupting something?" Dylan asked from behind Quade.

Talia gave Quade's waist one more squeeze before she stepped back and looked at Dylan. A scowl turned down his mouth, almost as if it angered him to see Quade holding her. "No. You aren't interrupting anything. Quade, thank you for your concern. I appreciate it."

"Anytime."

Talia walked past Dylan, but didn't make it more than two steps when he held her arm to stop her. "Why are you crying?"

She jerked her arm away from him. "None of your business."

Dylan turned his scowl toward Quade. "Did he hurt you?"

"Of course he didn't hurt me! How could you ask such a thing?"

Dylan's scowl faded, to be replaced by confusion. "Then why are you crying?"

Talia stopped herself before she stomped her foot in frustration. "It's *none of your business*. Just leave me alone." She spotted Paige coming toward her with the paper bag of vodka and another, smaller bag. *Perfect timing.* "Paige. I'm gonna get a blanket out of my car for us. I'll meet you by the river."

"Okay."

She left the garage without looking at either man again.

"What's wrong with her?" Dylan asked Quade.

"She wouldn't tell me."

"What makes you think something's wrong with Talia?" Paige asked.

"Because she was crying." Dylan pushed his hair back from his face. He hated knowing Talia hurt and he couldn't help her.

Paige touched his arm. "I'll take care of her, Dylan. I promise."

He glanced at the paper bag in Paige's hand that obviously held a bottle of liquor. "With whatever's in that sack?"

"Yep." She grinned. "We girls are going to par-tay." She waved at both of them. "See y'all later."

"I don't like this," Dylan muttered. "Talia shouldn't be drinking when she's upset."

"Maybe not, but she won't listen to anything either of us says."

"Do you have any idea what happened to make her cry?"

Quade shook his head. "She was crying when she came out of the kitchen."

"So someone in there must have upset her."

Fists clenched, Dylan stormed toward the door that led into the kitchen. Laughter greeted him when he stepped into the room. Someone laughed while Talia cried? *Oh, no. That's not the way it works.*

He stepped around the corner to see Maysen and Clay having a water fight. The faucet ran while each of them flicked drops on the other one. "Hey! What the hell are y'all doing?"

The laughter abruptly died. Clay hurriedly turned off the faucet, wiped drops from his face. "Just cooling off a little."

It had to have been Clay who upset Talia. He couldn't imagine Maysen ever saying anything to hurt anyone. He walked up to within inches of his chief. "What did you do to Talia?"

"What did I . . ." He blinked, as if trying to understand Dylan's question. "What?"

"She came out of the kitchen crying. What did you do to her?"

Maysen stepped next to Clay. "Dylan, we haven't even seen Talia lately. Clay did nothing to her." She motioned toward the tray of dirty dishes on the counter. "Someone brought in that tray, but we didn't see who. It might've been Talia."

"How could you *not* see who brought in a tray piled up with dirty dishes?"

"Someone must have brought it in while Clay and I were kissing a few minutes ago." A becoming blush spread over Maysen's cheeks. "We didn't see or hear anything then."

Clay slipped his arm around Maysen's waist. "I'm sorry if

Talia is upset, but it isn't because of us. So how about if you take a couple of steps back?"

Ashamed of accusing Clay of hurting Talia, Dylan did as asked and moved back. "Sorry, Chief."

"No problem."

The door opened behind him. Hoping it might be Talia, Dylan turned his head to see who entered. Disappointment flowed through him all the way to his toes when he saw Lucia and Keely.

Lucia set another tray of dirty dishes on the counter. "This is the last of it, Chief. Everything is cleaned up and put away. Wanna have a drink with the other gals, Maysen? Paige brought a bottle of sweet-tea vodka."

"Yeah, but only one," Keely said, rolling her eyes. "I can't believe she thought one bottle would be enough. I sent Nick to the liquor store for another one."

Maysen looked at Clay. "You can finish up in here, right?"

Clay chuckled. "Yeah. Go have fun with the gals."

Smiling broadly, she gave him a quick kiss. "See you later."

Once the women left, Clay turned to Dylan. "Wash or dry?"

Dylan blew out a heavy breath. "Dry."

The feminine chatter and laughter reached Dylan as soon as he stepped out of the kitchen and into the garage. The sun had set over two hours ago, meaning he couldn't see the women at the edge of the river. He didn't have to see them to know their exact location.

Only a few cars remained in the parking lot. Several of the male firefighters had already left, maybe to spend the rest of their Saturday night with their dates. Or perhaps they headed to Boot Scootin' to shoot pool, or O'Sullivan's for darts. Dylan could do the same. He knew he'd be welcome at either place.

Or he could wander across the street and check on the ladies.

Grabbing one of the last cans of Coke in the ice chest, he took several sips while strolling toward the river. The closer he got to the women, the more he recognized voices. He clearly heard conversation among Talia, Lucia, Paige, Maysen, Keely, Julia, and Rayna. But then he heard male voices. Apparently not all the firefighters had left.

Streetlights along the walking path by the river gave him enough illumination to make out everyone. Kirk and Kory Wilcox had managed to worm their way into the ladies' party. So had Royce Underwood and Judd Hamilton. Royce sat between Talia and Lucia. The youngest firefighter in the department at twenty-three, Royce joined the team a year ago and made it his mission to sleep with all three of the female firefighters. Paige and Lucia had given in—according to Royce—but he'd never mentioned being with Talia.

She had more intelligence than to submit to a guy who only wanted to carve notches in his bedpost. Or she normally had more intelligence. If she kept knocking back shots of vodka, she might be persuaded to do something she wouldn't normally do.

He made his way around the circle, saying hi to everyone who greeted him, to where Rayna sat and squatted beside her. He gestured to the can of Dr Pepper in her hand. "Guess you're off the hard stuff until the baby comes, huh?"

"Yes, but I don't mind." Even in the dim light, he could see her face light up as she placed one hand over her tummy. "This little one is worth it."

Dylan glanced at Talia to see her watching him as she downed another shot. "Any idea why Talia is drinking so much?" he asked softly.

Rayna's smile disappeared. "No, and I'm afraid she's going to pay big time in the morning. There's nothing wrong with having fun, but she seems to be punishing herself."

"She can't drive after drinking so much."

"She won't. Julia, Keely, and Maysen have a way home with

their fellows. Marcus and I will make sure the other gals get home safely."

"Good." Dylan felt better knowing Rayna would take care of everything. "Thanks, Rayna."

"Hey, Dylan," Judd called out, "wanna shot of this vodka? It's mighty fine."

"Thanks, but I'll pass." He lifted his half-full can of Coke. "I'm on the soft stuff now."

"Ooh, ooh, look!" Paige exclaimed. She pointed across the river. "The moon's coming up."

It had been full five days ago, but still made a magnificent sight as it rose over the water. Dylan's bedroom faced east, so he could lie in bed and watch the moon or sun rise.

It had been a long time since he'd shared that view with anyone.

Dylan turned back to the group to find Talia gone. Concern skittered down his spine. She didn't need to be alone after all she'd drunk. "Paige, where's Talia?"

Paige shrugged. "Don't know. She said she'd be right back."

"Probably had to potty," Lucia said with a giggle.

Dylan ignored that piece of too much information and stood, searching the area for her. He didn't see her anywhere. She wouldn't have had time to cross the street to the fire hall to use the ladies' room.

He did see Clay, Marcus, Nick, and Stephen making their way toward the group. They would probably collect their ladies and head for home.

Marcus walked behind Rayna, leaned over to give her a kiss. "You ready to go?"

"That depends on Paige and Lucia. I promised I'd get them home safely since they can't drive."

"I can drive," Lucia said before she hiccupped.

"Yeah, right." Clay reached out his hand to her. "It's almost midnight. Enough partying for the night. Maysen and I will drop you off on our way home."

"What about my car?"

"It'll be here tomorrow. You can pick it up after you get over your hangover." Clay looked at Dylan. "Quade is locking up the fire hall. Will you help him get the equipment back in the bays?"

"Sure thing, Chief."

One by one, everyone stood and strolled toward the parking lot. Or waddled, depending on how much they'd drunk. He hadn't seen Royce and Judd drink that much; they'd mostly flirted with the ladies. If Clay and Marcus hadn't insisted on taking Paige and Lucia home, Dylan would have. Even though they both lived only a few miles outside of town, he wouldn't let them drive after indulging.

Dylan scanned the area again, but still didn't see Talia. His concern began to morph into fear. Removing his cell phone from his belt, he keyed in Quade's number.

"Yo," Quade answered.

"Did you see Talia in there?"

"Nope, not recently."

"She said she'd be right back, but the group is breaking up and going home. I don't know where she is." He looked up at the sky as his fear grew. "I'm worried about her, Quade."

"I'll check around in here before I come over to help you move the equipment."

Desperate to find Talia, Dylan dialed her cell phone number. The call went directly to her voice mail.

"Damn it," he muttered. "Where the hell are you, Talia?"

Quade walked toward him. "Did you find her?" Dylan called out before Quade made it halfway across the street.

"No. I even went inside the ladies' room after I knocked. She wasn't there."

"She isn't answering her cell."

"She probably turned it off while she was serving and forgot to turn it back on."

"Yeah, maybe."

Quade laid a hand on Dylan's shoulder. "She probably caught up with Clay or Marcus and caught a ride home with one of them. Her car is still in the lot, so she didn't drive anywhere. That's a good thing, right?"

"Yeah. The way she was tossing back shots of vodka, she shouldn't be behind the wheel of a car."

"Let's move the equipment. That'll give Talia time to get home. Then you can call her there."

It sounded like a good plan to Dylan. "Okay. I'll start with the tanker."

"I'll take one of the brush trucks."

Dylan opened the door to the tanker and stood on the running board. His gaze swept the area one more time. No sign of Talia.

"Be on your way home," he whispered. "*Please* be on your way home."

4

The rumble beneath her ear woke Talia. She lifted her head from a hard surface and blinked her eyes into focus. She remembered downing a few shots of the sweet-tea vodka Paige had brought. After that, she began to get sleepy, which always happened when she consumed more than one drink. Deciding a walk would help her wake up, she'd wandered away from the group and . . .

She released a squeak of surprise when the hard surface beneath her moved. Having no idea what would happen next, she threw her arms straight out to give her more balance. Only after she'd blinked a few more times to stop her head from spinning did she realize she lay on top of the ladder truck.

She remembered now what she'd done. She'd become sleepy, but she'd also wanted to get away from Royce's wandering hands. The man didn't understand the word *no*. She had no desire to go out with him, much less sleep with him, yet he couldn't seem to get that through his thick, conceited brain. She'd decided hiding would be the best thing to do. And what better place to hide than on top of the ladder truck?

The truck stopped, then that annoying *beep-beep-beep* sound flowed to her ears, a signal that whoever drove decided to put the truck in reverse. Talia flipped to her back and watched the sky disappear as the driver backed the truck into the garage bay.

Home again, home again, jiggety-jog.

She giggled. What a silly time to think of a nursery rhyme. She must be more tipsy than she'd thought.

The big garage door clanged shut. "I'll walk out with you," she heard Quade say.

"I gotta grab my leftovers from the fridge," Dylan said. "Go ahead. I'll finish locking up."

"Okay. See you later."

Silence, then she heard a door open and close. After that, lights began to go out over her head. She'd be completely in the dark soon if she didn't let Dylan know she was here.

She scooted to the side of the truck and looked down. Dylan stood next to the set of light switches by the entrance to the kitchen. The remaining light shone on his head, highlighting his dark hair.

Damn, you are one fine-looking man. "Pssst."

He froze, looked around him. "Is someone here?"

"Pssst!" She waved one hand to draw his attention. "Up here."

His gaze swung her way. "Talia? What the hell are you doing up there?"

"I was sleeping until you moved the truck."

"You were *sleeping?*"

"Yeah. And hiding from Royce. I think that guy is part octo . . . octo . . . that sea thing with all the arms."

"Octopus."

"Yeah, that's it."

She could see Dylan's lips twitching. Shaking his head, he walked over to the ladder truck. "I think you'd better come down and let me take you home."

"Nope. I like it up here."

"Talia, you can't stay up there all night."

"Sure I can. Toss me a pillow and blankey and I'll be all co-cozy." She leaned a bit farther over the edge. The liquor she'd consumed gave her the courage to say exactly what she wanted to say. "I'd be even cozier with you up here with me under that blankey."

"Not gonna happen." He gave her a come-here motion with his fingers. "Time to go home."

"Nope." She flopped to her back, curved her arms beneath her head. "I'm staying here."

"Talia. Don't make me come up there."

She grinned. As if his stern tone could scare her.

"*Talia.*"

"You want me down, you have to come get me."

"Shit," he muttered.

Talia's grin widened when she heard his footsteps cross the floor. The stepladder on the side of the truck made a squeaking sound as he lowered it. His boots clomped on the ladder, then across the top of the truck until he leaned over her, a cross be-tween a scowl and laughter on his face.

"You're drunk."

"I am not. I'm just tipsy."

He held out one hand to her. "C'mon. I'll take you home."

"I told you, I'm not moving."

Dylan blew out a breath. "Talia, I'm willing to carry you over my shoulder, but I don't think your stomach or head would like that."

He had a point. Her stomach gave a lurch at the thought of her hanging upside down in a fireman's hold. "Not a good idea."

"That's what I thought, too." He tugged her hands from be-neath her head. "Let's go."

234 / *Lynn LaFleur*

Instead of allowing him to pull her up, Talia gave a hard yank on his hands. He fell on top of her with a loud *oomph*.

"See?" She wrapped her arms around his neck. "Isn't this better than getting down?"

He rose to his hands and knees, but she tightened her arms around his neck so he couldn't go any farther. "Talia, it's time to go."

"Nope. I like it here." She tugged on his neck, trying to bring his mouth closer to hers. "Kiss me, Dylan."

"Talia, you're drunk. You don't know what you're doing."

"I told you I'm not drunk. I know exactly what I'm doing." All traces of humor disappeared from her voice. "I've wanted you from the first time I met you, Dylan. Please don't turn me away again."

"Talia, we—"

Her mouth cut off whatever he'd started to say. Finally, *finally*, she had her first taste of Dylan. A hint of spice mixed with a bit of wintergreen, as if he'd recently eaten a breath mint.

Delicious.

He grabbed her wrists, yanked them away from him, and held them tightly. "Stop it."

His reluctance made her angry. She'd swallowed her last bit of pride and thrown herself at him, and he'd rejected her. Again. "Why? Why should I stop? Why don't you want me?"

"I never said I don't want you."

"Then what is your problem?"

He hung his head, sighed heavily, then looked into her eyes again. "Talia, I can't get involved with you. I can't get involved with *anyone*."

"Why not?" A sudden thought occurred to her, something she'd never considered. Perhaps he'd been injured and couldn't get an erection. "Can't you get hard?"

He barked out a laugh. "No, getting hard isn't a problem.

There are other, more complicated reasons why I can't get involved with anyone."

His hold had loosened on her wrists while they talked. She slipped them from his grip, ran her fingers into his hair. "There's no involvement here, Dylan. There's just you and me. I want you." She tugged his head closer. "Don't you want me?"

She covered his lips with hers in another kiss. She felt him tighten, as if he meant to pull away from her again. Then, suddenly, a low moan came from deep in his throat and he kissed her back.

Heaven.

Dylan lifted his head. He caressed her cheek with one thumb. "Yes, I want you," he whispered. "But you aren't acting like the Talia I know. I think the liquor is talking for you, and I don't want you to regret anything tomorrow."

His obvious concern made her fall even more in love with him. "I promise you, Dylan, I won't regret *anything* tomorrow."

His gaze slowly swept over her face as he continued that hypnotic glide on her cheek with his thumb. When it passed over her mouth, she parted her lips and touched it with the tip of her tongue.

"God, you're beautiful," he said in a husky voice.

This time, *he* kissed *her*. Talia's head spun, but not from the alcohol. She'd waited two years to experience Dylan's kiss. He caressed her lips softly at first, but his kiss soon turned deeper, more passionate. He slipped one arm beneath her, one leg between hers. She could feel the firm bulge of his cock against her hip.

He definitely had no problem getting hard.

The ten-inch difference in their heights didn't matter when he held her so close to him. Their bodies fit together like two pieces of a puzzle, just as Talia knew they would.

She suspected they would fit even better together when they removed their clothes.

Dylan abruptly ended the kiss, pulled away from her, and sat up with his back to her. "Shit," he mumbled as he drove both hands into his hair. "We can't do this, Talia. *I* can't do this."

No way was he going to kindle a spark and douse the flame instead of fanning it to life. "Yes, you can." Grabbing the back of his T-shirt, she jerked him down to the truck on his back. She would've smirked over the surprised look on his face if she hadn't been so hungry for his taste. Before he had the chance to respond, she climbed on top of him and kissed him again.

It pleased her to hear him groan. It pleased her even more to feel his arms wrap tightly around her. She didn't waste time with soft kisses, but dove right into ravishment. She moved her mouth one way, then the other, taking everything she could from Dylan's mouth.

Kissing him had to be one of the sweetest things on Earth and she hated to stop, but they wore way too many clothes. After giving him one more drugging kiss, she sat up, straddled his hips. His hard shaft pressed against her pussy. Staring into his eyes, she began to unbutton her blouse.

His gaze dropped to follow the movement of her fingers. When she freed the last button, she unfastened the tie at her waist, let the blouse slip off her shoulders. Dylan laid his hands on top of her thighs and squeezed.

Talia had a weakness for pretty lingerie. Her bra and panties set today consisted of mostly sage-green lace with just enough satin to hold the lace in place. She knew Dylan could easily see her nipples through her bra, even in the dim lighting.

She unhooked the front fastening of her bra, tossed it to land on her blouse. Dylan drew in a sharp breath through his nose. "Damn."

Talia had always wished for bigger breasts, but Dylan didn't seem to mind their small size. He cradled them in his palms, scraped his thumbs across the nipples. "Perfect," he whispered.

His compliment made her feel perfect. Needing some of his clothes off now, she pushed up his T-shirt to under his arms. Dylan lifted his torso a few inches off the truck, enough to let her pull the shirt over his head. It landed somewhere in the vicinity of her clothes.

She'd seen Dylan without a shirt many times at the fire hall. She'd never seen him this close, or had the chance to touch his bare skin. She did so now, running her fingers across his collarbone, his pecs, down the center of his stomach, to his navel. The light dusting of dark brown hair tickled her fingertips.

"I can't believe I'm finally touching you."

Dylan couldn't believe it either. He should stop this before it went any further. Talia's bravery had to come from the vodka. He couldn't equate the sweet, easygoing woman he knew with the temptress who dragged her fingernails down the center of his torso. He hissed at the slight bite of pain.

Her lips curved up in a siren's smile. "I like scratching."

"Good to know," he managed to rasp. He had a difficult time concentrating with her hands on him, much less saying no to something so pleasurable. The warmth of her pussy covering his cock felt wondrous because he wanted her so much, and also torturous because he knew he shouldn't have her.

It would be easier if he could think of Talia as just a lay. Not happening. He cared deeply about her and would never intentionally do anything to hurt her. The bliss they'd achieve having sex wouldn't accomplish anything other than making their hormones do a happy dance.

His hormones *really* wanted to do that happy dance.

She scooted back on his thighs, unfastened his belt buckle, and released the button at the waistband of his jeans. The rasp of the zipper sounded loud in the quiet garage. Dylan hissed when her soft hand slipped inside his briefs. His eyes drifted closed at the intense pleasure.

He'd hungered for her touch for two long years. He didn't want to deny himself—or Talia—any longer.

"You're so hard," she whispered.

"Yeah." His voice sounded like a frog croaking. He couldn't be expected to speak correctly when Talia had her hand wrapped around his dick.

She scooted back a few more inches, taking his jeans and briefs with her until his bare cock lay on his stomach. She ran her hands all the way up to his shoulders, then down to caress his thighs. Dylan had almost reached the point of begging her to touch his cock again, when she did exactly that. Wrapping one hand around it, she pulled it straight up. Happy to let her do whatever she wanted, he folded his arms beneath his head and watched her.

"Do you like me touching you?"

"Yeah. Very much."

"What about if I . . ." She swiped her tongue across the head. "Lick you?"

"Sweetheart, there isn't a man alive who doesn't love to have his cock licked."

She grinned at his comment before she dragged her tongue down the entire length, from the crown to the base. She repeated her action from base to crown, then took the head in her mouth.

"Sweet Jesus," he muttered. Talia's mouth felt like a wet furnace. Heat and moisture engulfed his flesh. He arched his hips off the truck, trying to capture even more of the delicious sensation.

"I guess you do like this." Her tongue swirled around the crown, the same way she would lick an ice cream cone. "I like it, too."

This time when she dragged her tongue down his length, she swept it across his balls before she nuzzled them with her nose.

"I love the way you smell."

The combination of abstinence and her expert mouth drove up his desire the highest he thought it had ever been. He had to have more of her. Now.

Dylan rose enough to grab her upper arms and pull her on top of him. Holding the back of her head, he urged her closer for a long, deep kiss.

Still holding her, still kissing her, he rolled them over so she lay on her back. The feel of the zigzag pattern in the truck's surface had him reaching for their shirts to place under her to protect her skin.

Having his jeans and briefs halfway down his thighs made moving difficult. Dylan quickly removed them, along with his socks and shoes, and helped Talia slip the clothing under her butt and legs. Once satisfied she wouldn't be poked by the design, he moved over the top of her again.

Her lips parted beneath his, her tongue dueled with his. Dylan filled his hands with her breasts while he made love to her mouth. Somehow during their shifting of positions, she'd lost her sandals. Her bare heels pressed into his ass as she hunched her pussy against his cock over and over.

A few more moments of her movements and Dylan would lose it long before he wanted to. He kissed her once, twice, then rose to his knees between her legs. The elastic waistband in her capris made it easy for him to tug them off, and her panties. He touched the mound of her bare cunt with his fingertips.

"So pretty." One finger slid between the feminine lips to find them slick with her cream. "Now it's my turn to lick."

5

Talia let her eyes drift closed, lost in the pleasure of Dylan's touch. Only one finger caressed her, but that one finger did more to her than other men had done with a whole hand. *Two* hands. And a mouth. And a penis.

Being in love made all the sensations brighter, more intense.

Her eyes popped open when she felt his warm breath on her pussy. He continued the caressing with his finger while he blew on her clit. Talia spread her legs wider apart, wanting more of the delicious foreplay.

He kissed the inside of each thigh. "I love the way you smell, too."

An orgasm loomed, ready to rush through her body with the slightest graze to her clit. Instead of the direct stroke she needed, Dylan continued to rub her juices all over her labia. She opened her mouth, ready to give him detailed instructions of what she wanted, when he plunged two fingers into her channel.

The climax shot out from her core to her limbs and back again before she could even draw a breath. Stars flashed behind her eyelids. Completely taken by surprise, she couldn't speak or think clearly. She'd never come so quickly in her life.

Leaving his fingers inside her, Dylan leaned over and braced himself on his elbow. "Your pussy walls are milking my fingers."

"No shit."

He burst out laughing. Talia would've laughed with him, but she didn't have the strength.

He leaned closer, until their lips almost touched. "I like that you come so quickly."

"I don't usually do that."

"Yeah?" A smug grin spread across his lips.

"Don't get cocky."

"Sorry."

His grin faded, but she could still see the twinkle of humor in his eyes.

His fingers began to slowly move in and out of her again. "How do you feel about multiple orgasms?"

"I think they're lovely, but I rarely have them."

"Then I guess I'll have to work a little harder, huh?"

Before she could respond, he kissed her. She'd already felt as if her bones had melted with her orgasm. Adding his kiss to the mix made her even weaker. But not so weak that she couldn't respond to the delightful thing his long fingers did inside her. He pumped them in and out, then curled them and rubbed her G-spot. Talia began to move her hips in the same rhythm as his caresses—sometimes side to side, sometimes up and down, depending on what he did with his fingers.

He kissed his way to her breasts as his thumb joined in the play. It flicked her clit while his tongue flashed over her nipples. Talia could hear the wet, sucking sounds his fingers made as they moved in and out of her channel.

"Mmm, love how wet you are. I think I need a taste."

He pulled his fingers from her, lifted them to his mouth. Staring into her eyes, he thoroughly licked every bit of her juices from the two digits.

That had to be one of the sexiest things she'd ever seen.

"Just as delicious as I suspected you'd be."

He rubbed her pussy again, raised his fingers to his mouth for a second taste. The third time he gathered her juices, he held his fingers in front of her lips.

"Taste yourself for me."

Holding his hand, she stared into his eyes as she ran her tongue over his fingers. Heat blazed in his blue irises, his nostrils flared. He leaned over and gave her the most passionate kiss she'd received from him. His lips coaxed, his tongue stroked. He pulled her lower lip between his teeth before he covered her mouth with his again.

Talia tunneled her hands into his hair, kissed him harder. She wrapped her legs around his waist and pumped her mound against his cock. Two seconds from reaching between them and guiding his cock inside her, Dylan ended their kiss.

"No fucking yet," he said as though he'd read her mind. He nipped the side of her neck, the point of her chin. "I'm not through tasting you."

He settled on his stomach between her legs and began to lick her . . . slow, gentle strokes of his tongue that caressed her clit and feminine folds. She propped herself on her elbows so she could watch him. With his hands beneath her ass, tilting up her pelvis, she could see his tongue moving over her flesh. He stared into her eyes as he made love to her with his mouth.

It looked incredibly sexy. It felt even better.

She couldn't believe how quickly desire climbed once more. Talia hadn't had a vast number of lovers, but enough to know her body and how it reacted during sex. No man had stirred her, satisfied her, the way Dylan did.

Another orgasm exploded when Dylan suckled her clit. Her

elbows lost their strength and she lay back on the truck. Warmth spread to her toes, her fingers, the top of her head. No stars behind her eyelids this time, but that didn't make the sensation any less powerful.

A gentle swipe of Dylan's tongue across her tender clit made Talia moan. "No more. I can't."

"Oh, I think you can." Another lick, another pass over her clit. "I think you can come again and again and again."

"Not without you." She slipped one hand beneath his chin. "Fuck me, Dylan."

"You don't want to come again on my tongue?"

"Not now. Inside me. Please."

After one more long lick of her labia, he tugged his jeans from underneath her enough to withdraw his wallet from a back pocket. A tear of plastic and he sheathed his cock with a condom. Stretching out on top of her, he palmed her ass, lifted her hips, and drove inside.

Talia moaned at the same time that Dylan did. At last, at last, she had the man she loved stretching her, filling her. He buried his face against her neck and withdrew almost all the way before plunging back into her sheath.

"God, Talia, you feel so good."

She couldn't think of a strong enough word to describe how incredible it felt to have Dylan on top of her, inside her. She let her hands sweep up and down his spine as his thrusts picked up speed. He hooked one of her legs over his arm, drove even deeper. Every surge of his cock brushed her clit.

Needing a bit more stimulation, she dug her fingernails into his ass to guide him. Dylan picked up on her silent command and shifted his hips into a different rhythm . . . a rhythm that soon had Talia reaching for that height of sensation once more.

She came mere seconds before Dylan's body tightened and he released a long groan.

Sweat dotted his skin, and hers. The garage hadn't had the

chance to cool off from the heat of the day, and it had to be at least ninety degrees in the enclosed space right next to the ceiling. With any other man, Talia would get away from his sticky skin as quickly as possible. With Dylan, she tightened her arms and legs around him, determined to hold him close as long as possible, despite the heat.

Soft, warm kisses fell on her cheek, her neck, her shoulder. "Wow," he whispered.

She smiled at the sound of wonder in his voice. "I second that."

"We're stuck together."

"I don't care."

He lifted his head, looked into her eyes. He didn't say anything else for several moments. "Talia, I . . ." He stopped.

She waited for him to finish his statement. When he didn't, she gently prodded, "You what?"

"I still want you."

A flex of his hips showed her his cock remained hard. A surprised look passed over her face, quickly followed by a pleased one. His temptress still wanted him, too. That realization sent more blood into his dick, making him even harder than before he'd come. He didn't think that could be possible.

He kissed her sweet lips, the curve of her cheek, the sensitive place beneath her ear. He moved slowly down her body, not wanting to move too quickly and pull her skin where they stuck together. He licked down the center of her throat, across her collarbone. Each nipple received a thorough lap of his tongue and tug with his teeth. He kissed his way down the center of her stomach, circled her navel, continued to her mound. The musky scent of her pussy enticed him to linger between her thighs.

First, there were other parts of her body he planned to explore.

Dylan helped her turn over onto her stomach. She folded her arms beneath her cheek, released a long breath as if settling in to accept whatever he did.

After removing his condom and setting it aside to dispose of later, he pushed her long hair away from her neck. Dylan lay on top of Talia, propping himself up with one arm so as not to squeeze the air from her lungs. That special area where neck met shoulder deserved his attention. He gently nibbled on it while he settled his cock in the cleft of her ass. The perspiration on her skin made it easy to slide his firm flesh over her butt while he dropped kisses across her upper back.

Talia arched her pelvis, as if trying to get closer to his shaft. "You like my cock against your ass?"

"Yes."

"So do I."

He bit her nape, and smiled to himself when she moaned. He'd suspected Talia would be an amazing lover, but her reaction to him far surpassed anything he'd anticipated.

Although only about five-three, Talia had a long torso and beautiful back. She had the type of creamy complexion that tanned easily. The golden glow of her skin proved she'd taken advantage of the sun's rays over the summer. He slid his hand down the center of her back, admiring the color and softness. He continued his exploration over the firm globes of her ass, coasting his palms over both several times.

Very nice, but more would be better.

Dylan rose to his knees between her thighs. Using both hands, he kneaded her buttocks, pulled them apart to see her anus. He'd been with women who liked anal play, and some who hated it. He hoped Talia fell into the first category.

Grabbing her hips, he pulled her to her knees. He used his thumbs to spread her cheeks apart and gave her anus a slow lick.

"Oh, God!"

Dylan took her exclamation to mean she liked what he'd done. He licked her anus again, darted his tongue past the rosette. Talia buried her face in her arms, arched her back. Pleased at her reaction, Dylan began fucking her ass with his tongue while he fingered her clit. He'd stop all movements, then lave the sensitive area and dart his tongue inside her again. He would love to fuck her with his cock instead of his tongue, but he didn't have any lube and he wouldn't take the chance of hurting her.

Instead, he donned the last condom he had in his wallet and rammed his dick into her wet pussy from behind. Talia threw back her head and cried out. Afraid he'd been too rough, he didn't move while he caressed her back.

"Talia, you okay? Did I hurt you?"

"No. No, you didn't hurt me. It just . . . *God*, it feels so good to have you inside me!"

Her confession raised his desire a few more degrees. He gripped her hips tighter and remained still for several moments, simply absorbing the pleasure of her tight channel surrounding his hard flesh. When she started rocking back on her knees to meet his thrusts, he started pumping again. Soon he pounded into her as fast as he could. She took every hard ram into her cunt and pushed back at him for more.

"Ohgodohgodohgod. Don't stop, Dylan!" She reached back and dug her fingernails into one of his thighs. "Right there. Move a little . . . Oh, yes. *Yes!*"

Her pussy walls milking his cock brought on his second orgasm. It shimmied down his back, through his balls, and out the head of his dick. Dylan leaned over Talia's back, cradled her breasts, while the pleasure went on and on.

Talia wilted to the truck. Dylan followed, stretching out on his side next to her. Sweat poured off him. He desperately needed something to drink, but no way could he move to take care of that.

After a couple of attempts, he managed to roll to his back and remove the condom. Talia scooted over to him, draped one arm over his waist, and rested her head on his shoulder. "That was amazing."

Sweat covered her skin as heavily as it covered his. She had to be as hot and thirsty as he. A gentleman would offer to get off the truck and find them cold drinks. "Yeah."

"I'm thirsty," she muttered.

"Me, too." He could barely get the words out with his thickened tongue. "I'll get us something in a minute."

He wrapped his arm around her shoulders, laid his hand over her arm at his waist, and closed his eyes.

6

Talia frowned as she moved her tongue inside her dry mouth. A herd of some kind of critter must have marched through there last night and left piles of really nasty stuff. She didn't think her mouth had ever tasted so bad, and she'd had many occasions of super-duper morning breath.

Consciousness slowly seeped into her brain. She lay on something a lot harder than her comfortable mattress. Her back, butt, and thighs seemed to be stuck to something sweaty. And warm. A piece of cloth covered her torso, but her legs remained bare.

It took three tries to pry her eyes open. Talia looked out over what appeared to be the fire hall garage. The dim lighting must mean the sun had barely risen. She could see the tanker, brush trucks, ambulances. It shouldn't be possible for her to see anything clearly with her nearsightedness, unless she'd slept in her contacts. Which, apparently, she had, since her eyes felt as dry as dust.

Moving her head a bit to the right, she saw the huge ladder above her from the ladder truck.

What the hell . . .

She started to sit up, but quickly stopped when the band belted out in her head, complete with big bass drum. With a groan, she laid her hand on top of her head, hoping to keep her brain inside her skull where it belonged.

"You okay?" a raspy voice asked from behind her.

The sweaty, warm thing behind her was a man. She lay on top of the ladder truck in the fire hall's garage with a man. And if the feel of skin against her indicated anything, neither of them wore a stitch of clothing.

The warm skin separated from her as he moved. "Talia? You okay?"

Dylan lay with her on the truck? How . . .

The previous evening came rushing back to her—Paige bringing a bottle of sweet-tea vodka, drinking with the other gals and some of the guys by the river, climbing up on the ladder truck to get away from Royce's wandering hands. Then riding the truck into the garage while Dylan drove it. Him trying to coax her off it and her refusing. Her initiating their first kiss, which led to many kisses, then a lot more than kisses.

He slipped his arm around her waist and leaned over her. "You gonna be sick?"

Her skin must be pale for him to ask that. Truthfully, she didn't know. "I . . . don't think so. Not unless I move too fast."

He chuckled. "A little hungover?"

"Yeah." She closed her eyes, but quickly opened them again when the room spun. "I'm going to kill Paige for bringing that vodka."

"You can't blame Paige. She didn't pour it down your throat."

Talia glared at him over her shoulder. "Do *not* side with her if you want to live."

"Sorry."

His grin proved he wasn't the least bit sorry. She started to snap again, but a good look at him froze her words. His hair appeared sexily tousled, not stuck out in all angles the way it should look upon awakening. Dark stubble dotted his cheeks and the area around his luscious mouth. He had full, well-shaped lips in the barest shade of rose. His eyes reminded her of the color of a lake under a blue sky.

His grin abruptly faded. His gaze dropped to her lips and lingered, his hand spread wide over her stomach. She felt the stirring of his cock against her ass.

Instead of acting upon the obvious condition of his body, he pulled away from her and sat up. "I doubt if anyone will come in here on a Sunday unless there's a fire, but we should go."

Talia knew he was right, that they didn't need to stay here any longer. Yet it hurt how quickly he'd pulled away from her after what they'd shared last night.

"What time is it?"

Dylan pressed a button on his cell phone. "Almost seven-thirty."

"When did we . . . go to sleep?"

He shrugged. "I'm not sure. Probably around three."

Four hours of sleep on top of several shots of sweet-tea vodka. No wonder she felt like hell.

Talia sat up, and immediately grabbed her head as she sucked in a sharp breath. The bass drum player added a kettle-drum and tom-tom while dancing around in her brain.

Dylan dropped his T-shirt before he donned it, rose to his knees, and grabbed her shoulders. "What's wrong?"

"Tell the drummers to stop playing in my head."

He had the nerve to chuckle again. The bum.

"You'll feel better after some breakfast."

The thought of food made her stomach lurch. "Uh, no, I don't think that will help."

She lowered her hands, which gave her a perfect view of

Dylan's body kneeling before her. The impressive erection made her swallow.

He gave her shoulders a gentle squeeze before he released her. "Get dressed and I'll take you home."

She'd thrown herself at him last night, he'd accepted—twice—and now he planned to simply drop her off at her house. So much for a morning after cuddle. "I have my car."

He slipped his T-shirt over his head. "You shouldn't drive if you don't feel well."

"I'm fine."

Talia struggled into her bra, then searched for her panties. She found them beneath her butt. Getting them on wouldn't be easy when every movement made the band play louder and her stomach churn. She slipped the lingerie over her feet and up her legs as far as she could. Raising one cheek and then the other, she managed to get her panties situated where they should be.

The blouse slipped on easily, although it took her three times as long as usual to close the buttons since her fingers refused to cooperate. Leaving the tie dangling, she tugged her capris from beneath her. She stared at them and sighed.

"Here, let me help you."

A fully dressed Dylan knelt before her again. He took the capris from her and slid them up her legs to her thighs. "Lift."

She did as he said, resting on her hands so she could raise her butt. He settled the pants at her waist and reached for her sandals. She watched his long-fingered hands as he glided the shoes onto her feet. Memories of how he'd touched her with those fingers last night filled her mind, made her yearn to feel his caresses again.

"Ready to go?" he asked.

She thought she saw desire in his eyes, but she must be mistaken. He couldn't wait to be away from her. "Sure."

He went down the ladder first, then placed his hands on her

waist to help her. Talia appreciated the help since her legs still wobbled. "I don't know why I feel so bad when I was only tipsy."

"You aren't used to drinking."

"That's for sure. Other than a sip of champagne at my wedding, I'm never drinking alcohol again."

His eyebrows shot up to disappear beneath his tousled hair. "You planning on a wedding soon?"

"No, just making a statement. God, even my fingernails hurt."

He slipped his hand beneath her hair, squeezed her nape. "Let me take you home. I'll get your car to you later."

Being with him any longer would only make her want even more time with him. "I'm okay, Dylan. I can drive myself."

He didn't look convinced, but Talia wouldn't budge. His concern touched her, yet she knew he cared about her as a friend, not a loved one. She'd go home, shower, and work on the new curtains for her bedroom.

Or maybe not that last part. Running a sewing machine probably wouldn't be a good idea until the band decided to finish the concert in her head.

Talia headed for the exit with Dylan right behind her. She waited by the door while he locked it. With one hand on her lower back, he guided her toward her car. She didn't see his pickup anywhere. "How did you get here?"

"My truck's in the Methodist Church's parking lot."

It was only two blocks away, but she saw no reason for him to walk when she could drive him there. She fished her car key from her pocket, pressed the button on the fob to unlock the doors. "Get it. I'll drop you by your truck."

She slid behind the wheel and he rounded the car to the passenger side. While he fastened his seat belt, she pulled her cell phone from its compartment and checked for messages. One from her mother, one from her sister, Carolyn, and two from girlfriends. Nothing she couldn't handle later, after her head cleared.

Talia glanced at Dylan as she started the car. He sat with his hands hooked at his waist, staring out his window. She'd give up a week's commission at Janelle's to know his thoughts.

The short ride to the church took only moments. Talia pulled into the space next to Dylan's pickup and left the motor running.

"Thanks for the lift," he said, finally looking at her.

"You're welcome."

Not one word about what happened between them last night. Dylan obviously thought it had been a mistake for them to make love. Talia didn't. She'd treasure the memory of being in his arms for the rest of her life.

Dylan rubbed the spot above his lips. She waited—prayed—for him to say something else, something that would give her hope that he felt the same way as she. Instead, he unbuckled his belt and opened the door. "See ya, Talia."

A huge lump formed in her throat as she watched him climb into his pickup and drive away. "Yeah," she whispered. "See ya."

Dylan got tired of pacing in his living room, so he moved to the kitchen to pace in there. He couldn't believe how stupid he'd been this morning. He hadn't told Talia how much their lovemaking had meant to him. Oh, no. Mr. Smooth said "see ya" and walked away from her without talking about what they'd shared last night.

He'd showered, put on clean clothes, and scrambled a couple of eggs. The eggs had filled the empty spot in his stomach, even though he hadn't felt like eating. Then he'd puttered in his garage with his fishing gear to kill some time and take his mind off Talia.

The puttering hadn't worked. He thought about Talia constantly and worried about her . . . if she'd made it home, if she'd gotten sick, if she'd eaten anything. Her complexion had looked more green than ivory when he'd gotten out of her car. He'd had a few hangovers in his lifetime and knew how miserable they could make a person feel.

Opening the refrigerator, Dylan stared at the meager contents. He wanted something, but didn't know what. Maybe a beer would taste good. He reached for a bottle, then changed his mind and selected a Coke instead. He glanced at the clock on the stove as he downed half the can. The Cowboys played at three-thirty today, so he still had almost two hours to kill before the football game.

Dylan crushed the empty can, tossed it in the recycle container. He didn't want to be here, alone in his house. He wanted to be with Talia. She hadn't looked well when he left her. He should drive over to see her and make sure she'd made it home safely.

The decision made, Dylan grabbed his cell phone and keys and headed for his pickup.

Talia lived three blocks from the downtown courthouse, in a small, two-bedroom house that she rented from Janelle Hunt, her boss. Dylan made it there in under ten minutes. He pulled into her driveway, parked in front of the closed garage door. He noticed the drawn living room curtains. Perhaps Talia had gone somewhere else instead of coming home.

No, as badly as she felt, he had no doubt she'd come home and probably gone right to bed. Dylan didn't want to bother her if she slept, but he had to know she was okay. He turned off the ignition, got out of his truck, and walked to her front door.

He smiled at the sound of Westminster Chimes when he pressed the doorbell. She'd had the new doorbell installed shortly after she rented the house. Talia had said several times she wanted to visit England.

When the door didn't open in a minute, Dylan pressed the

doorbell again. Another minute passed with no Talia. Deciding she must still be asleep, he turned to walk back to his pickup.

He'd taken no more than three steps when he heard the front door open behind him. Turning toward it, he saw Talia leaning against the doorframe. She didn't look quite as green as she had a few hours ago, but still didn't have the appearance of the friendly, perky woman he usually saw. "Hey."

"Hey. Sorry I took so long to answer. I was in bed."

Just as he'd suspected. "I'm sorry I bothered you. Go back to bed."

"No, it's okay. Actually, I was awake, but too lazy to get up. Come in."

Dylan stepped over the threshold into Talia's neat living room. He'd often teased her about being such a neat freak and needing to have everything in its place. She'd told him she kept what people saw in order, but he could never look in her closets or cabinets. She didn't know what might be growing in them.

"I made fresh tea after my shower. Do you want a glass?"

"Yeah, that sounds great."

Dylan admired the way her ass looked in her denim cut-offs as he followed her to the kitchen. She had her hair pulled up in a ponytail on top of her head. The end swept across her upper back as she walked, drawing his attention to the scooped-neck purple tank she wore. No shoes, no jewelry, no makeup.

She didn't need makeup to be gorgeous and sexy.

"Do you want to sit in here or in the living room?" she asked, taking two glasses from the cabinet.

"Wherever you want to sit is okay with me."

She took ice trays from the freezer, filled each glass, then added tea. "The couch will be more comfortable."

And give him the chance to sit closer to her. "Works for me."

Dylan accepted the glass from Talia, then followed her back to the living room. He waited until she sat in one corner of the couch before he took the other. He sipped his tea, admiring the slight taste of lemon in the sweet beverage. "Good."

"Thanks. Although I doubt if you came over to compliment my tea." Talia drew her knees up on the couch. "Why did you come over?"

"To check on you. You look so much better now than when I left you this morning."

Her lips twisted to the side. "Thanks a lot."

Realizing he'd insulted her without meaning to, Dylan quickly backtracked. "I mean, you weren't feeling well this morning, so your complexion was a little green. You aren't green anymore."

She smiled. "I knew what you meant and you're right. I was a mess this morning. It's amazing how much good a person can get from a shower and a nap." She placed one hand on her stomach. "I'm even starting to think about food."

"You haven't eaten anything yet?"

Talia shook her head. "Food didn't appeal to me at all when I got home. The only thing I wanted was to shower and sleep. Now I think I'm ready." She swirled the ice cubes in her glass. "Have you had lunch?"

"No."

"I forgot to bring my barbecue leftovers home. I usually shop on Monday, so I don't have a lot of food in the house. I can order a pizza."

"Do you think your stomach is ready for something spicy?"

"Yeah. Pizza sounds really good. Does that work for you?"

"I can always eat pizza, but don't feel like you have to feed me."

"I'm not. I'm having it delivered." She grinned. "I like sausage and onion and green pepper. Will that work for you?"

"Add some mushrooms and extra cheese and it'll be perfect."

Her grin widened. "You have a deal."

7

Dylan had many traits that Talia appreciated, including his ability to keep a conversation lively and entertaining. They'd spent time with friends, laughing and talking, so she'd already learned a lot about him in the last two years. But only about his adult life. She knew little about his childhood since he never talked about it. She knew he had no siblings, and his mother died during his early teens, but that's all she knew. Whenever she would steer the conversation toward his growing up years, he would promptly guide it back to her or to something that concerned one of their friends.

Obviously, something happened during his childhood that had hurt him and he didn't want to talk about it.

Talia understood that. She never talked about losing her father, or about how her mother married and divorced two awful men before she realized she could live better without a man in her life than with the wrong one. Once she realized that, she met her Prince Charming. Talia adored her stepfather, yet sometimes she still yearned for one of her daddy's hugs.

Even with the ease of conversation while they devoured

most of the large pizza and several bread sticks, Talia felt a weight on her chest from what they *didn't* talk about—their lovemaking last night. She'd caught Dylan deep in thought several times and assumed he would bring up the subject. He never did.

So she had to do it.

Talia tossed her piece of crust into the pizza box and wiped her hands on her napkin. "Are we going to talk about the elephant in the room?"

Dylan froze with a new piece of pizza raised halfway to his mouth. His eyes widened when he looked at her. Then, slowly, he lowered the piece back to the box. "I, uh, didn't notice any elephant. It must be hiding in the closet."

His attempt at a joke fell flat. "Don't play dumb with me, Dylan. You're far from dumb and so am I." She lifted her feet to the couch, wrapped her arms around her raised knees. "We made love last night. Don't you think we should talk about it?"

He wiped his hands on his napkin, laid it next to the pizza box on the coffee table. Turning toward her, he stretched his arm along the back of the couch. "It was incredible," he said, his voice soft and low.

"Yes, it was. So why last night? We've spent time together. I've asked you out, but you always said no." Now that she'd started this conversation, Talia decided to be completely honest. "I fell for you the first time I met you, Dylan. That's the reason I joined the fire department. Yes, I wanted to help people, but more than that I wanted any opportunity I could get to be close to you."

He remained silent for several seconds. "Talia, I . . ." He stopped.

"You what? *What?*" she said again, more forcefully, when he didn't respond to her question. "Tell me what you're thinking, what you're feeling. Be honest with me."

A look of anguish crossed his face. "I can't."

"Why not? Why can't you talk to me?"

"I just . . . can't."

Every time Dylan had turned her down, a little piece of her heart broke off. That heartbreak couldn't begin to compare to the pain now. It engulfed her entire body, until she wondered how she could breathe with the crushing weight on her chest.

She swallowed twice, pushing aside the lump of tears in her throat. She refused to cry in front of him. "Then I guess there's nothing else I need to say either." She stood, picked up the pizza box and her empty glass. "You know your way out."

Without looking back, Talia walked to the kitchen. She'd barely set her items on the counter when Dylan grabbed one arm and spun her around. Before she could say or do anything, his other hand cradled the back of her head while his mouth slammed down on hers.

He couldn't expect her to melt at his feet just because he kissed better than any man she'd ever kissed. She put her hands on his chest, intending to push him away, when his lips softened against hers. He slid his hands across her shoulders, up her neck, to frame her face. His lips glided over hers, coaxing a response from her.

Instead of pushing him away, Talia curled her fingers into his T-shirt and parted her lips. Dylan moved his mouth over hers one way, then the other, then back. His tongue tickled the corners of her mouth, swept across her bottom lip, before he kissed her again. His kisses moved from sweet to passionate and returned to sweet. She felt dizzy from the bombardment of sensations he generated.

"I'm sorry." He kissed the side of her neck. "I didn't mean to hurt you." He kissed her jaw again, then her cheek. "I *never* want to hurt you." He pressed his forehead against hers. "I love you, Talia," he whispered. "I love you so much."

She couldn't stop her tears at the sound of his precious words. She wrapped her arms around his waist, laid her cheek against his chest. "I love you, too."

* * *

Dylan held Talia close to him, savoring her nearness and her declaration of love. He hadn't meant to tell her of his feelings. He'd planned to keep them deep inside so she wouldn't expect more from him than he could give her. But it tore him apart to see the pain in her eyes when he wouldn't talk to her. He had to be honest. Talia deserved nothing less.

"Will you talk to me now?" she asked.

With one finger, he lifted her chin so he could look into her eyes. His heart lurched in his chest to see her eyes glittering with tears. "Yes. But let me make love to you first. I need you."

"I need you, too."

She interlocked their fingers and guided him to her bedroom. He smiled at the sight of at least a dozen throw pillows in various colors and sizes propped against her headboard. How very much like Talia. He could easily imagine her making her bed every morning, arranging the pillows just so.

Now, he didn't want to imagine anything. Reality stood before him, looking at him with love shining in her eyes.

She tugged his T-shirt from his jeans, pushed it up until it bunched under his arms. Dylan sucked in a sharp breath when she kissed the center of his chest. Her lips skated over each nipple, her tongue followed the same path. Wanting more of her luscious mouth on his skin, he pulled off his shirt and let it fall to the floor. Talia kissed her way up the center of his chest, his neck, until she reached his mouth.

Dylan reached behind Talia's head and pulled out the band holding her hair. He tunneled his hands into the long strands, releasing the clean fragrance of her shampoo. Every time he'd gotten close enough to smell her hair, desire had curled in his stomach. He'd pictured that mane spread over a pillow while he thrust inside her. Or spread over his stomach as she took his dick deep in her mouth.

She reached for his belt buckle. Dylan laid his hands over

hers to stop her. "I took off my shirt. I think it's only fair that you take off something now."

He took a step back to give her more room. Grasping the bottom of her tank, Talia pulled it over her head and tossed it on top of Dylan's shirt. She wore a lacy purple bra almost the same shade as her tank. She looked into his eyes as she reached behind her.

"Wait. Let me."

Talia turned her back to him. Dylan unhooked her bra, slid his hands beneath the cups. Her warm breasts filled his palms.

"Mmm, these feel good."

"They aren't very big."

"They're perfect." He nudged aside her hair so he could kiss her shoulder. "Your whole body is perfect."

He dropped kisses along her shoulder as he removed her bra and unfastened her cutoffs. He tugged down the denim enough so he could slip one hand into the front of her panties while his other played with her breasts. His cock jumped at the feel of her smooth, creamy pussy. He danced his fingertips across her clit and along the slit. One finger ventured inside her channel. "You're so wet. I love that." He pushed his finger farther inside her, pressed against her G-spot. "What do you need me to do? I want you to come."

Her head fell back to rest on his shoulder. "You're doing fine."

He smiled at her breathless tone. "I could do better. Maybe you'd rather have my tongue than my hand?"

She whimpered. Dylan nipped her shoulder. "How about hand now and tongue later?"

"Stop teasing me."

"A slow buildup is nice. We didn't have that last night." He added a second finger inside her. "I want to make love to you for the rest of the afternoon."

He plucked at her nipple until it peaked. More cream oozed from her channel. He spread the moisture over her clit, circled the swollen nub with a fingertip. Her breathing grew heavier, more labored. She spread her legs and arched her hips toward his hand. "More," she breathed.

Dylan pressed his denim-covered cock against her ass. It ached from being so hard, but Talia's needs came before his own. He rolled her nipple between his thumb and forefinger while he pushed two fingers back into her channel as far as he could. "Come for me, darlin'."

He'd barely uttered the words when the walls of her pussy clamped onto his fingers, milking them with each contraction of her climax.

"*Ohhhhhhhhhh.*" Her entire body shuddered. "Dylan. *Yes!*"

He held her as she came down from the heavens, his hand on her breast, his fingers still inside her. He kissed the side of her neck, beneath her ear. "You okay?"

"No. All my bones melted."

Dylan smiled. He liked that she could tease even while the aftereffects of her orgasm flowed through her body. "Then it's a good thing I'm holding you."

His fingers slipped from inside her when she turned to face him. Running her hands into his hair, she tugged his head down for a kiss. She swiped her tongue across his lips, plunged it inside his mouth to touch his. Dylan clasped her ass and pulled her tight against his shaft. He didn't know how much longer he could wait to be inside her.

The abrupt end to their kiss surprised Dylan. Talia pushed hard on his chest, hard enough that he lost his balance and fell back on the bed. Before he could move, Talia removed her shorts and panties and straddled his hips.

She gave him a wicked smile. "Now it's *my* turn to tease."

Dylan had given her a staggering orgasm with his fingers, but she desired more. She wanted to see his body, touch it, feel his hard cock slide into her pussy the way it had last night.

But first, she planned to play.

She stared at his wide shoulders, broad chest, muscled arms. Between fighting fires and his work at Clay's station, he'd developed a lot of strength in his upper body. He tanned easily. The light brown tone of his skin proved he'd been outside a lot this summer without a shirt. Dark brown hair sprinkled over his chest and narrowed down his belly to swirl around his navel. Talia ruffled it with her fingertips. "I love hair on a man's chest. It's so sexy."

She moved her hands over his stomach, his chest, and up to his shoulders. Starting at his collarbone, she dragged her fingernails down his body to his belt.

Dylan hissed and arched his back. "Hurt?" she asked, even though she knew she hadn't scratched him hard enough for pain. The heat in his eyes proved that.

"You told me you like to scratch."

"I do." Once again, she dragged her fingernails down his skin, this time journeying across his nipples. They beaded beneath her nails.

"*Damn,* Talia."

"Too much?"

"No." He cradled her breasts in his hands, thumbed her nipples. "Not enough. I need to be inside you."

"You will be. Soon."

She scooted back on his thighs, which caused him to release her breasts. "Hey! I wasn't through touching you."

"Tough."

"You realize I outweigh you by a hundred pounds."

"Yes, I do. I don't care."

She unfastened his belt and button on his jeans. His chest rose and fell with his deep breathing as she reached for the zipper. Instead of lowering it, she laid her hand over the hard bulge behind his fly. She ran her palm along the impressive width and length, reached between his legs and gently squeezed his balls. "Very nice. I'm going to enjoy playing with this."

The fire in his eyes almost scorched her. He clenched his fists at his sides when she slid down the zipper. "Lift your hips," she commanded as she moved to his side. Jeans, shoes, and socks landed on the floor. He lay on her bed wearing nothing but a pair of black briefs that outlined his shaft and left nothing to her imagination. Not that she needed imagination. She remembered every vein, every curve, every texture of his luscious cock.

She straddled his hips again, slowly lowered her torso until her breasts grazed his chest. She leaned down until her lips were a whisper from his. "Your body is amazing."

"So is yours." He gripped her ass, lifted his hips to rub his cock against her mound. "The most beautiful I've ever seen."

Talia doubted that, but thought it sweet for him to say so. She brushed her breasts over his chest again, earning her a soft moan from Dylan. "You like this?"

"Oh, yeah." He squeezed her ass before sliding his hands up her back to between her shoulder blades. Pressing gently, he urged her closer until her breasts flattened against his chest. "I like this better." Tangling his fingers in her hair, he outlined her lips with the tip of his tongue. "And this."

He kissed her deeply, hungrily, outlining her lips again before darting his tongue into her mouth. Talia sucked it farther inside, nipped it with her teeth. Dylan drew in a sharp breath through his nose. The next instant, Talia found herself on her back with Dylan lying between her legs.

"I promised myself I'd make love with you." He kissed her mouth, her jaw, beneath her ear. "I didn't want this to be a fast fuck." His mouth covered hers in a kiss that stole Talia's ability to think. "You aren't making it easy for me to keep my promise."

"Good," she managed to say once she recovered her voice. She pulled his bottom lip between her teeth, soothed the bite with her tongue. "Fuck me, Dylan."

8

Dylan rose to his feet long enough to shuck his briefs. Talia sighed at the sight of his fully aroused cock. Long and thick with a slight curve at the tip, it fit perfectly inside her.

A drop of pre-cum formed at the slit. She yearned to lick it off, then keep licking the entire length of his hard flesh and tight balls.

Instead of joining her on the bed again, he grasped her ankles and tugged until her hips lay on the edge of the bed. "I made you come with my fingers," he said, parting her labia with his thumbs. "Now I'm going to make you come with my tongue."

Talia longed to feel his cock thrusting into her channel, but couldn't find a reason to complain about his statement. After all, they had the rest of the day to make love. There could be many, many orgasms between them.

She sighed at the first stroke of his tongue. It came gently, as if he knew her clit would still be sensitive from her climax. He licked up and down the folds with the same easy touch. A finger entered her channel, another breached her anus. He didn't move them, but left them still while he lapped at her clit.

Talia hooked her hands behind her knees and spread them wide.

"That's the way. Give me lots of room to eat this pretty pussy." He kissed the inside of each of her thighs. "You're beautiful here. Pink. Wet. Swollen." He swept his tongue across her clit again. "Delicious."

Now he settled in to feast. His fingers pumped in and out of her body while his teeth and tongue did wicked things to her cunt. He placed his lips directly over her clit and sucked.

The top of Talia's head blew off when the orgasm hit. Or that's the way her head felt. Her body jerked, goose bumps erupted all over her skin. She cried out when the intense pleasure raced through her body, then settled in her womb. Her pussy and anus pulsed around Dylan's fingers.

Her arms trembled so, she couldn't hold up her legs any longer. They fell to the bed as she tried to catch her breath. Dylan slid his hands beneath her ass and continued licking her. Only after she'd regained control of her heart and lungs did she slip one hand beneath his chin and guide his mouth away from her.

"Fuck me. Now."

She backed to the middle of the bed while he picked up his jeans, removed his wallet from the back pocket. He opened it, and froze. "Shit," he muttered. "Shit, shit, shit."

"What's wrong?"

"I didn't put any more condoms in my wallet." He dropped the useless piece of leather to the floor. "Do you have any?"

The hopeful look he gave her would normally make her laugh. Not now, not when she wanted him so much. "No." She rose to her knees, laid her hands on his chest. "Do you trust me?"

A confused look crossed his face, as if he didn't understand how she could ask such a question. "Of course I do."

"I'm on the pill and I haven't been with anyone in over a year. I'm clean, Dylan."

He tunneled his hands into her hair. "I'm clean, too. I swear it."

"Then there's no reason to stop, is there?"

He didn't answer her question with words, but with a kiss. Holding her tightly, he lowered them both to the bed. Talia immediately parted her legs and made a place for him between them. His firm cock pressed against her belly.

"I need to thrust, darlin'," he said between kisses. "I need to thrust hard and fast. You okay with that?"

Most definitely okay with that, Talia lifted her hips to accept his entrance. Dylan had said he needed hard and fast, yet he slid his shaft into her one slow inch at a time. Once fully seated, he lay still while he kissed her, over and over.

"You aren't moving," she whispered against his lips.

"I'm savoring. It's been years since I've made love without a condom."

"Me, too." She smiled. "It feels really good."

"*You* feel really good." He pulled his hips back a few inches, then thrust forward. He repeated the action while nibbling on the spot where her neck met her shoulder. "Mmm, yeah. So good."

He still didn't start thrusting the way he said he needed to. To urge him in that direction, Talia gripped his ass, dug her fingernails into the firm flesh. "Move."

Dylan gasped, then laughed. "Pushy, aren't you?"

"*You're* the one who said you needed to thrust hard and fast. So *move.*"

His smile faded as he began to do just that. He propped himself on his hands, stared at the spot where their bodies joined together. Talia did the same, loving the way his cock looked covered in her juices. He pulled it all the way out of her, then pushed back in to his balls. After repeating that process three times, he settled on top of her again. Burying his face against her neck, he began to pump.

Talia shifted her hips a few inches to get the perfect stimulation to her clit. *There. Oh, yes, there.* Each of Dylan's thrusts brushed all the sensitive parts of her pussy. Despite the glorious orgasms she'd already had, another one built inside her, ready to gallop through her body.

Then, he stopped moving.

Talia came crashing back to earth before she had the chance to fly to the heavens. She slapped one of his butt cheeks. "Why did you stop?"

"I'm too close to coming."

"So was I, until you stopped."

"I'm sorry." He kissed her softly. "It feels so good inside you. I don't want to come yet."

Her frustration disappeared. She understood exactly how he felt. "There's no reason why you can't come more than once, is there?"

"Hardly."

"Well, then . . ." Gripping his ass, she lifted her hips while she nipped his chin. "Move."

He did as she ordered, his thrusts slowly picking up speed until he pistoned into her. Talia's pleasure quickly built again, until it peaked in a toe-curling climax. She held tightly to Dylan while he continued to pump. Perspiration beaded his skin, he breathed in and out of his mouth. His hot breath brushed her ear, causing goose bumps to pebble her flesh again.

"You're so tight. *God,* Talia, you take me perfectly."

His movements stopped, then his body gave a hard jerk and he groaned loudly. Talia could feel his cock pulsing inside her as he filled her with his cum.

Dylan didn't move, other than to brace his weight on his forearms. Talia caressed his back and butt while his heart slowed from its fierce pounding. Her own heart coasted back to its normal rhythm, her lungs no longer fought for air.

The things he did to her body amazed her.

Dylan gently pulled out of her and rolled to his back, eyes closed. His cock lay against his thigh, somewhat relaxed but not completely soft. Talia couldn't resist running one finger over it, liking the way it felt wet with her cream.

"Don't even think about it," he said with his eyes still closed.

"I can't touch you?"

"As long as you don't want sex again for about three weeks, you can touch me."

She rolled to her side toward him. "*Three weeks?* No way, buddy."

He cracked open one eye to peer at her. "You're heartless, do you know that? You damn near killed me and you want more?"

"Hey, you said you could come more than once."

"I didn't mean in ten minutes."

"You didn't have any trouble coming a second time in ten minutes last night."

A smug grin turned up his lips. "Yeah, that's true."

Three orgasms should've been enough. Her body felt deliciously tired and sated, yet the sight of Dylan lying nude on her bed made her want him again. She drew a figure eight on his chest with the finger that had caressed his cock, leaving a thin trail of her essence on his skin. "Maybe a little help would speed up that three weeks."

He opened both eyes. "What do you have in mind?"

She leaned over and covered his mouth with hers. Cradling his jaw, she rubbed his cheek with her thumb as she kissed him. She caressed his lips with hers slowly, gently, in no hurry to stop.

He slid one hand up and down her back and over one buttock. Talia traced his lips with the tip of her tongue, nipped at the pulse that once again fluttered in his neck.

A deep growl came from his throat.

Talia traveled down his body, dropping kisses along the way. She whisked her tongue over each nipple, bit the firm muscle of his breast. The soft hair on his stomach tickled her lips. She licked and nibbled his stomach, darted her tongue into his navel.

"Talia." His voice came out low and guttural.

Continuing her journey south, she ran her tongue down his happy trail, through his pubic hair, until she reached his hardening cock. Gripping the base of it, she swept her tongue around the head. She slid her mouth down his length and back to the tip. One more path around the head and she took him in her mouth, sucking hard as she moved her lips up and down his shaft.

Dylan drove the fingers of one hand into her hair. "Damn, you are really good at that."

She looked into his eyes as she continued to lick his now fully hard cock. Wanting to add to his pleasure, she wet one finger and slid it beneath his balls to circle his anus.

His hand fisted in her hair. "You need to stop before I come."

Ignoring his command, Talia continued to move her mouth up and down his shaft. She tickled his anus with her finger another moment, then pushed it inside his ass. Dylan hissed.

"Oh, yeah. Go deeper, darlin'."

Talia added a second finger, pushing them as far inside his ass as she could reach. Dylan's body jerked. "Fuck!" he muttered. He arched his hips, squeezed his eyes closed. Warm semen hit the back of her throat. Talia greedily swallowed every drop.

She rose to her knees between his legs. Dylan slowly opened

his eyes. They burned with desire, even though he'd just climaxed. That look made even more moisture flood her already wet channel.

Dylan touched his mouth. "I want your pussy right here."

Obeying him instantly, Talia climbed up his body and did as he commanded. Clutching the headboard, she waited for what he would do.

Dylan gripped her buttocks and spread them far apart. His talented tongue flashed over her clit, dove into her sheath, skittered across her anus. His tight hold on her ass kept her from moving more than an inch or two. He held her in place and licked her pussy easy, unhurried, letting her desire climb again.

It took mere moments for the direct stimulation to those sensitive nerves to push her over the edge. A keening moan rippled from her throat when the pleasure galloped up from her toes to envelop her entire body.

Too weak to move, Talia hung on to the headboard to hold her upright. The bed dipped as Dylan scooted from beneath her. He wrapped his arms around her from behind, guided her back to the bed. He lay on his side, tugged her into the circle of his arms. "Love you," he whispered before kissing her nape.

"Love you, too," she said, and closed her eyes.

Dylan silently cheered when the Cowboys made a touchdown. He didn't want to make too much noise and wake Talia. They'd both fallen asleep after making love, but he awoke after a few minutes. Covering her with the light blanket at the end of the bed, he'd gathered up his clothes and left the bedroom.

He had no doubt she'd want to talk when she awoke. He'd told her he'd explain about his hesitance to get involved with her, yet he didn't know how he could do that. She'd hate him when she knew about his past.

She'd hate him anyway, when he broke her heart.

You've fucked this up big time, Westfield.

Soft hands slid down his chest while warm lips kissed him beneath his ear. Dylan turned his head and smiled at Talia. "You're awake."

"Why didn't you wake me when you got up?"

"You looked so pretty sleeping, I didn't want to bother you."

She rounded the couch and sat by him. Dylan wrapped his arm around her, tucked her next to his side. She rested her head on his shoulder. "Who's winning?"

"Redskins, but only by two points."

Talia reached across him, picked up his beer bottle from the end table, and took a drink. He couldn't resist teasing her about drinking his beer without asking. "Oh, so it's going to be that way, huh? A guy tells a gal he loves her and suddenly everything he has is hers?"

"Yepper, that's the way it works."

Her eyes sparkled with happiness. A hard kick to the stomach couldn't hurt him any more than the pain he would experience when he told her the truth and she turned away from him.

She must have sensed his unease for the joy faded from her eyes. "What's wrong?"

"I, uh, promised I'd talk to you after we made love, about why I avoided you for two years."

Talia straightened. "Why did you?"

"To protect you."

"Dylan, why would I need protection from you?"

He picked up the remote from the coffee table and turned off the TV. He supposed the best way to start would be with his mother. "I was fourteen when my mother died. She got sick with a really nasty virus and went downhill quickly." He rubbed his forehead, where sweat began to form. "I think she willed herself to die so she could escape from my father."

Talia lightly touched his arm. "Did he abuse her?"

Dylan nodded. "Yeah. It wasn't so bad when he didn't drink,

but he was a mean drunk. She used to tell me to hide when he came home. She took whatever he gave her to protect me."

Unable to sit still, Dylan stood up to pace. "I begged her to leave. I told her the two of us could just disappear. But I'd heard him tell her many times that if she ever left him, he'd hunt her down, tie her up, and make her watch while he beat me." He pushed his hair off his forehead. "He'd never hit me in my life, just her. That changed when she died."

He glanced at Talia. It didn't surprise him to see tears glittering in her eyes.

"After she died, he needed a new punching bag. He didn't count on me fighting back. The first time he took a swing, I wasn't fast enough. After that, I learned to avoid him whenever he started drinking."

He stopped by the window, parted the curtain, and looked out at the neat houses across the street with their painted shutters and pretty flowerbeds. "He snuck up on me one day before I could get away. He gave me a black eye, swollen jaw, and fractured my left wrist. I decided that was enough. With him yelling at me to get back in the house, I took off on my bicycle and rode seven miles to the police station."

Talia remained silent, wiping away any tears that fell. He wanted to hold her so badly, but had to get everything out while he had the courage.

"CPS wanted to put me in a foster home since I didn't have any relatives. My mom's parents were dead and my dad's parents lived somewhere in Europe. They had a lifestyle that wouldn't have room for a fourteen-year-old kid. I figured a foster family would be better than the way I lived.

"My best friend's parents came forward and said they wanted me to live with them. It was the best thing that could have happened to me. All I had was the clothes I wore that day and my bike. Mrs. Thompson took me shopping and bought me clothes and shoes, and I borrowed stuff from Andy since we were the same size. I took any odd jobs I could find to help pay them back for the clothes and any food I ate at their house." He smiled at the memory of meals at the Thompson house. "She was a terrific cook."

His smile faded and he turned to face Talia again. "I left San Angelo right after I graduated high school. As far as I know, my dad still lives there, but I don't know for sure. He might be dead. Either way, I don't care. He's out of my life forever."

"I'm glad." She held out her hand to him, palm up. Dylan walked to her, took her hand, and sat next to her. "I'm so sorry all that happened to you and your mother. But I'm so glad you told me about it. Now it's behind us and we can move forward with our lives."

"Not together, Talia. We can't be together."

Pain flashed through her eyes, mixed with confusion. "I don't understand. Why can't we be together? We love each other."

Dylan stared at her soft hand clasped in his. He lifted it to his mouth, kissed the back of it. "Because I'm just like him."

9

He didn't mean it. Dylan would never hurt a woman. "That isn't possible. You're *nothing* like your father."

"Yeah, I am," he said softly, disgust evident in his voice. "I hate it, but I am."

"You've never hit a woman, have you?"

"No, but I came close."

Talia blinked, unable to comprehend or believe what Dylan said. "What?"

Dylan rose again, took several steps away from the couch. "I was involved with someone three years ago when I lived in Fort Worth. Patricia. She was sweet and kind, but a little flighty and forgetful. She'd be late every time she was supposed to meet me. One night, I made a special dinner for us and she was almost an hour late." He stuffed his hands in the pockets of his jeans. "I kept getting her voice mail when I called her cell, which wasn't unusual since she often forgot to turn on her phone. Every time I called and didn't get her, I tossed back another shot of whiskey. Just like my old man."

Talia saw his body shudder in distaste. She started to rise and go to him, but he threw out a hand to stop her.

"Let me finish. I have to get everything out."

She folded her hands in her lap and remained on the couch.

"She was full of apologies when she got there, as usual. She'd gone shopping with girlfriends, lost track of time. She laughed it off like it was no big deal that she'd put her cell on vibrate and dropped it in her purse. I was livid. I asked her what if there had been an emergency and no one could reach her? She gave me that no-big-deal look and continued to chatter about the good time she'd had with her girlfriends."

He stared across the room, apparently thinking about whatever had happened in his past. "I lost it. Between worrying about her and the shots I'd drunk, I lost it. I yelled at her about her forgetfulness and selfishness and a bunch of other things. She stared at me, her eyes wide and her mouth hanging open. No apology, no saying she'd try to do better. She just stared at me. That's when I . . ." He ran one hand over his pale face. "I grabbed her by the front of her blouse and drew my fist back to hit her." Dylan looked at her with tears in his eyes. "Just like my dad did to my mom."

Talia couldn't sit still any longer. She had to touch him, to comfort him. He backed away from her when she tried to wrap her arms around him.

"No! I don't deserve your sympathy."

"Dylan, you didn't hit her. You stopped, right?"

He nodded. The torment in his eyes broke her heart. "I caught myself in time. I told her I was sorry and to go home. She couldn't get away from me fast enough. I gave notice at my job the next day, packed up my stuff, and moved to Lanville. I needed a fresh start." He backed up two steps, stuffed his hands in his pockets again. "That's the last time I drank whiskey. I'll drink a beer now and then, but I haven't drank hard liquor since that day."

"So you *aren't* like your father. Don't you see that?" She moved closer to him, laid her hands on his chest. "You stopped the cycle before it could consume you."

"But I can't know that for sure. That's why I haven't gotten involved with another woman. I've dated now and then, but I couldn't take the chance on falling for someone in fear of hurting her." His gaze passed over her face. "I didn't plan on falling in love with you, Talia, but I couldn't help it. You're so caring and sweet and beautiful. I would rather jab a knife into my gut than hurt you."

"I believe you, and I also believe you would never hurt me." She grabbed his hands, held them tightly when he tried to jerk them away from hers. "I've known you for two years. I've been with you in a lot of situations when you could've lost your temper. You never did. You don't have the anger festering inside you like your father did. You're nothing like him."

He shook his head fiercely. "I can't take the chance. I'm sorry. I just can't."

He hurried out the front door before Talia could grab his arm and stop him. She ran outside to see him striding toward his pickup. "Dylan! Come back."

Tears fell down her cheeks as she watched him speed away in his truck. She could call his cell, beg him to come back, but she knew he wouldn't. Whatever demons chased him, he wouldn't let her help him fight them.

She walked back into the house and curled up in a corner of the couch. She didn't believe in giving up when something mattered to her, and Dylan definitely mattered to her. She'd waited two years to have him in her life. No matter what happened in his past, she knew him to be a caring and loving man.

The department had practice fires Tuesday night at two old buildings on the same property in the country. A plan began to brew in her mind of a way to prove to Dylan she knew he

278 / Lynn LaFleur

would never hurt her. It might take a little trickery, but she'd use that if necessary to show him they belonged together.

Talia enlisted the help of Clay and Quade in her plan to get back together with Dylan. She couldn't tell them exactly what she planned since things depended on how Dylan reacted, but she asked them to go along with her. They both agreed.

Fifteen of the volunteer firefighters showed up for the practice fire. Talia worried that Dylan might decide not to come. Relief flooded through her when she saw him with Stephen and Nick as the three men donned their turnout pants and coats.

Two teams would fight the fires. Talia made arrangements with Clay to be on the same team as Dylan. Now she simply had to wait for the opportunity to make Dylan argue with her. Everything depended on him becoming boiling mad at her.

The opportunity arose when Dylan had his turn holding the fire hose. Talia used a pickax alongside Quade to tear away the burning wood of the old barn. Knowing she would get knocked on her ass, she purposely stepped in front of the hose so the streaming water hit her square in the back.

She stood several feet away from the hose's nozzle, but the force of the water still sent her sprawling to the ground. Quade immediately took her arm to help her stand. "You okay?"

"Yeah. Is Dylan coming?"

"On his way."

"Shit, Talia, what are you doing?" Dylan yelled as he grabbed her other arm.

Time for my Academy Award performance. "What am *I* doing?" She jerked her arm away from Dylan. "Why don't you watch where you aim the hose?"

"You stepped right in front of the stream."

"Oh, sure, blame me for your mistake. It won't be the first time you've done that."

Confusion mixed with the concern on Dylan's face. "What the *hell* are you talking about?"

"Hey, hey, what's going on?" Clay asked. He stepped next to Talia, Dylan, and Quade.

"Dylan's being a jerk." She answered Clay's question, yet kept her gaze fixed on Dylan's face.

"I'm doing *what*?"

The fire of anger flashed in his eyes. That's exactly what Talia wanted. She took the few steps necessary to be right in front of him. She punctuated her next words with jabs into his chest with her finger. "You heard me. You're being a jerk. You made a mistake and you're blaming it on me. Again."

"I didn't make the mistake, *you* did. And I've never blamed you for *anything*."

"Oh, no? What about the schedule mix-up last month? You didn't show for your shift to cover the phones and you blamed me."

"You offered to switch shifts with me! *You're* the one who didn't show up."

"Look, guys," Quade said, "I'm sure—"

"Stay out of this, Quade," Talia said, frowning at him. She hoped Quade remembered this was an act and she wasn't really angry at him. In her peripheral vision, she saw the rest of the firefighters creeping closer. "Maybe hitting me with the water was your way of getting back at me for that 'supposed' mix-up."

Dylan's scowl would've made anyone cringe. Not Talia. She wouldn't give up now. She couldn't.

"You're being stupid."

"Don't call me stupid!"

"I didn't call you stupid! I said you're *being* stupid. I would never purposely hit you with the water!"

"Why should I believe that when the proof is running down the back of my coat?" She glanced at his hands to see them clenched into fists. She gestured to them. "What's with the fists? You gonna hit me, Dylan?"

"*No!* I would *never* hit you! I would never hurt you for any reason. I love you!"

Her love for him expanded her heart until she wondered how her chest could hold it. She gently cradled his cheek in her palm. "I know you do. And I love you."

All traces of anger faded from Dylan's face. Comprehension flared in his eyes. "You fought with me on purpose," he said in a voice low enough that she could hear, but the other firefighters surrounding them couldn't.

Talia nodded. "I wanted to prove to you that you wouldn't hurt me, no matter what."

Dylan took her hand from his cheek, kissed her palm. His eyes looked suspiciously moist. Not wanting him to appear less than macho in front of the other guys, she smiled at her friends. "I heard a rumor there will be Bunkhouse barbecue with all the fixin's at Clay's house after we get through here."

A cheer went up from the firefighters. They headed back to their posts to finish the exercise.

"Kiss her and then get back to work, Westfield," Clay said with a grin.

Dylan waited until Clay and Quade walked away before he spoke. "You want to go to Clay's after we're through here?"

The teasing glimmer in his eyes told her he didn't care one bit about going to Clay and Maysen's house. "Well, barbecue does sound really good."

"I could pick some up for us and meet you at your house. We can have a private picnic."

"With or without clothes?"

He flashed her a wolfish grin. "I've never had a naked picnic. Sounds like fun."

"Yes, it does." Talia rose on her tiptoes, gave him a soft kiss. "See you later."